BOOK OF BLACK

BOOK OF BLACK

E. S. Abbott

This book you're reading is a work of fiction. Characters, places, events, and names are the product of this author's imagination. Any resemblance to other events, other locations, or other persons, living or dead, is coincidental.

Copyright © 2024 E. S. Abbott

The author reserves all rights to be recognized as the owner of this work. You may not sell or reproduce any part of this book without written consent from the copyright owner.

First paperback edition August 2024

ISBN-9798334656239

DEDICATION

To everyone who believed in me and contributed to helping me realize this world I've created. You know who you are. Thank you.

Table of Contents

Chapter 1 1
Chapter 2 16
Chapter 3 37
Chapter 4 52
Chapter 5 76
Chapter 6 103
Chapter 7 136
Chapter 8 164
Chapter 9 188
Chapter 10 211
Chapter 11 226

Chapter 1

Jenna gripped Lucy tight as the banging started up again. The storm raged outside, its fury sounding as if it was tearing the world apart. The light from the fireplace waltzed across Daniel's face as he stared into the blackness of the other rooms. He sat at the edge of a recliner, tense with listening. The banging continued, as did Jenna's tears, tracing the familiar salty tracks.

"I think it's coming from the front door," Daniel said slowly getting to his feet. "Maybe it's the man Father Frank was sending to help us."

Jenna sat on the floor with her back against the couch. Lucy slept in her arms clutching her doll that she received for her fifth birthday only a month prior before this nightmare started. They resembled nesting dolls. A woman holding a child holding a baby.

"Please be careful," Jenna whispered as Daniel slowly moved to the doorway of the foyer.

The banging stopped. Daniel stood at the front door straining his vision through the etched glass but it was too dark to make out any details. He reached for the door knob and froze as he heard the sound of little feet swiftly moving up the stairs behind him. He turned to peer up into the dark void. There was no denying what he was hearing. Amidst the rain and wind came the sound of a child laughing.

Daniel's spine turned to ice as he heard the shrill sound of a child's words, "I want to play! Don't you want to play with me anymore?"

Daniel knew with a father's certainty, that wasn't his daughter's voice. From behind came a crash of thunder. Daniel spun around and stumbled back coming down on the stairs. In the flash of lightning, he had seen a silhouette on the other side of the front door.

BANG! BANG! BANG!

Each impact sent a shudder through Daniel. "Who? Who is it?" The words barely escaped his throat. Daniel got to his feet and reached for the knob again.

While Daniel was in the foyer, Jenna sat trying to push the events of the past few days from her mind. She was exhausted, but every time Jenna closed her eyes she feared that something evil was watching and tore them open again. She stared into the fire and listened to the rain. The flames performed to the beat of the storm and a warmth came over her. Her eyes grew heavy as the elements seemed to bewitch her and the evil she feared grinned in the darkness.

The fire grew dim and the house creaked and shivered. From the corner of the room the shadows opened up for a pale face with an unnaturally wide mouth turned upward into a smile. The face seemed to float in the darkness.

Lucy roused from her sleep and felt the draw of the white face. She crawled off her mother's lap and stood looking at the pale faced man. He moved a few feet closer to her, pulling the shadows with him, engulfing more of the room.

"Molly wants to play with me?" Lucy whispered. "What about mommy?... Later?... Downstairs? Okay, I guess so."

A thin pale arm reached out of the shadows. The house groaned and the face's smile seemed to stretch even wider, pushing deep grooves into its cheeks. Lucy reached out to take hold of the near skeletal fingers that slithered towards her.

"No!" Jenna cried out and yanked her daughter back down to her so hard that Lucy dropped her doll.

The thin hand slipped back into the shadows. "You filthy sack of meat!" hissed a voice that seemed to come from all corners of the room. She sat frozen, holding Lucy so tight that she nearly squeezed the life out of her. The white grinning face lowered down to Jenna's level and slowly moved towards her, the shadows spreading out as if its whole body was filling the room.

Daniel turned the knob and as the bolt slipped from its home the wind blew the door in nearly catching him in the head. In the doorway stood a large black figure. Daniel's eyes made out the details of a man's face glistening with rain as it streamed off the tip of his nose. The storm beat down on the man and threw his hair and hood about so that it seemed it would tear away from him.

The man had a cold look in his eyes as he spoke, "Frank sent me." They stood for a moment in silence. "You gonna let me in?"

Daniel opened his mouth to speak but was interrupted by a scream. "Jenna!" He cried out as he turned and ran to the living room leaving the saturated stranger in the open doorway. In the past few days Daniel had witnessed horrors that had pushed his mind to near madness but what he saw bearing down on his wife and child overwhelmed him.

Daniel stood as stone, petrified just like his wife. A great mass of darkness moved closer to Jenna and Lucy led by an ivory face and two pale arms. The creature was now close enough to snatch them and as it reached out one long bony arm for Lucy's strawberry blonde hair it froze.

The pale face turned in Daniels direction, its huge grin now inverted. Daniel felt his legs about to give out on him. He knew his family was in danger but his body refused to move. *How can I stop something like that?* Daniel's thoughts raced. *What even is that?*

Daniel felt a firm hand grip his shoulder and before another thought could cross his mind he heard the stranger speaking. "Sorry, I let myself in and I didn't want to track in any mud so I left my boots at the door."

Who is this guy, Daniel thought. Does he even know what's happening right now?

The stranger narrowed his eyes on the pale grimacing face looking in his direction. "I think you've overstayed your welcome." The stranger advanced towards the creature muttering something under his breath. The fire which had been reduced to glowing embers burst back into life. The entire room was showered in light and the creature let out a shrill painful scream and retreated back into the corner it originated from and faded into the shadows.

The stranger inspected the corner until he seemed satisfied and turned to the frightened family that was now clutching each other and staring at him.

"It had no eyes," Jenna mumbled, trembling as she spoke. "Just darkness."

Daniel stared into the corner the monster had retreated to. His nerves felt frayed and he cleared his throat before speaking. "Thank you, um, Father Frank didn't tell us your -"

"Black."

"Are you another priest?" But Daniel knew the answer before he even asked. Aside from wearing all black he looked nothing like a priest. He was tall and broad shouldered. He wore black jeans, a thick black coat that went down to his knees with black fur around the collar and hood, and under that was a black t-shirt. His eyes were cold and gray. His hair was dark and shaggy.

"No, I'm ...something else. A specialist in these kinds of matters," Black replied.

Jenna wiped some tears from her eyes and asked, "is it gone?"

Black nodded his head, "For now." He gestured to the recliner, "Do you mind?"

"No, of course." Daniel moved his family around to sit on the couch.

Black sat down in the recliner, relaxing into it.

Daniel pulled his wife close. "What was that thing?" His voice shook as much as his hands.

Black stood up again for a moment, removed his coat, and laid it across the back of his chair. "It's a weak, pathetic creature frightened by the light," he said as he sat back down and gestured to the fire. There was a hint of bitterness in his words. "It builds up strength from your fear. I imagine this past week has been full of startling moments as it played its little tricks."

Jenna's eyes widened, "it's been dreadful."

"But what is it?" Daniel inquired. "Like a, uh, poltergeist?" His mind flashing back to the movie he and Jenna had seen in theaters a few years prior.

"Something darker. This thing isn't just trying to annoy you for its entertainment." Black's eyes fell on Lucy. "This was a demon manifesting itself without a body. It would have broken you down mentally and gathered strength until it could possess the weakest of you. This would give it a physical form in this world...and then it would likely kill you all."

Jenna gasped and clutched Lucy tighter.

"Why us," Daniel cried out. "And how do we get this thing out of our house?"

Black stood up and walked over to the fireplace and stared into the flames for a moment. The shadows on his face made him appear quite frightening but considering what they had all just witnessed it was diminished a bit. He glanced back at Lucy in Jenna's arms. Black crouched down in front of Lucy.

"You've been very brave haven't you?" Black looked into Lucy's large green eyes as she nodded. "That's a pretty dolly you have there." He gestured to the toy on the floor. "Was it a gift?"

"Yes," Lucy said hesitantly. "Uncle Patrick gave it to me for my birthday."

"I see"

Daniel shifted a little, his spine returning to his body at the mention of uncle Patrick's name. "I don't see what this has to do with anything."

"Not a fan of Uncle Patrick, eh?"

"My brother showed up to her birthday party drunk," Jenna spoke up. "We didn't even expect to see him. We don't get along very well, since my father died."

Black looked back at Lucy and her doll. "I think we should talk about my fee for getting rid of your demon."

"Well," Daniel stood up and looked down at Black. "How much do you want, or normally charge for this kind of thing?"

"Not much," Black glanced from Daniel to the doll. "I'll take that doll."

Daniel chuckled for a moment, "seriously, how much is it going to cost?"

Black stood up and fixed an icy gaze on Daniel. "The doll is my price and I don't negotiate."

Black's eyes glared at Daniel before he felt a chill weaken his spine again. "Fine."

Black picked up the doll from where it had fallen earlier. "Molly," Lucy squeaked from behind her mother's embrace.

"Don't worry honey," Daniel assured his daughter. "We'll get you a new one." As Black examined the doll for a moment Daniel noticed strange tattoos on Black's forearms that resembled some form of Arabic writing but not quite anything he'd ever seen before.

"Well then," Black said while reaching for his coat. "I should be on my way."

"What if that thing comes back!" Daniel said, glancing at his wife excitedly.

"It won't be coming back."

"But you just got here and you haven't even done anything yet," Jenna gasped.

"I have work to do elsewhere and it sounds like the storm is letting up." Black pulled on his coat and moved swiftly to the foyer where he slipped on his boots.

The whole family followed him to the door. "Well thanks?" Daniel said questioningly.

Jenna and Daniel looked at each other in confusion. *Did he even do anything?* Daniel thought.

"One more thing before I go," Black wavered for a moment after opening the front door.

The family stood expecting some advice or further explanation pertaining to the terrible events they'd undergone.

"Jenna, right?" he said, gesturing to her.

"Yes."

"What is your maiden name?"

Jenna looked shocked by such a peculiar question. "Stuert."

"Thank you," Black said as he turned and started off down the sidewalk and into the setting sun beginning to spill through the clouds.

***

Johnston heaved himself out of his favorite armchair and glanced out his front window. "Looks like the rain has passed," he said, letting his crimson curtains fall back into place. He glanced down at an American bulldog almost as plump as him and said, "Alright Colonel, I suppose I'll take you out one more time before we call it a day." Johnston leashed up Colonel and they set out the door.

The sun was halfway below the horizon, the fading light glistening off the raindrops that were still clinging to the leaves and grass. They made it about a block when he noticed Colonel perking up at attention. Something had caught his dog's eye across the street on a corner. Johnston beheld an unusual sight. Several large crows were perched on the power lines looking around in all directions and a few more had nestled perched on top of an old phone booth. One was looking up the street and another was looking down the street, but a third was looking at him.

Johnston froze. At that moment he witnessed what could only be described as peculiar. Within the phone booth were two more crows and it looked as though one of them was turning the pages of a phone book while the other was reading it. "Must need to make an important call," he nervously chuckled to himself.

He watched for a moment longer before the two inside turned and flew out, with the rest falling in behind them, except for the one that had been watching him. It lingered for a moment before letting out a shrill squawk and following after the others.

Johnston and Colonel both stared into the sky until Johnston finally muttered, "I must be losing my mind."

***

Another late night, barely able to drive home. Patrick fumbled with his keys at the front door. After putting a couple new scratches around the door knob he stumbled in. Patrick stood in the front room for a moment with the door still open. How much did I spend on that slut, he struggled counting on his fingers and dropping his keys. Twenty or thirty dollars? The whores I was fucking in Hong Kong last month barely cost that. He bent over and picked up his keys letting out a long burp. Another bitch not giving me what I deserve. It should have been my money and I should be getting laid tonight.

He shut the door and flicked the light switch, but nothing happened. "Shit!"

"Just more bad luck," he mumbled to himself as he meandered towards the kitchen. He opened a cabinet and pulled out some bread and started towards the table when he froze.

The moon was large and shining through the window. Its silvery gaze blanketed the kitchen table and a little girl's doll that sat facing him. Its face was hidden in shadows, but lit a match of recognition in Patrick's mind.

The bread fell out of his hand and he looked around nervously. He caught some movement in a shadowy corner to the left of the window. "Did it work?" He asked wildly. "Is that bitch and her snobby family dead?" A large grin spread across his face. "I told her she'd pay for cheating me out of the old man's money!" He laughed. "It should have been mine!"

Patrick stopped laughing as a creak came from the figure in the corner and silver eyes reflecting the moonlight blinked into existence. The figure stepped into the light spilling through the windows and fear washed over Patrick.

Patrick saw immediately that he wasn't normal. Aside from the glowing eyes there was something else. The whites of his eyes, he cringed. Are black! The figure's hair seemed to grow paler the closer it got to his roots until it was completely white. And his mouth too had a strange shape that bothered him.

"You," the stranger spoke with a disgusted look on his face. "Smell terrible."

Patrick realized what bothered him about the man's mouth now. His canines were too long. Too pointed. "Who are you?"

"My name is Black and you, Mr. Stuert," Black pointed a finger in Patrick's face. "Tried to have your sister and her family killed. And over petty sibling jealousy."

As Black spoke Patrick could see a dark haze fill the translucent fingernail and it began to grow out to a point.

Black's hand closed and fell back to his side. He clenched his teeth into a snarl. "You tried to kill a little child!" He took a step closer. "Where did you get this doll?"

"A man I met in China," Patrick spoke, now drenched in sweat. "Somehow he knew what happened and he offered to help. He did something strange to my arm and then I didn't hear back from him again until I returned home and he was just waiting in my house for me one night."

Black snatched up Patrick's arm in a steel grip and turned his wrist face up. At first it looked normal but as Black focused his gaze on it a searing hot brand started to shine through. Patrick was squirming and whimpering as Black examined the ringed design.

Finally Black let go and the mark faded away. "What else?"

"He told me the doll was cursed and it would do what I wanted-"

"Murder them," Black interrupted.

Patrick nodded reluctantly and said, "I never even saw his face."

"What was his name?" Black growled.

Patrick threw his hands up, "he just said his name was Mr. B. That's all I know, I swear!"

Black seemed to relax for a moment. "Normally, I would let the police deal with murderous scumbags like you, but given the nature of things," he gestured towards the doll. "You're under my jurisdiction."

The doll burst into flames and at that Patrick watched frozen by fear as Black's clothing seemed to constrict into his skin and white hair poked through. In less than thirty seconds Patrick was staring into the jaws of an enormous white wolf as big as a small horse.

As the beast wrapped his jaws around his head the smell of urine filled the air along with one short but extremely loud scream. The neighbors reported hearing it followed oddly enough by what sounded like a whole flock of crows squawking as they ascended.

As Black's many wings pounded against the night sky one thought consumed him, who is Mr. B?

***

20 years ago in the forests of another world

As a boy Black spent his days with the animals of the forests. He would occasionally go into the villages of the elves when the winters got too cold. He learned language from them, normally watching and listening from a distance. Sometimes he'd received clothing from them, but his time with them was always temporary. He never felt like one of them. His place was running through fields with deer, chasing rabbits, or catching fish from the stream. He loved to feel the dirt beneath his feet and sleep under the open sky.

It was a typical day. He'd gone swimming in a lake and worked up quite an appetite, so he went looking for some food. He'd eaten fish for the past three days and was in the mood for something else. As he strolled through the forest his ears caught a rustle up ahead of him. He immediately crouched down and scanned the forest floor. Out hopped a fat rabbit.

No fish tonight, he thought.

Black slowly but silently crept closer towards his next meal. The rabbit nosed around in the grass unaware that it was being stalked. Black inched closer almost in range to pounce.

Suddenly a crack in the trees above echoed. The rabbit turned quickly and met Black's eyes. They both sat frozen until another snap came from above and Black's dinner turned and bolted.

Those squirrels, Black thought as he gave chase.

The rabbit was all white and easy to spot through the green of the vegetation. Black was close behind. Ahead of him he spotted a fallen moss-covered log. The rabbit scurried under it while Black planted a hand and cleared it in one leap keeping pace.

Black was vaguely aware of the rustling and cracking that seemed to be trailing behind him in the trees above. He was gaining on his prey, just a little closer and he'd have him. His lungs burned and his legs ached but he pushed even harder, stretching out his hand and tumbled.

Black rolled through a bush and came to rest with his back against a tree. He set, catching his breath for a moment, then raised up his prize, the plump rabbit. While savoring his victory he suddenly heard what sounded like something falling through the trees above. He looked up the trunk just in time to see a green scaly face full of teeth coming straight down at him. It let out a hiss as he dove to the side, losing his prize in the process. He turned back to see the creature descending down the trunk and snatching up his dinner in its jaws.

The wingless dragon dropped to the ground and watched him through yellow slits as it swallowed the rabbit whole. Black's heart pounded against his ribs trying to break free and then he was on his feet running again. This time as the prey. He weaved in and out of trees as did the dragon like a great serpent. It may not of had wings but was surprisingly swift on all four squat legs.

Black could feel it closing in. His bare feet kicked up dirt as he pushed everything he had into his legs. It wasn't enough, the calamity behind him closed in. Its jaws hissed as it stretched out for him. Its tongue licked his bare back as it prepared to strike. Black heard a rip as his pants tore off.

Did its teeth catch me, Black thought. No! He was on all fours running. Black didn't understand but he looked down and saw white furry paws. He was pulling away. He could out run it now!

He'd never run so fast or felt so strong. He bounded over some bushes and heard the dragon behind him crashing through but falling behind. He was going to outrun him but then he hit a wall. A staggering rock face reaching fifty feet into the air. He spotted it just as he flew over a row of thorn bushes. He tried to stop but slid sideways slamming into the rocky edifice. His whole right side cried out in pain but he managed to stay on his feet. Turning just in time, he came face to face with the monster after it tore through the thorns. Black considered maybe he could still try and bolt but as he applied pressure to his right front leg he felt it falter. Running was no longer an option. The dragon closed in prepared to strike. Black heard the alien sound of a growl rumble from his own throat.

This is it, Black thought, taking notice of the dragon's jaws, big enough to wrap around his body. Black bared his teeth despite his growing dread.

The dragon drew itself in, poised to strike. Then Black heard a flapping like laundry in the wind and a shadow cast from above as a figure fell from the sky. The man landed with his knee firmly in the would-be killer's back smashing its torso to the ground. The beast was sprawled out and letting loose a painful screech. The man stood up, grabbed the dragon by the tail and with a great feat of strength flung it into the trees.

"Find something else to eat!" The man turned towards Black. He took a step forward and wobbled for a moment on the leg that had dealt the painful blow.

He winced as he picked up a cane that must have plummeted down with him. "I've gotten too old to be jumping off cliffs and tossing wyrms around."

Black realized he was staring at an old man. He might have been 80 years old by the looks of him. He bent over his cane as he walked. His beard was gray and matched the color of his hair pulled back into a ponytail.

He pulled off a backpack and rummaged through as he spoke. "You can change back, boy. I'm not going to hurt you." He pulled out a blanket and threw it on him. He returned his bag to his back and looked at him for a moment. "What are you waiting for?"

Black realized he didn't know how. He tried to speak but it only came out as a pathetic whimper.

"You can't speak," the man muttered to himself. "And you can't turn back can you?"

There was another whimper from Black.

"Maybe I can help you," the man knelt with a crackling of joints and another wince. He reached out and Black recoiled for a moment. "Relax," the man assured him. "It won't hurt, I promise."

He placed his hand on Black's head and a calmness washed over him. "Close your eyes and imagine yourself as you were."

Black pictured his reflection looking back from the surface of a placid lake.

Sensing Black had relaxed a bit the man continued, "Good, now don't just see yourself. Feel what it is like to be you. What it's like to stand up on your own two legs and to reach out with fingers to climb and grip the branches of a tree."

Black could feel it. He clenched his fists tight before opening his eyes. He was naked but human again. The old man stood holding the blanket out to him.

"Cover yourself up boy. Maybe someday you can learn to shift your clothes too." The old man smiled at him.

Black wrapped the blanket around his waist. "Who are you," he asked.

"My name is Mazurus Flannigan." Mazurus gave him a little bow. "The elves told me there was a human boy with a bit of magic in him living savage out here." He raised a bushy eyebrow. "But they failed to mention more than that. I suppose that's common of their folk" He stroked his beard now. "They don't share much with outsiders. For instance, they didn't tell me you had a totem in you."

"A totem?" Black looked confused.

"The wolf spirit inside you. How'd you think you changed like that? But I reckon that's the first time it's happened to you."

Black nodded his head.

"Of course," Mazurus said with a warm smile. "Do you know who your parents are or how you got here?"

Black shook his head.

"Well, how would you like to travel with me? I sense that you've got great potential in you and there's more adventure than what you can find in this forest."

Black thought for a moment. "Could you teach me how to use my totem?"

Mazurus smiled. "Oh, I could teach you a great deal of things."

Black smiled back. "Okay then. M-Mazurus."

"Oh, and how could I forget." Mazurus whacked himself on the head. "So old. What is your name, boy?"

"I've heard the elves call me Black because of my hair." He pointed to his long unkempt mane.

"Well that's only half a name." Mazurus put his hand on his shoulder and studied him for a moment. "For now on you are... Amadeus Black."

Chapter 2

Present

Rinx strolled down the middle of the Bleeding Bazaar. Named for the fact that it existed in Tír na nÓg while also existing in the Earthen Realm and could be easily entered by anyone with a bit of magic in their blood or a special token for those unfortunate enough to be born without magic.

She appeared a bit out of place among the sages, sorcerers, and witches catching a few eyes with her deep crimson hair, red shorts, and white tank top sporting a popular brand's logo. But as out of place was her style, it was what she had trailing behind her that really got the merchants and customers interested. She wore a pair of black fingerless gloves with a shiny metal band across the knuckles and clenched in her right hand dragged a long old chain.

Rinx strutted up to a vendor.

A man with black greasy hair in a purple robe looked from a dusty tome. "What do you ne-" he began to say with an equally greasy voice but stopped. He made a face resembling a rat as he studied the red headed woman for a moment.

Rinx casually put a foot on the edge of the counter and wiped a smudge off the end of her black black and white trainer. The mage studied her further as she leaned in close.

Her right hand was hanging the chain over her shoulder while her left elbow rested on her raised knee.

She gave him her sweetest smile looking up at him with auburn eyes. "Nictus Prothers?"

"Yes, who are you?" Nictus asked, squirming uncomfortably so close to the attractive young woman.

"The name's Rinx Quint," she stated flatly. "And I was sent to drag you before the Guild on suspicion of practicing forbidden blood magic." As she said this an emblem representing her authority from the Guild of Ravens appeared to illuminate on her cheek and then faded away. The emblem, a crescent moon surrounded by five stars, was bestowed upon all members of the Guild and served as a badge.

Nictus recoiled at the sight of the emblem and stumbled back. He mumbled a few words and flicked his hand in Rinx's direction releasing a grapefruit sized fireball. Rinx swung the chain, slamming it into the projectile, turning the flames blue for a moment and scattering sparks to the ground. The stand was cleaved in two by the force of the chain and the discarded embers caught the debris on fire. Rinx grabbed one half of the stand and effortlessly tossed it behind her as she stepped behind the row of merchants. Nictus had a good head start pushing his way past several witches and wizards.

"You're lucky I have orders to bring you back alive," Rinx called after him with a fire in her eye. "Or I'd show you a real fireball!" She waved her hand for all the people to get out of her way as she lined up with the fleeing criminal. She bit her lip and dug her right foot in the ground. In the next moment there was a red blur and Nictus was swatted to the ground by the heavy chain. The chain glowed with blue runes and coiled itself around him.

Rinx rolled Nictus on to his back. Bound, he spat some more incantations at Rinx but nothing happened. Rinx poked him in the forehead.

"Oh, shut up and go to sleep." And at her command the chains glowed again and he was unconscious. His eyes rolled back, closed, and he began drooling in the dirt.

The many onlookers realizing the fight was over went back to their business. Rinx mused at their indifference, They are used to seeing a couple of sorcerers going at it every now and then, you just have to be careful you don't catch a stray spell in the crossfire. She took a deep breath, "Another lovely day at the Bazaar."

Rinx tossed Nictus over her shoulder with ease and began making her way back. She paused when a figure caught her eye perched on a low rooftop.

Rinx used her free hand to shield against the gleaming sun and let a smile slip across her face. "Did you enjoy the show, Deus?"

"Well," Black said as he dropped down brushing his dark hair out of his face at the same time. "I would've jumped in if I thought you needed it."

"I've done pretty well on my own for a while now," she responded, trying and failing to keep a serious face.

Rinx carelessly tossed the unconscious Nictus to the ground and with the same serious look on her face she became rigid and the Guild symbol flushed on her cheek. Black put on his own serious face and snapped to attention raising his left hand, the back of which flashed the same symbol.

They stood for a moment facing each other before Rinx started laughing and ran up and gave Black a hug, lifting him off his feet a couple of inches and setting him back down.

"It's been too long," Rinx said looking up at him with the faintest glisten of a tear in her eye.

"I know, I'm sorry," he paused for a moment, scratching the back of his head. "But look at you. So tan, did they have you scaring off kappas on a beach somewhere?"

"I wish, try hunting down some grave robbers in Egypt. One of them got a hold of an Earthen Realm golem, too."

"Well I bet those old enchanted gloves came in handy for that," he grabbed one of her hands but quickly let go.

"Yeah, super strength is pretty good for tearing a golem's arm off and beating him with it. But god, sand everywhere!"

"I see you got some new shoes too," he nodded down at her feet.

She gave him a smile and in two red blurs moving at a ninety degree angle she was behind him. "Super fast," she laughed.

"And super dangerous," he added. "At those speeds it's difficult to react."

"Don't lecture me on safety. I know you have some rune tattooed on your body somewhere that does the same thing." She made a real serious face at him.

Black raised his eyebrows and a little smirk appeared on his face. "Maybe you can finally keep up with me."

Rinx scowled at him for a moment and swung a right hook to his gut but only hit air. A dark blur lingered in front of her a moment before she turned to face Black who was now directly behind her.

"Thought so," she said with a slightly crazed smile.

Black managed a smile back and put his hands up in surrender. The annoyance faded from Rinx's face and was replaced with a sad distant gaze.

She turned her head as she spoke, avoiding his eyes. "Rumor is that you killed a man. Some normie"

"It was a mercy," Black said, looking down at her with wonder at how someone can be so delicate and powerful at the same time.

And Black knew that she was powerful. There were only a handful of magic folk he had ever encountered in his life with the raw magical talent of Rinx. She had been a prodigy like him and in some aspects of the craft she had certainly surpassed him. Her mastery over the element of fire was an obvious example. She had advanced to the point of not needing an incantation to use fire spells, which finally assured her a position as one of the Elite ranked Battlemages in the Guild. The same as Black but he'd never managed to master an element to that degree. His talents laid elsewhere.

"How much trouble are you in," she said, still not looking at him.

"Just a slap on the wrist, given the circumstances."

"What circumstances?" she demanded.

Black ran his fingers through his hair. "Someone tricked the bastard. They made a soul pact with him in exchange for a demon cursed doll so he could kill off his family.

"Soul pact?" Rinx turned to Black with an inferno burning in her eyes. "Dirty, evil magic. And demons." She spit the last word out like it left a bad taste in her mouth.

"Well it is one of the worst crimes you can commit," he said, surveying the stalls. "Trading for someone's soul and he was no saint, but still," he spoke more to himself.

Rinx mirrored his gaze. "I just don't understand how someone could…" she trailed off. "Well I supposed he didn't know what he was getting himself into."

"Right. He was a rotten man but I couldn't condemn him to that fate. Better to kill him before the one behind it claimed his soul. Let him take his chances with the afterlife. Maybe the gods will have mercy on him." Black let out a sigh. "The Guild was only upset that I didn't bring him back for questioning first, but he didn't know anything. Only a name, 'Mr. B'."

"So are we going to find this 'Mr. B'?" Rinx's voice had an edge of rage to it.

"I'll find him," Black responded, feeling her inner beast tugging at his own.

"Are you going to kill him?" Rinx focused on cooling the rage burning inside her. She had earned a place as a Battlemage because of her skill and love for hand to hand combat but her overwhelming talent at elemental magic could have earned her a position as a Guild Sorcerer. Despite reveling in a good fight she normally tried to avoid taking a life.

Black knew the pain she was feeling and the old wounds that ached at the mention of the dark deed, evoking memories from the Great Calamity all those years ago. He placed a firm hand on her shoulder and gave her a warm smile.

"Of course. But first I need to fish around for some information," he said, explaining why he was in the area.

He decided to pause his investigation just long enough to accompany Rinx back to the Guild of Ravens in the capital city. Black reached for Nictus, threw him over his shoulder, and gestured with a little bow. "After you."

Rinx took the lead looking back over her shoulder to Black. "We'll take the Gate up ahead to Tuatha Dé."

As Rinx and Black made their way towards the end of the Bleeding Bazaar they passed several interesting booths. One had dried lizards hanging from it and another a jar with several different eyes suspended in a pink jelly-like substance. One had a collection of shrunken heads while another of the more popular booths had hanging bird cages filled with pixies. There was a sign hanging next to them that read; CAUTION PIXIES BITE! But what was really drawing a crowd was a large cage containing a dragon the size of a sofa. It had a muzzle chained to its snout so the best it could muster was a few sparks shooting out of its nostrils.

Black watched the dragon as they passed. He noted that the creature was a different breed but almost as big as the first one he'd encountered as a boy. He smiled fondly thinking of the day his master had saved him.

***

Past

"You can't run from every fight Amadeus," Mazurus shouted as he rounded a kick just missing Black's head. "If your opponent continues to pursue you, you must find an opening and attack."

Black couldn't reach Mazurus with his strikes. He was too small and his arms too short. The old man's reach gave him a huge advantage even with him holding back against the boy. Black thought to himself, *If I could get inside his reach then Mazurus would be at the disadvantage.*

Black feigned exhaustion and lowered his guard a bit. Mazurus took the bait.

"Keep those fists up!" He cried as he threw a quick jab at Black's face.

Black dodged inside, taking his master by surprise. Black's arm drew back to strike a blow on his chin when he felt a crack against his nose. Mazurus couldn't get a clean punch with him so close so he shortened his reach by using his elbow. A few drops of blood rocketed from Black's nose as Mazurus followed up with a knee to his belly. He dropped to the ground gasping for breath.

"Way to use your head my boy." Mazurus handed him a rag to wipe the blood from his face. "It's been six months and you've shown great improvement."

"You're still too fast and strong. Why can't you give me a rune like the one you use?" Black sat kneeling on the ground dabbing at his nose.

"You've got to learn to control the strength you already have first." Mazurus walked over to a stump and picked up an old gourd. Black admired the runes tattooed down the old man's bare back. Mazurus pulled a cork out of the gourd and took a drink. He held it out towards his ward but Black shook his head. "These enchanted runes can be dangerous to your body when used improperly. You could tear your own muscles and bones apart. Besides, you've already learned how to take the form of a wolf when you like," he continued. "Now you need to learn how to tap into the strength without changing all the way. You must find a balance."

Black thought it was impossible. The change always happened like tipping over a glass of water. Once it started it went all the way and quickly. What Mazurus wanted was for him to change partially, keeping his human shape, to balance the glass on its edge and hold it.

"Try and lift the log again, my bones are aching and I need a break."

"But I'm exhausted," he whined.

"That's when the beast is most awake." Mazurus sat on the stump taking another drink.

Black stood drenched in sweat and crossed the field they'd been sparring on the edge of the forest where an enormous log rested. He gripped it firmly and attempted to heave it off the ground. All the muscles in his body strained as he tried to lift it. He focused in his mind trying to balance the glass on its edge.

After about an hour of no success the sun was nearly behind the horizon. Mazurus had started a fire and made his way over to him aided by his cane again. "That's enough, son. I have dinner ready. We should get to sleep early tonight. You can work on enchanting some scrolls while I get us breakfast tomorrow and then we're going to meet an old friend of mine."

"Who are we going to see," Black asked, resting against a log.

"Her name is Rhiss Quint. She's going to help you with your totem. She's more experienced with them than I am."

As they ate, Mazurus told Black stories of wicked sorceresses and elven wars fought against goblin clans. And after Black had had his fill of food and his eyelids began to sag. Mazurus muttered some words, the fire went out and they drifted off to sleep.

The next morning they rose with the sun and packed up their sleeping rolls and blankets.

Mazurus headed towards the forest to catch a couple of squirrels for breakfast. "Don't forget to feel the magic flow through you and into the parchment as you copy down the runes," he called back. "And just stick to water spells. Don't want you accidentally burning the forest down."

The spell Black was trying to recreate was supposed to produce a powerful jet of water. According to Mazurus very few magical folk could properly enchant. He boasted his mastery of the craft and believed it the best lesson to pass on to Black. And so, Black's tutelage in magic had commenced. He taught the young pupil that storing spells on scrolls was the first step in learning to enchant. You could use the stored spell instead of a lengthy incantation by flowing a little bit of magic through the object to activate it.

Black finished copying his runes and was ready to give it a try. He held the scroll pointed away from him and focused a little magic into it. He felt the paper become damp in his grasp and saw a few drops of water drip to the ground.

"That's pretty good," Mazurus said, returning with breakfast swinging over his shoulder. "But you need to focus more magic into it. I know you don't have a lot yet but I feel it growing in you every day, so really pour it in there."

"I'll try," Black replied, staring disappointedly at his pathetic enchantment.

Black dug another piece of parchment out of his bag and set to work again while Mazurus cooked their meal. He finished the spell just as Mazurus finished the food.

"Ok, think this is the best one I've ever done," Black boasted.

"Give it a shot," Mazurus said, taking the squirrels off the fire.

Black again pointed away from their camp and focused. A weak stream shot out about two feet from the paper and continued until he cut off his flow of magic.

"I did it," Black gleamed. "It's not much but it's a working spell!"

"Not much? I've seen seasoned mages that couldn't do any better." Mazurus patted him on the shoulder. "Enchanting is a hard skill to learn. Son, you've done a terrific job." Mazurus handed him his food. "Eat up, now. We've got a long march ahead of us."

As they traveled through the day, Mazurus, as was his custom during their hikes, would continue Black's education. He'd point out poisonous berries along the path or pause for a moment to dig up some roots they could chew, giving them energy to march through lunch. He'd point out anything that he thought was relevant to survival in the wilderness. Sometimes he would share stories about rare magical creatures.

"Now, you were lucky the dragon that tried to eat you was only a forest wyrm," he explained while hopping across a small stream and stopping a moment to rub his aching knee after he landed. "If it had been a fire-breather like a red dragon or zmey, then you would have had some real trouble. A Zmey can even have more than one head and boy are they some nasty business."

"Have you seen a zmey?" Black followed behind chewing on another piece of root.

"Oh yes, and let me tell you, once is enough." Mazurus let out a hearty laugh.

"Are all dragons bad?"

Mazurus leaned against a tree for a moment. "No, not all of them. There used to be a group of mages called the Garabonciás. They were able to tame flying serpents called Zomoks. They were supposed to be the most powerful of the magic folk. Had no masters and traveled the world on the back of a Zomok searching for the wicked and bringing justice for those who needed it."

"What happened to the Garabonciás?" Black sat down in some cool grass.

"They were hunted down one by one by a very powerful and evil sorcerer. By the time the others knew what was happening six of their brothers and sisters were dead. The remaining six rallied together to face the murderer."

"Did they beat him," Black asked with wide eyes.

"They did," Mazurus replied.

"But they gave their own lives to do it," came a mysterious voice.

Black jumped to his feet and saw standing in the middle of the path an enormous fox. Mazurus looked casually towards the creature.

"Or so the legend goes," came a voice that emanated from the fox, though its mouth never moved to form the words.

"So it goes," Mazurus echoed.

The fox walked up to Mazurus and spoke again in that unnatural manner. "You two alerted every creature in the forest carrying on like a couple of chattering chipmunks."

"Well I thought we'd be safe in your domain. Besides, haven't you been guarding us for the last hour or so," Mazurus said with a little smile.

Black had never seen a fox look embarrassed before, or maybe it was annoyed. Either way he let a little snicker escape him.

The fox brought its gaze to him. "See just like a chipmunk."

Black became aware that something was familiar about this fox but he wasn't sure what it could be. Before he could think on it anymore the fox took a couple of steps toward him and as it moved it changed into a beautiful woman in a long white dress. Black could see her feet were bare as she advanced upon him.

"When you should be acting like the wolf you are," she said, meeting his eye.

"Amadeus, this is the Red Witch, the sorceress Rhiss Quint." Mazurus made a gesture towards the woman.

Her crimson eyes lingered on him as she gave a slight head nod.

They followed Rhiss through the forest towards her home. Mazurus and her spoke like old friends as they went. They occasionally brought up the name Myoto. Black soon realized that this was Rhiss's husband and from how they spoke of him he must have died. As they made their way Black quietly trailed behind, mesmerized by Rhiss's long apple-red hair and how it fell down to her waist. She had a graceful stride and although she didn't smile much like Mazurus, as they caught up with one another, he could sense that she had a great deal of respect for him.

The day was winding down and Black's stomach was beginning to rumble. The roots he'd eaten earlier in the day were no longer enough to hold back his hunger. His stomach made a loud groaning sound.

"See, he even growls like a wolf," Mazurus laughed.

"Don't worry, boy," Rhiss assured him. "Our home is just ahead and I can already smell dinner in the air."

A few minutes later they stepped into a clearing and Black began smelling a delicious aroma as well. In the clearing was a grass covered hill with windows and a door set into it. Black noticed also, a chimney coming out of the top with a wisp of smoke trailing off into the dimming sky. There was also a tranquil pond next to a little shed.

Rhiss turned towards Black as they approached the house. "Why don't you take a bath in the water over there." She turned back to Mazurus. "No offense, but your companion is filthy."

Black hadn't really considered his hygiene when it was just him and Mazurus but he supposed she was right. He and Mazurus had spent a short time in an elven village where he received the only clothing he had and the rest of their time had been spent in the wilderness. Black was about to apologize but the conversation had moved on.

Mazurus and Rhiss continued on to the house while Black jogged over to the water's edge, anxious to be done so he could have some of whatever smelled so good. He removed his clothes and slipped into the water. He felt right away that the water was very warm and was likely a hot spring. As the evening cooled a fog settled just over the surface of the water.

Black found his muscles relaxing after traveling all day. If not for his appetite he'd have no desire to leave the soothing water.

Suddenly, Black heard a little squeak behind him in the grass. He turned quickly to see a nervous little boy carrying some clothes and a towel.

He looked to be a few years younger than Black and spoke very timidly. "Mother asked me to bring you out some clean clothes. She said your old ones smelled like troll dung and should be burned." The boy never took his eyes off the ground as he spoke. He sat the bundle down and ran back up to the house.

"Uh... thanks," Black shouted to him wondering if he should be insulted.

Mazurus sat at a long table near one of many fireplaces in the house. The night was going to be chilled and Mazurus was happy to have a warm house to spend it in.

Rhiss came from the kitchen and glanced out the window to see her son carrying the clothes to their young guest. "I sent Mhimo out with some clean clothes for the boy and Rinx is still finishing up dinner." She looked from the window to Mazurus. "It's been a long time since the great Mazurus took on an apprentice."

"It's been a long time since the great Mazurus was called great," he said with a smile.

"Those of us who matter still remember what you did," she gave a nod. "But what made you decide to take him on, why not leave him with the elves?"

Mazurus gave her another smile. "You mean aside from all that natural power he has?"

"Yes, aside from that."

They both paused their conversation for a moment as Mhimo scurried into the front room which separated them from the kitchen. Mhimo looked in at his mother and the stranger for a moment and then ran to the kitchen to help his sister.

Mazurus continued. "I'm getting old." his face hardened and he grew serious for the first time since Rhiss had joined them in the forest.

Rhiss pulled out a chair to sit near him. "You've beaten death enough times in your life, why not this time too?" For just a moment she allowed the faintest signs of a smile to show.

"I'll be 153 in two months." Mazurus still had a look of stone. "Even for magic folk that's old." He stared into the fire and continued as the light danced on his face, now making him appear older than ever. "Besides, I don't intend on outliving another student."

Rhiss looked away. "Rinx should be finished with dinner." She stood up and walked back to the window. "And your student is finished as well."

Black left his dirty clothes outside and let himself in. He stood in the doorway for a moment before he heard Mazurus calling from the room to his right.

"We're in here, son. Come in and have a seat."

Black did as he was told and took a seat next to Mazurus. As soon as he sat down his stomach began growling again. As if his stomach had sent out a summons, in walked the boy from earlier carrying a tray with a large loaf of bread set upon it. Behind him was no doubt Rhiss's daughter, made obvious by the color of her ruby red hair. She was carrying a large pot with something that smelled delicious. There were already bowls and silverware on the table and once the food was sat down everyone else took a seat.

They all took turns filling their bowls. Rhiss and Mazurus sat at opposite ends of the table. Rhiss's daughter sat across from Black. Mazurus helped himself to the contents of the pot first.

"What are we having for dinner," Mazurus asked.

Rinx answered. "Rabbit stew and I baked some bread too."

"That sounds great," Mazurus replied. "Rinx, do you remember the last time I saw you?" He spoke as he tore away a chunk from the bread loaf.

"No, not really," she said as she got some stew for herself. "But mother has told me stories about you."

"Well, I suppose you were only about three." Mazurus looked at Mhimo who seemed to shrink closer to Rhiss. "And you were only a couple of months old."

Rinx took a big bite of stew and said, "Mother says you and father used to go to the Earthen Realm and that you fought some vampires there." She then focused her attention on Black and gave him a scowl. "So who's this kid? Is he your servant or something?"

Rhiss gave her a fiery look. "Have some manners, Rinx. That's Mazurus's apprentice. And you're going to be helping him learn how to use his totem properly."

Rinx made a disgusted face and opened her mouth to speak but thought better of it and remained silent.

Black was also put off by this, wondering how this girl could help him with his totem. She didn't look any older than him and he'd thought Rhiss would be the one to instruct him.

"That's correct," Mazurus confirmed. "Black is struggling to use his totem's power properly."

"That's easy," Rinx said, holding back her laughter.

"Well," Rhiss cut in. "Since you just learned to control yours you should be able to give him some guidance. Easy."

Rinx's face turned red at the last comment. She didn't speak another word for the rest of dinner. Once it was over Black was feeling quite full and ready for a good night's sleep.

Mhimo showed Mazurus and Black to a spare bedroom. The room's fireplace was already stacked with timber. Mhimo silently crouched down in front of the fireplace and with his palm out made three attempts at some incantation that resulted in little more than a small wisp of smoke rising from the logs.

Mazurus put his hand on the child's shoulder. "Let me give it a try."

Mhimo stepped back and Mazurus extended his hand towards the logs and repeated the same spell. There was a crackle as the logs erupted into flames.

"Well, I'm sure you had them warmed up for me," Mazurus said with a wink.

There was only one small bed in the room so Black began to make a spot on the floor after Mhimo left but Mazurus stopped him.

"You can have the bed, son." Mazurus looked back as he walked out of the room. "I still have some matters to discuss with Rhiss so I'll be up late.

Mazurus entered the dining room aided by his cane. Rhiss was waiting for him, staring out the window again. He took a seat at the table silently. Rhiss turned from the window to speak. "So why else have you come here?"

Mazurus looked at her solemnly. "Have some matters to take care of in the Earthen Realm."

"And you'd like to leave the boy here," Rhiss chimed in.

"He'll stand out too much there and we wouldn't be able to get much training in. Besides, he could learn a lot from being here." Mazurus laid his cane across his lap.

"You want him to learn elemental magic, too?"

Mazurus nodded his head. "He's a natural with enchantments and hand to hand combat, but I'd like him to be well rounded. I want him to join the academy with Rinx. They look to be about the same age."

Rhiss made a bitter face. "I haven't decided if I want her to go to Tuatha Dé's academy yet. Too much politics. Too much corruption."

"But that's the world we live in, Rhiss. Better they learn how to defend themselves against it at an early age. Besides," he smiled. "You seem to have benefited from their teachings."

"Maybe, but they still have almost two years before they are old enough." She said with a faraway look.

Mazurus tapped his cane on the floor. "Well they still have a lot to learn. You know how competitive it can be. They can't be too prepared."

***

Black awoke late the next morning. He rolled over and gently opened his eyes to see Mhimo silently standing over him. Black sprang from his bed. "What's going on? Why are you watching me sleep like that?"

Mhimo shuffled his feet a bit. "Your breakfast is cold and Rinx said that if you didn't get up in fifteen minutes she was going to eat it and that was thirteen minutes ago."

Black stood in just some baggy pants staring at Mhimo for a moment and then he bolted out the door. He popped his head back in the room and said, "Thanks, Mhimo." Then he was gone again.

Black found his food waiting for him and intact. There were two hard boiled eggs, a piece of bread with a small jar of honey, and some dried apple chips.

Black dug in. His mouth was stuck together with bread and honey when Mhimo walked in with a pitcher of water and a wooden cup.

"Thank you." Black tried to say as Mhimo poured the water. After he had taken a big, cool gulp Rinx walked in and sat down across from him.

"Alright Deus, Mother says I have to teach you how to use your totem but I have my own stuff I have to do so I'll give you some pointers and then you're on your own."

Black finished one of his eggs. "My name is Amadeus, but I'd rather you called me Black."

Rinx waved her hand. "I'd rather call you Deus and since you're my student that's what I'm going to call you now."

Before Black could even respond Rhiss spoke from the doorway. "You'll be learning from him, too." Black hadn't even heard her come in. "Mazurus taught him how to use martial combat. He'll be teaching you those skills."

Rinx had a grin that swept across her face. "Finally!" She erupted and turned to Black. "You really know how to fight?"

Black nodded.

"Yes! Maybe you won't be so useless after all."

Black looked around the room for a moment. "Where is Mazurus?"

They both looked to Rhiss for an answer. "He had some business he needed to attend to in the Earthen Realm," she said. "He'll be returning in spring to collect you. Until then he wants you to continue practicing your enchantments." She motioned towards a bookshelf. "We even have a book of basic enchantments you can use."

Black looked hurt for a moment. "Why didn't he tell me or say goodbye?"

Rhiss seemed to soften her usually hardened expression. "He did, but you were sleeping and he thought it was important that he took care of his business right away. He'll be back before you know it." She forced a smile and then left the room.

Rinx fixed Black with a curious look. "I wonder what business he had to take care of so suddenly?"

"He didn't tell me anything," Black replied.

"Perhaps he's fighting some more vampires!" Rinx had that look of excitement back. "Come on! Let's go do totem stuff and then you can start showing me how to fight."

They trained every day for a month. The first half of the day was devoted to totem training. Rinx proved to actually be a great teacher and could explain things in ways that Mazurus could not. After a week Black could speak in his wolf form. Rinx taught him how the change was more of a fusion than a transformation. He was joining his power with that of the wolf spirit, so he was able to command the spirit to speak for him. Since the spirit is ethereal in nature and only manifests itself physically through him, the voice appears disembodied. She explained that the totems are guardian spirits that watched over certain families and are passed down through bloodlines but were rare.

After lunch they would spar in martial combat. Black was surprised with how eager Rinx was to fight. She had some skill.

"Mother used to forbid me to learn any martial arts or physical techniques," she said between heavy breaths during one of their first sessions. "But I found one of father's books on battlemage combat and taught myself a few things when she wasn't around."

Black had reservations about fighting a girl at first, but soon he had to put those aside. Rinx had realized early on that Black was holding back on her and had punished him for it. He was just going through the motions and before long realized that Rinx was getting a lot quicker and her kicks and punches a lot harder. Before he knew it, it was taking everything he had to defend himself. That's when he realized through the flurry of attacks that her hair looked thicker with white tips at the ends and sticking up from the top of her head were two triangular fuzzy ears with the same white tips. Rinx dropped and swept his feet clean out from under him.

As he was sprawled out on the ground Rinx had made her point. "That's what happens when you hold back on your opponent!"

Rhiss would watch them practice from the window and occasionally she would come outside and silently spectate. Black also noticed that she would mysteriously disappear for a day every two weeks or so. Black asked Rinx about her mother's strange behavior.

"I don't know what she does out there," she admitted. "She's been doing that for as long as I can remember. What do you think Mhimo?"

Mhimo always seemed to be around but was so easy not to notice. He shook his head. "I don't know anything," he said quietly.

"Do you want to spar with us a bit, Mhimo," Black asked. "You're always watching, why don't you join?"

Mhimo's face turned red. He quickly shook his head and ran away.

"He's not very good at that kind of stuff," Rinx said as they watched him run off into the woods. "Someday he'll find something he's talented at." She looked a bit sad and distant.

In the evenings Black continued practicing his enchantments. If it was raining he would even practice some fire enchantments outside. He'd learned how to consistently enchant parchments to create some weak spells, but nothing too intimidating, a squirt of water or a few little flames that quickly died.

At the end of the month Black finally had some success. Rinx had been bragging. She had triumphantly turned her clothes with her body into a fox. "Well, at least one of us is good at using their totem," she beamed as she threw a kick at Black's head. She continued to assault him while still partially changed. He struggled to keep up with her enhanced speed and agility. "If only you could get some control over your totem, maybe this would be more of a challenge for me."

Black continued to defend trying to anticipate her moves. Suddenly all the noise around him faded into silence followed by a booming voice. At first he didn't know where it was coming from. As Rinx continued pummeling him he listened.

"Stop letting that kit push you around!" The voice growled inside his mind. There was a second voice too that Black couldn't make out. It sounded muffled and far away. "Feel my strength bleeding through your muscles," the first commanded.

Who are you, Black demanded.

"You already know me," the voice responded.

The name came to Black without him needing to hear it. Fenrir.

"As you say."

Who is the other I hear?

"He is not important," Fenrir roared. "Fight now!"

Black could see another one of Rinx's kicks flying towards his head. He grabbed her by the ankle and with an unfamiliar swiftness and strength he kicked her other foot out from under her. With his grip still tight on her ankle he flung her to his left with ease.

Rinx hit the ground and tumbled right back to her feet but she wore an expression of shock. She stared at Black. His eyes had an icy glow and his dark hair was white as snow. "You did it," she gasped. "You've taken full control of your totem!"

Black gave her a fanged grin. "Looks like I'll be able to take it easy on you again."

"Oh no," she said. "Now we can get serious."

Chapter 3

Past

Rinx was true to her word. The sparring had intensified. Each kick and punch had enough power to splinter wood and probably bone if delivered to a normal human. Black had her beat in pure strength and endurance and his technique was disciplined and focused, but her agility combined with an unorthodox fighting style that was not above sneak attacks, made her a worthy challenge for him. Since he had mastered his totem injuries healed much quicker. Black would go to bed bruised and cut up and awake the next day with hardly a mark if any at all.

Nearly two weeks later he'd learned to turn his clothes with his body. Rinx looked at Black as a snow-white wolf void of tattered cloth and declared.

"I'm impressed, Deus," Rinx said with a look that reflected it. "There is nothing more I can teach you."

That proved to not be true. The very next morning as they ate breakfast Rhiss sat down to join them.

"You've made quick progress with your totem mastery," Rhiss said with her usual stony expression. Her eyes followed a wisp of steam as it rose from her tea cup and vanished. "Rinx, I'd like you to begin teaching him elemental magic this morning before sparring."

Black expected Rinx to protest but she remained silent.

Rhiss continued. "However, first I would like to determine if you have any sort of affinity towards one element or another."

"What do you mean," Black questioned.

Rhiss took a drink of her tea and Rinx spoke up to answer for her. "Some people have natural talent with one element over others. Like with mother and I ours is fire and our totem happens to have an affinity for fire as well, so while we can use other elements, we are especially good with fire."

"It comes easier for us," Rhiss took over again. "Our affinity for fire may even come as a result of our totem. But even people without a totem can have an affinity and become extremely powerful."

"Do you know what master Mazurus's affinity is," Black asked curiously.

Rhiss looked away drawn into her memories. "He seemed to always lean towards lightning. Quite difficult. But he had clever ways of making it easy." Black thought he'd almost caught a smile on Rhiss's face for a moment.

Black's mind drifted back to when he first heard Fenrir's voice. "If my totem is a wolf then what do you think my affinity will be," Black asked, beginning to get excited.

Rhiss watched another wisp of steam fade away. "Well, it's not guaranteed that you'll possess the same affinity, but the wolf spirit is a guardian of the forest so it would command the power of the earth and life that grows from it."

Black let a smile spread across his face. "Ok," Black said. "What do I have to do to find out?"

Rhiss finished the last of her tea and stared across the table with dulled eyes and after a moment of silence she spoke. "When I first met you I was able to see your totem was a wolf immediately because it was so close to the surface of who you are, but to see this I must go much deeper. The tea that I just finished was brewed with a special kind of toadstool that allows me to accomplish this." Rhiss turned her head as if she caught something in the corner of her eye but then stopped herself. She appeared to refocus and continued. "All you need to do is relax and don't fight me. Just let me glide through like a spectre."

Black nodded his head as Rhiss reached across the table and clenched both his hands.

"Close your eyes and relax," Rhiss said as she settled back in her chair. Rinx watched wide eyed and silent.

Rhiss projected herself into Black's mind and beyond. She resembled a tiny ember falling through the currents of raw magic. Finally, she came to rest among the blue and white streams of ether before an enormous gate. Rhiss heard a growl from behind her. It was the great form of Fenrir circling around Rhiss, stopping between her and the gate.

"You do not belong here," the wolf snarled.

Rhiss took a moment to marvel at the enormous white beast. Its fur had the ethereal qualities of smoke and seemed to twist and trail off into nothing. Rhiss gathered and willed herself into a form she was more familiar with. She resembled her usual slender and pale reflection but her hair and gown were rolling flames. They danced with red, yellow, orange, and the occasional blue.

"Stand down guardian," Rhiss commanded. "Your master has given me safe passage." Rhiss stared unflinching at the monster.

Fenrir flashed an enormous set of dagger sized teeth at her and then gave a snort.

"I suppose he has," Fenrir said as he stepped out of the way. His silvery eyes flashed and the mighty gate released. "But you are watched," Fenrir said with a frightening grin as Rhiss glided through the opening.

Rhiss continued on her journey making her way to the core of Black's magic. The magical currents were growing thicker and she could feel a kind of pressure pushing in on her as she got closer. It was as if she was sinking to the bottom of an ocean. The flames that had been so defiantly blazing from

Rhiss shrunk the deeper she went. Then she saw it. It was the source, a giant swirling ball of glowing blue magic with silver streaks. As Rhiss approached it she suddenly became aware of another presence. Before her sprang into existence a giant black eye. Rhiss did not recognize this as the wolf spirit she'd previously encountered.

"Who blocks my path," Rhiss demanded.

"We are many," came a harmony of disembodied voices speaking as one. The eye twitched and moved as if in an invisible socket. There was no white, just black with a slightly darker pupil. "We are the messenger, the watcher, and the old man."

"What is your name," Rhiss demanded again. She had not expected to encounter something like this but she knew she was speaking to a second totem, something she didn't think possible. She'd never heard of anyone possessing two totems.

"We are many," the voice repeated. "And so are our names. We have been named Trickster, Morrighan, Huginn, Muinnin, and Death."

"Corvus?" Rhiss asked with awe in her voice.

"Yes," the voice replied. "We have been named Corvus and that name does suit us."

Rhiss remembered her task. "I must pass to determine your master's elemental affinity if he possesses one." Rhiss said as she began to press on, but was stopped by an intense magical pressure that made her shutter and her flames nearly extinguished.

"The boy has far to go," Corvus bellowed. "Before we call him master. But we will protect him as we protect ourselves. You may come no closer."

Rhiss could feel that her own power in this place was draining quickly. "I only seek to know what his magical affinity is." Rhiss said calmly.

"To aid our vessel we will share our knowledge." As soon as Corvus finished its sentence a mass of black feathers exploded out from behind the unblinking eye forming two giant wings. The wings began beating powerfully, snuffing out Rhiss's flames and carrying her swiftly back to her own body.

Rhiss now back in the dining room was staring across the table at Black. Her eyes were wide for a moment as she absorbed everything she had witnessed.

Rinx had never seen her mother make such an expression and she hesitated before she spoke. "Mother? Does he have an affinity?" Rinx and Black waited with anticipation as Rhiss's usual emotionless veil swept back across her face.

"Wind," Rhiss said plainly. "His affinity is for wind. A rare element but not as rare as lightning or quite as difficult." Rhiss stood up and stared into her empty cup on the table for a moment. Then she looked as if she had come to some kind of decision. "Rinx, fetch me the shears from the kitchen, we're going to Tuatha Dé. Amedeus needs a haircut before we leave."

Rinx looked ecstatic and cried out as she ran to the kitchen. "Tuatha Dé! I can't wait!"

Minutes later Rhiss stood outside cutting Black's long hair off skillfully, leaving just enough on top to lay down. Black was brushing himself off when Rinx brought out brown cloaks for each of them. The air had been getting cooler with the approaching winter and they would need something to keep the chill out. Rhiss walked over to Mhimo standing in the doorway to the house.

"He's going to be missing out," Rinx said as Rhiss spoke with Mhimo. "He doesn't like crowds very much, but who wouldn't want to visit Tuatha Dé.?" Rinx looked at Black with excitement. "Have you ever been there?"

"No," Black admitted. "I've never even heard of it. What is it?"

Black had never seen such a look of shock on Rinx's face before. Her mouth hung open until she finally spoke. "I can understand not having ever been there since you grew up near the elves but not knowing what it is... Mazurus never told you about the city of Tuatha Dé?"

"He'd mentioned that there were some large cities in Tír na nÓg and even bigger ones in the Earthen Realm but I don't think he ever mentioned a Tuatha Dé by name."

"It's the capital of Tír na nÓg," Rinx explained. "And it's full of all kinds of people. Like wizards and witches, sometimes elves and goblins and all kinds of magical creatures. It's where the Academy is. Where you can start training for different professions."

"So why are we going?" Black asked.

"Because I have some business there and it would do you good to have a break from your training," Rhiss said as she passed them and made her way towards the forest edge. "It should only take us about two hours with the aid of our totems." And with that Rhiss changed into her fox form and bolted ahead of them. Rinx and Black gave each other a quick look and then did the same.

Despite how large Rhiss was, she moved gracefully through the forest. Rinx looked like a miniature version of her mother trailing Rhiss's shadow and Black kept pace behind them both. He enjoyed the run and reminisced on his days living in the forest near the elves. He now moved with a swiftness he never knew in those days but it all felt so familiar. The cool air blew through his fur and the changing seasons left the trees painted red, orange, and yellow. Black took in the sight and felt at home.

Finally they came upon a clearing and in the center stood a shiny stone of ebony. The stone was intimidating, looming over them at ten feet tall. As Rhiss stepped into the clearing she stood up taking her human shape again. Rinx and Black followed behind, shifting back as well.

"What is it," Black asked.

Rinx started but Rhiss spoke first. "The Gates are points of old magic that are bound to the Earth itself. They allow someone with magic to travel between them almost instantly.

They also allow a person to move between Tír na nÓg and the Earthen Realm freely without any complicated rituals or spells that most people don't have the power to perform anyways. As for Tuatha Dé, it's the physical seat of power for the Guild of Ravens. It has a large fortress that serves as training grounds for new recruits, center for magical politics, and academy for furthering science and the magical arts." She turned quickly towards Rinx and Black. "Also, it is extremely dangerous and full of corrupt, power-hungry vultures, so keep your eyes sharp and do not trust anyone." Rhiss gave them both a sharp look and then continued towards the Gate.

The two children watched as Rhiss placed one of her slender hands on the stone. The wind was blowing gently, moving her cloak around. Golden leaves rained down upon them in a steady flow from the surrounding trees. One of the star shaped leaves caught in Rhiss's fiery hair as she turned towards the children again.

"Rinx, hold his hand going through the Gate. You'll have to pull him through since he's never been to Tuatha Dé, like I did for you and Mhimo your first times." Rhiss addressed Black. "Once you've been there once you can always travel back." Rhiss placed her hand on the Gate, pushed through and disappeared, leaving behind what looked like a ripple across a surface of black water.

Rinx took Black by the hand and stepped towards the Gate. He had taken countless blows from this hand but only at that moment realized how soft it really was. He squeezed it firmly.

Rinx looked back at him and said, "You don't need to be nervous."

"I'm not," Black responded.

"Do you have any questions before we go," Rinx asked, returning his gaze.

"Just one," Black said as they stood still holding hands. "Who is the Guild of Ravens?"

Rinx shook her head as she turned towards the gate. "You don't know anything," she muttered as she pulled Black through.

As Black glided through the ebony stone there was a shimmer and a familiar feeling tugged at him for a moment and then he was standing outside again holding Rinx's hand and staring at five other Gates. There were three on each side of a brick road. The road was gray like the sky and led under a large archway with enormous stone walls on either side.

"The great fortress city of Tuatha Dé," Rinx said, dropping Black's hand.

There were many people coming and going. Some used the Gates, others entered the fortress, and a few moved away from the city, past the Gates, following the road to a group of houses and buildings gathered around a winding river. They wore many different styles. Some were dressed in robes and cloaks made from all different materials. Some wore turbans and masks, elaborate jewelry, armor, and a few even wore modern clothes from the Earthen Realm.

Black had never seen so many people in one place before and as they ran to catch up to Rhiss, Black realized he'd also never seen a structure this big before. They entered under the archway and an enormous city stood before them. Off in the distance stood what looked like a castle.

They paused in a courtyard just inside the walls with several streets branching off in different directions as people and the occasional elf or goblin, hurried about them.

Rhiss set her gaze on Rinx and Black. "There's an individual I need to speak with," Rhiss said as she raised her eyebrows and focused her attention on Rinx. "I want you two to stay in the square until I return." Rhiss turned to walk away but spun back around. "And don't talk to anyone." Rinx and Black both nodded and she went on her way down one the street.

"Let's go look at some of the shops," Rinx squealed with a huge grin on her face.

They both hurried over to a stall that had several dead animals hanging from it and bowls and jars filled with all manner vile things. On the other side of the counter stood a hooded figure with long gray strands of hair hanging down. Black thought he saw a twitch from the figure as he and Rinx were examining the wares but paid it little attention. He found a jar sitting next to the stall with a dead snake coiled in it. The jar was filled with a brown liquid. It was large, as was the snake that was decorated with black and white stripes. Black looked back to see Rinx smelling a shriveled salamander. He returned to examining the snake and noticed that its eyes were open. The eyes were bright red with black slits and were clearly visible despite the brown preserving liquid in the jar. He leaned in closer to get a better look at them.

Suddenly the hooded person threw back their head and inhaled sniffing at the air. Rinx and Black jumped to attention as the figure's hood fell off and a withered old woman continued sniffing in their direction. Her left eye was milky and surrounded by burn scars and her hair was stringy and patchy.

"Y'two gotta quite o'bit o' power in yo? Yessss." The old witch said as she kept sniffing the air. She licked her cracked lips and spoke again, "How'a 'bout y'two trade a spell wit me. Sharla give yo a powrful spell dat make yo into great sorcers." She licked her lips again and smiled revealing a row of worn and broken teeth.

"Great sorcerers don't use the kind of spells you're peddling, witch," came a voice from behind Rinx and Black.

Both of them turned to see a boy about their age smiling at them. He had ebony curls that nearly hid his dark eyes and he wore a brown leather overcoat with green trim that fitted his small stature neatly as it descended to just below his knees.

He stood with his hands behind his back and spoke with a slight accent. "She was imprisoned a while back for draining magic from students at the academy." Rinx and Black looked back at Sharla to see her pulling her hood back up and returning to the lifeless state they had found her in.

The boy continued, "my father gave her that scar on her eye." The smile had left him for a moment. "She tried to hit him with an acid spell. Some of it bounced off his Aegis and back into her ugly face." The boy grimaced at his own words.

Rinx stepped away from the stall. "I've read of the Aegis," Rinx said, turning to Black. "They are shields that nullify the arcane arts. They are worn by members of the Guild who don't have magic."

"Very good, but we technically are independent from the Guild," the boy said with a nod and a smile back on his face. "My name is Damascus Mageese." And with his arms still behind his back he gave a slight bow.

"My name's Rinx," she replied.

Black nodded back to Damascus. "Amadeus Black."

***

Present

"As an Elite Battlemage you answer directly to us!" Boomed the voice from one of twelve robed figures.

They stood before Rinx on top of a platform at the end of a long corridor lined with stone pillars. The corridor's only illumination came from lanterns filled with blue flames that hung from the ceiling.

"So any assignment given to you is important," continued the figure.

Rinx had been staring at the checkered floor but now raised her head. "Forgive me, Premier Geist, but I was not questioning its importance only pointing out that it did not require the attention of an Elite rank. I earned my rank by being one of the best Battlemages the Guild has in the field and I feel that my talents are wasted on these… amateurs."

Rinx noted that one of the thirteen seats was empty. "I see Premier Barnabas is absent again."

Premier Valen spoke up, "yes, Barnabas has been quite ill lately."

"None of your concern, Rinx," chimed a smoky projection of Premier Roth. He stood as the center member of the thirteen. "What we thirteen do is none of your concern." Roth had a bird-like face. His eyes were narrow and his pointed nose looked like a beak. Although his skin was wrinkled and his hair was gray, like most people with magic, it was difficult to determine his age.

Valen smiled as the blue light reflected off his smooth head and jolly cheeks. "Oh, I think having concern for our health falls well under her duties as one who has sworn to protect us and the people." Valen smiled at her again warmly.

Roth glared at Valen.

"I believe we've strayed from the matter at hand," an elegant voice broke the tension.

Roth turned his gaze to a masked woman seated to his left. The elaborately decorated mask hid the upper half of her face and had tinted glass over the eyes so that they were obscured from sight.

"And to speak of 'wasted talents' when you threw away your chance in the Sorcerer's division is laughable," the woman continued. "Like mother, like daughter I suppose."

Rinx felt her face flush with anger but she bit her tongue.

The woman paused for a moment anticipating a retort and then continued when it didn't come. "But again we stray from the matter at hand. Roth, can we proceed with what we discussed?"

The smoky image of Roth projected from a jewel embedded at his feet and its match hung around his neck. These allowed him to attend his meetings remotely and each Premier owned one. It was rare to see all the Premiers physically in attendance.

"Of course. You are correct, Margret, thank you." Roth spoke while offering a respectful nod to the masked woman. "We are not here to chastise you. On the contrary we wanted to reward you for your loyal work." Roth cupped his hands together. "We are giving you three months leave and..." Roth dragged out the last word, obviously pleased with himself. "Upon your return we will place you on freelance status."

Rinx was speechless and realized for a moment that her jaw was hanging open.

Valen spoke next. "Yes a long time coming but a well earned honor."

Rinx regained her composure. "Yes, an honor indeed. Thank you Premiers."

Geist gave Rinx a sneer. "So you can choose who is fit for your talents but don't forget," Geist raised a sausage-like finger. "That you are still at the Guild's disposal should we call upon you."

Rinx had forgotten her anger. "Apologies Premier Geist, if I was out of line earlier."

Geist simply folded his arms over his burly chest.

"This offers you autonomy. Something that only a handful of Battlemages have. Do not disappoint us," Margret said sternly.

"Very well," Roth rubbed his hands together. "If there is nothing else then I believe we can adjourn."

The other premiers echoed his suggestion.

"Then we are adjourned." Roth announced and his image faded away.

The handful of Premiers in attendance shuffled off the stage to adjacent chambers but Valen gave Rinx a wave as he approached her.

"A moment of your time my dear," he said with a pleasant smile and the blue light still dancing across his round bald head. "A very eventful meeting today."

Rinx relaxed, "I'd agree. I hadn't expected this."

"Well I can imagine that since they aren't the friendliest bunch," he chuckled.

"Premier Morgu really has it out for me."

"Margret is just a little sore you didn't join the Sorcerers. You know she has a special interest in them." He rubbed his smooth chin. "Geist is admittedly a bit rough around the edges and Roth…well he's a politician through and through."

Rinx replied, "They say that about you." but she immediately thought better of these words. "Sorry." She felt at a loss.

Valen simply laughed, "Is that what they say? Well then maybe it's true then."

Rinx couldn't help but smile.

"So my dear, how do you plan to spend your time off?"

Rinx ran a hand through her hair. "I'm not certain. I suppose I could spend some time at home. See my mother."

Valen nodded his head. "Yes, that sounds like a great idea. I understand that it has been quite some time since you've had a holiday and even longer since you visited your lovely mother. Oh, she must be so lonely living like a hermit."

"It's true," she agreed. "It has been too long."

"Well it's settled then," he exclaimed. "When do you plan to leave?"

"Well, I have grown tired of this stinking city. I just need to sort some things out this evening and then I could be on my way tomorrow," She confirmed. "You've always been kind to me, Premier Valen. Thank you."

"I suppose that it's just that you remind me so much of my own daughter." He grew suddenly somber. "But anyways, remember to relax and enjoy this time away. I'm sure there will be plenty of excitement on your return." Valen gave a little bow and took his leave.

***

Rinx returned to her modest apartment to find Black waiting. He had been leaning next to the door, arms across his chest, and head drooped as if he was in deep meditation.

"Oh, what a pleasant surprise," Rinx displayed her most charming smile. "To what do I owe this honor?"

Black stepped away from the wall. "Sorry if you're busy but I thought you might be able to help me out."

"Busy?" Rinx feigned a little dance. "My sweet Deus, I'm on holiday." She paused with a big grin on her face. "for three months," she said as she resumed her dance.

"Oh lucky you." Black couldn't help but smile to himself at the performance.

"Aren't I? And when I return from my time off." she leaned in close to Black shutting her eyes in another enormous grin. "I will be resuming as a freelancer." She finished her dance with a spin and arms wide.

Black clapped his hands together. "Well bravo! I should be congratulating you then."

"Save your congratulations," she responded with a shake of her head. "We should be celebrating." She put her hands on her hips. "But first tell me this favor you needed." She turned toward the door and as she gripped the handle several magical locks responded to her distinct touch and could be heard releasing from the other side.

"Well perhaps it can wait until tomorrow," he said as he followed her into her apartment.

"Nonsense," She said with a dismissive hand wave over her shoulder. She pulled two tumblers from a cabinet and a bottle from below. "Besides," she continued. "I've decided to go home tomorrow." They exchanged a glance and Rinx poured their drinks.

"I understand." he watched the liquid fill their glasses. "Well it's just information really. I met with an informant of mine to try and dig up something on this 'Mr. B.'"

Rinx corked the bottle and set it down on the table bringing her full attention to him. "And?"

"Well, my informant hadn't heard of him. But he told of someone peddling cursed objects who was recently operating in China until a couple of weeks ago when he relocated to the Bleeding Bazaar."

She put it together before he needed to say it. "And you can make cursed objects using blood magic. Our peddler is possibly that worm Prothers."

Black nodded his head. "My informant called him by name."

"Well I don't know much about him. It was a straightforward assignment. Bring him in. I was given a description and the location of his stall. Supposedly he had been witnessed by several individuals performing blood magic but I wasn't given any names or privy to any information on his prosecution." She sighed. "Pretty standard for those who aren't on freelance status. They say jump and you say how high."

"I remember," Black said, running his fingers through his hair.

She cocked an eye at him. "The timing on this seems too good."

"It does."

She rubbed her bare arm as if a sudden chill had come over her. "This is what I'm going to do." She reached for her glass and he did the same. "Before I leave tomorrow we can go ask him a few questions ourselves."

Black prepared a protest but could see from the look in her eyes that she would not be deterred from coming with him. "Sounds like a plan," he sighed as he raised his glass. "To your reassignment."

She touched her glass to his. "To catching this 'Mr. B' bastard."

They both threw back their drinks.

Chapter 4

Past

"Damascus!"

The three children turned to see a man in the middle of the street with the same dark features, matching attire of brown leather with green highlights, and arms folded behind his back. He was accompanied by two other men. One in a similar uniform and another in plain clothes pulling a cart. The two uniformed men carried short swords on their hips and one had a silver buckler strapped to his left arm.

"Come boy." Called the man with his arms behind his back as the other man eyed Rinx and Black with suspicion.

"Yes father." Damascus answered and turned back to the other children. "Well it was a pleasure meeting you both." he said with another bow before he turned and ran to his father.

Damascus's father placed a hand on the boy's head as he took his place by his side. The man gave a quick glance between the other two children and Sharla. It was a cold expression he wore. "Let's go," he commanded and they were on their way.

As the third man passed by pulling the cart they could see that it was full of an assortment of boxes, bags, jars, and crates. Some contents were visible. Dried husks, plants, mushrooms, and the like.

"What a strange boy," Rinx stated.

Black nodded in agreement. "His dad looked important."

"There was an image on that man's shield and etched in the leather on their backs." She squinted her eyes recalling the image. "It looked like some kind of animal with a snake in its mouth."

"I hadn't noticed," Black admitted.

The rest of their time passed without incident. They strolled the streets examining the different shops and stalls. Rinx spent a considerable amount of time in a store stocked with clothes from the Earthen Realm.

After a few hours of exploring they heard a familiar voice call to them.

"Children."

They turned from whatever knick-knack held their attention to find Rhiss standing before them.

"I have completed my errands. We'll return home now," she informed them.

"But mother can't we stay a bit longer," Rinx pleaded.

Rhiss barely gave her a glance. "We still have a couple hours journey ahead of us and Mhimo will have dinner started before we arrive."

Both the children realized at that moment that they hadn't eaten since breakfast and were awfully hungry.

There was no debate after that and they began their way back home. The trip back through the Gate and the run to their home was uneventful and they arrived home with stomachs roaring.

Mhimo had begun dinner as expected and the children gingerly assisted to speed things along. Rinx and Black shared the events of their day with the younger child while they enjoyed their dinner. Mhimo listened timidly and his eyes grew wide as they described their experience with Sharla the witch. Rhiss sat quietly in her own thoughts while the children laughed and ate their fill.

After they had begun to slow down and were near ready for bed Rhiss spoke up. "Tomorrow Amadeus will begin learning how to cast his first wind spell."

Black and Rinx shared excited glances.

"You will continue your sparring in the morning for two hours after breakfast. After that Amadeus, I'd like you to continue the lessons Mazuras instructed you on for the rest of the morning." She turned to Rinx. "You will continue your lessons as well. You can barely get a flame going so we'll need to be a bit more hands on with you."

Rinx appeared offended quickly followed by excitement again.

"And in the afternoon I will be guiding you," she continued looking at Black.

***

The two children continued their studies day in and day out with few exceptions. Black found some slight improvement with his enchanted scrolls. His water spell produced a steady stream that was useful in extinguishing some fires caused by Rinx. He started working on a wind enchantment that he was quickly picking up but so far only amounting to a short but pleasant breeze with only enough force to blow your hair back. Not really useful at all. The earth enchantment when he placed it on the ground would create what resembled a gopher mound a couple feet in front of him and his fire enchantment normally resulted in a few sparks and a hole burnt through the center of the parchment.

Rinx had been able to improve her ability to start fires by reciting an incantation and focusing on the object. Anything that wasn't easily flammable still remained impossible for her to ignite. She had also commenced learning an incantation to produce a fireball about the size of walnut in her hand. She could throw this but it normally fizzled out into a handful of sparks falling to the ground before it got too far. However, from a distance of a few feet she was able to knock over a small log on occasions leaving behind the slightest hint of a singe mark.

Black's ability in incantations still left much to be desired. Since discovering this affinity for wind magic he had focused on learning the same incantation equivalent to what he was using in his enchantment but so far he'd failed to produce the slightest breath of wind.

Rhiss assured him that it was understandable that he would find it challenging since he'd had no previous guidance in incantations prior but Black could not help but feel a sense of defeat every day he failed to produce the tiniest effect. Even Rinx took some pity on him, hardly teasing him at all.

The days wore on and the autumn leaves were soon hidden by a layer of fluffy snow. While outside belonged to the cold, inside was warmer than ever.

"In response to your persistence," Rhiss spoke with an air of annoyance directed at Rinx. "I will allow you the next few days off from your studies to celebrate Saturnalia."

Rinx exploded in excitement and even Mhimo let out a squeal of joy.

"You can spend today setting up the decorations. Rinx, you are in charge of gathering and decorating the inside of the house. Amadeus, you can assist Mhimo in hanging the lanterns outside." In a rare moment of parental concern she wavered for a moment and added still addressing Mhimo. "Make sure you dress warm."

Mhimo nodded his head obediently as Rhiss made her way to the kitchen.

"You've been talking about this Saturnalia thing for a week now but I still don't know what it is," Black questioned Rinx.

"It's a holiday," she responded.

Black stared at her blankly.

She rolled her eyes as she spoke, "Of course you didn't have holidays growing up in the woods like an animal." Rinx patted him on the head and Black quickly smacked it away. "It's a day for celebrating," she searched for some hint of understanding in his eyes. "Singing, eating sweet cakes, spiced drinks. It's the longest night of the year!" She threw her hands up in the air. "It's just a nice time to spend with your family."

Black thought it all sounded marvelous but felt a pain of sadness at her last point, thinking of his mentor, Mazurus.

"Well," she surrendered. "I have to gather some stuff to decorate." And she was on her way pulling on a heavy cloak and heading out the door.

Black looked to Mhimo standing quietly at his side.

Mhimo gave him a timid smile and spoke, "The lanterns are in the shed." He waited for Black to take the lead and gather his cloak before making for the shed.

Inside the shed, Mhimo pointed to the shelf with the many lanterns stacked on top of one another. "There are some stands to hang them from so we can line the path from the treeline to our door too." he said pointing to the black metal stands leaning in a corner.

For the most part they worked in silence starting by hanging the dark stands first. The sky was gray and the snow was falling gently in big clumps. Rinx would occasionally hurry by carrying some mistletoe or fir tree branches bundled in her arms to the house. At one point she ducked into the shed returning with several smaller lamps.

"It's nice to have you here." Mhimo's voice came so suddenly that Black nearly fell off the tree branch he was standing on.

Black steadied himself and finished attaching a lantern he was working on. "It's nice to be here," he confirmed, looking down at Mhimo for a moment. "I didn't have things like Saturnalia when I was living in the forest but I remember seeing the elves celebrating things sometimes so maybe they did."

"It's nice to have another boy here," Mhimo responded quietly. "And it must have been lonely... for you before I mean."

Black thought about it and couldn't say that he ever had felt lonely then. *It's just how it was,* he thought. How it always had been but now after this past year he'd doubted he could go back to just existing alone.

"You didn't have a dad either," Mhimo whispered, looking away now.

Black was painfully reminded again of Mazurus's absence. He couldn't see Mhimo's face but he knew what he felt; to have someone missing from your life but to know he wouldn't return. Black had never noticed before this moment but the boy was always watching him. Always looking up to him.

Black dropped down from the branch and gently placed a hand on the boy's shoulder. " No, but I do have you." He gave a gentle squeeze. "And your mom and your sister, too." He felt the truth of his words. They comforted him even while he tried to comfort the boy. "And that's so much more than I could have dreamed of."

There was a moment of silence except for the sound of Mhimo's unsteady breathing then, "Hey are you two almost done!" It was Rinx shouting from the house.

"Almost!" Black replied.

"Well hurry up! Mother is making something good," she cried as she shut the door behind her.

He sniffed the air and exclaimed, "Wow! Something does smell good." He patted the boy on the shoulder. "She's right, we should finish up."

Mhimo quickly ran his forearm across his face as he nodded and turned toward the next low hanging branch. They finished the lights shortly after that and made their way back to the warmth of home.

Inside they peeled off their boots and hung up their cloaks. The interior of the house had been transformed. Everywhere they looked they saw fir branches strung together and mistletoe and pine cones hanging here and there highlighted with several little glowing lamps. It was a beautiful sight. The air was filled with a spicy aroma combined with the scent of hot stew Rhiss carried in from the kitchen. Rinx followed her with a large spiced cake.

They ate their fill of both each child taking a double helping of the cake. When the sun had set they all went outside to watch with a hot mug of apple-spiced tea as Rhiss with a wave of her hand illuminated all the lanterns. It was quite a spectacle as the flames swept from left to right until they were all glowing brightly.

The next few days passed by quickly until Saturnalia had arrived. Rinx and Black spent part of the day racing through the snow trying to determine who was faster in their totem forms and the other part piling logs for a bonfire. Rhiss had been out early that morning twice. Returning once with a fat goose and a second time with an even fatter boar. It was to be a feast that night before the bonfire and she and Mhimo were busy all day in the kitchen. As the sun began to hang low in the sky Rinx and Black returned inside to set the table and help out where they could with the food.

Finally dinner was ready and the feast was paraded out onto the long table. They brought mashed cinnamon and brown sugar yams, hard-boiled peppered quill eggs with the gooey yolks, fluffy biscuits with a creamy butter side and two types of jam, strawberry and blackberry, seasoned brown rice, three different kinds of cakes, chocolate with a chestnut cream, spiced with a pumpkin cinnamon icing, and carrot, full of walnuts, an apple pie, a rhubarb pie, a bowl full of whole roasted chestnuts, sugar frosted cranberries, salted green beans, steamed carrots, and to bring it all together a juicy goose roasted with herbs and whole hog glazed with apple cider and honey.

Black's eyes were so wide they could have rolled out of his head. "I've never seen so much food in one place," he said as he inhaled deeply through his nose and wiped the small trickle of drool from his chin.

To drink, each of the kids had hot apple cider and for Rhiss, she helped herself to a tall pitcher of mulled wine of which she allowed the two older children a small glass of. "But no more," she stated, raising her index finger. "It is to be savored, not guzzled."

The children loomed on the verge of pouncing and filling their bellies to the point of near bursting when Rhiss suddenly raised her hand. They all paused, Rinx with her hand already gripping the spoon for the mashed yams.

"It seems," she spoke at an unhurried pace. "that we will need to set the table for one more."

The children set for a moment's delay as this information sunk in when a knock came at the front door.

"Amadeus, can you answer the door and you two prepare another place for our guest," she commanded.

Black pushed himself from the table and trotted to the foyer. He opened the door to discover a man with his back to him stomping his boots and shaking the snow from his shoulders. The man turned to reveal rosy cheeks and a frosted beard.

A cloud of steam escaped his mouth as he exclaimed, "My boy, Amadeus, how you've grown since I've been gone!"

Without a word Black rushed in and hugged the old man. His eyes squeezed tight like a levee against a storm.

"And grown stronger too," Mazurus groaned as he hugged the boy back.

After a long moment Black released him and he opened his mouth to speak but the words died on his lips.

Mazurus ruffled the boy's hair and rested his hand on his shoulder. "I didn't miss the celebration did I?"

"No," he responded, shaking his head.

"Grand!" he exclaimed. "Help me with my things." Mazurus passed the bag he carried on his back to Black which he quickly set down in the front room before returning to the opened front door.

Black could see that Mazurus had dragged a small sled up to the front of the house and was removing a long case with silver latches from it. He passed this onto Black as well. "I was concerned I wouldn't make it in time dragging all of this with me," Mazurus spoke with a laugh. "It was slow going. Snow up to my waist in some places."

He grabbed a sack from the sled and stepped into the house shutting the door behind him. He set the bag down and started to remove his gloves, boots, and cloak as the others joined Black in greeting the old man.

"Yo Saturnalia," he called when he saw them.

"Mazurus! Yo Saturnalia," Rinx returned grinning ear to ear and with one eye on the sack.

"Welcome back Mazurus," Rhiss greeted him. "I assume you received my letter."

"I did," he replied. "We can discuss it later, but first, what is that delicious smell?" he sniffed the air and rubbed his hands together. "Could have made the last half mile walking here blind just by nose."

"Of course," Rhiss gestured and they all made their way back to the table.

Mazurus let out a cry of joy upon entering the room.

Black spoke, "There's so much, right?"

"My lady," he said as he took a seat next to Black. "You have really outdone yourself." He poured himself a large glass of the mulled wine and held it with both hands under his nose. The steam rose up to meet him. "Nothing better after coming in from the cold."

Rhiss raised her own glass. "Welcome again and help yourself."

With that they commenced the massive undertaking of stuffing their bellies to maximum capacity. Black needed to taste everything. The green beans while not bad, he could only commit the tiniest portion of his stomach to. Unlike the smashed yams which he helped himself to on three occasions and of course he needed a slice from each cake and pie. They ate themselves to near sick. All but Rhiss who after one plate of brown rice, carrots, green beans, roasted goose and a meager slice of the rhubarb pie on the side only indulged in her occasional sip of the hot spiced wine.

After they were quite full and satisfied Black felt a light kick from under the table. He looked across to see Rinx mouthing the words to him, "Ask about the sack."

Black turned to Mazurus, "What was the sack for?"

"Oh, I'd nearly forgotten," he brooded, stroking the white hair on his chin. "Oh, nothing of any interest to any of you I'm sure."

Rinx made a face at Black that urged him on.

So he persisted. "Well maybe it is," he was unsure what to say.

"Well you know there is another Saturnalia tradition," he held his brooding look as he stared off into the distance.

Black was at a loss but quickly Rinx jumped in. "Gifts?" she squealed with a grin.

Mhimo, despite his attempt to hide it behind his hands, also had a large smile on his face.

Mazurus exploded into a raucous laughter. "Ah yes! Thank Rinx for the reminder. I do believe you are correct."

The children all laughed as Rhiss looked on with a hint of amusement and Mazurus rose to fetch his bag. He returned quickly doing a little jig along his way only pausing once to rub his knee. He dropped the sack on the floor and pulled three folded bundles of cloth that he passed to each of the children. They unfolded them to reveal new hooded cloaks. Rinx's cloak was fiery red with the face of a fox sown in white thread on the back. Mhimo too had a red cloak but he had triangular ears attached to the hood.

"Wow," Mhimo said as he pulled the hood up and tugged on the ears.

Black's expectantly was a deep black but like Rinx's cloak had a white face of a wolf sown into the back.

"They don't seem very warm," Rinx said with a puzzled look on her face.

"Of course not," Mazurus responded with a wink. "You're inside. These are special cloaks made by the elves. Magic. When it's cold, they feel warm but when it's hot. Well then they feel cool."

They all three stroked the material and Mhimo squeaked, "the elves?"

"That's right," he confirmed, nodding his head. "And one more thing they can do. If they are ever torn they will repair themselves in a couple of hours."

"Quite a gift," Rhiss chimed in.

Mazurus gave a wave of his hand. "Now for something a bit more fun," he said, reaching into the bag again and pulling out a small wooden dog. "Something for Mhimo." He passed the toy to the young boy.

The boy's eyes were wide and his mouth was in the perfect shape of an 'O'. "Thank you, sir," he said quietly.

"Now," Mazurus leaned towards him. "Hold it like this," he placed the dog on Mhimo's flat hand. "And try to channel just a little magic into it."

"I'll try," he responded. And after a few seconds of him pushing his eyebrows together the dog sat down on his hand and gave a little bark before returning to its original position. "Wow!" the boy exclaimed. "Wow, wow." Then another moment of silence as his eyebrows squeezed together and his forehead wrinkled, before the dog sat and barked again. "Wow!" he exclaimed one last time. "Thank you."

"Now something for Rinx." Again he rummaged around in the bag pulling out a box. "I hope they fit," he confided, passing the box to Rinx.

She opened the box and her draw dropped. She pulled out a bright red and white trainer. "They are so... I love them!" She cried and gave him a hug before she dropped to the floor and was tying them on. "I've never had shoes like this before. I've never had any clothes from the Earthen Realm before." She stood tapping the toe of her right foot to the floor. "They're beautiful."

"Well it's time for you my boy." he pulled out a pouch and passed it to Black.

The pouch smelled of old leather and Black poured the contents into his hand. Resting on his palm was a ring.

"It was made by the elves as well. From the Yew tree. The Yew is said to represent rebirth," the old man explained.

"And death," Rhiss added.

Mazurus gave her a quick glance and continued. "Well they believe it's a trinket of good fortune."

"Thank you," Black said as he slid it onto his finger and admired the visible grains in the wood.

"I also have a pouch full of elvish treats. Not that any of us could stomach them right now," he laughed as he passed them to the children. "And just one more gift left." he retrieved a little box from the deflated sack. "Did you think I would forget about you my lady," Mazurus turned toward Rhiss, his face illuminated with joy.

For the first time since Black had known her, Rhiss actually looked shocked.

"You shouldn't have," Rhiss said taking the red box tied with a black ribbon. She gently pulled at the ribbon loosing the bow and setting it to the side. She removed the lid froze. "You-," the words caught in her throat and it seemed to take effort to turn her gaze back to Mazurus. "You really shouldn't have."

"It's nothing," Mazurus responded with a twinkle in his eye and slight upturn at the corners of his mouth.

Rhiss raised the gift from its confinements. It shimmered in her hand. A silver chain held an intricately crafted silver medallion with a cat's eye sliver ruby adorning the center. The fire light seemed to dance across it and fill the ruby giving the illusion of self-illumination. "It's beautiful," the words barely escaped her mouth.

The children looked on in silence, mesmerized.

Mazurus spoke up. "It was crafted by the elves as well. They are remarkably talented."

Finally the spell was broken and Rhiss gathered her composure. "Thank you. This was too generous of you Mazurus."

"It's nothing," he repeated.

"Put it on, mother," Rinx called out.

"Of course," she responded. "Help me." Rinx ran behind her and buckled the chain around her mother's neck while Rhiss held her hair out of the way.

"It looks beautiful," Rinx took a step back and proclaimed.

Mazurus nodded in agreement, "It suits you quite well."

Rhiss shifted in her seat with everyone's eyes on her. "I think maybe now would be a good time to light the bonfire," she spoke suddenly.

"Let's do it," Rinx shouted.

They all topped up their hot drinks and made for the door. Each of them only paused along the way to slip on their boots. Rinx delicately removed her trainers and returned them to the box.

Black marveled as he made his way to the pile of logs opening and closing his cloak, "It feels so light but you really can't feel the cold at all when it's closed."

Rinx was testing its effectiveness by exposing her bare arm and then securing it back into the folds. Mhimo simply pulled his hood up so that the ears were erect and scurried to a seat near the bonfire. After everyone had found a seat Rhiss waved a hand and the pile of wood ignited into a pillar of fire. The flames were so intense that the layer of snow that had settled upon them sizzled and evaporated instantly. The heat slapped their faces and then eased off. They sat in silence for a time. The snow fell gently and the air was thick with the scent of the fire's breath and spice. The flames waltzed and tangoed and after some time Mazurus disappeared into the house returning with the contents of the case he'd brought with him. He sat down with a stringed instrument and after a moment of tuning he began to play. Black had never heard such magic. His jaw hung slack for so long that he had to remind himself to close his mouth.

After the first song ended another began but this one was more melancholic and shortly after it had begun a voice began to sing. Rhiss had joined in. The children looked on and not a word was spoken. Black believed that it was the most beautiful thing he'd ever heard. Their eyes had begun to grow heavy and once Mhimo had nodded off, nearly slipping from his seat. It signaled that it was time for them to go to bed.

The children dragged themselves back to the house and into their warm beds. Mazurus and Rhiss said their good nights and watched the children leave.

"So?" Rhiss asked. "What did you discover?"

"He's a descendant, he has to be." Mazurus stared deep into the flames. "The elves were as tight lipped as ever but they said enough to add to the evidence." Mazurus stroked his beard. "I had my suspicions when I found the boy but know… with his powers it can't be any other way."

"Are you sure you're not seeing what you want to see?" Rhiss searched the old man's face.

"By the gods, I can see it in the boy's face." Mazurus looked to the sky and closed his eyes.

"So what do we do?"

"We keep this secret to ourselves and we keep that boy safe." Mazurus exhaled a plume of steam.

***

Present

The rain had begun its onslaught well before Black had dragged himself out of bed. Too many drinks celebrating Rinx's advancement and too few hours of sleep ensured a late start that morning. He made his way hurrying through the back streets to save time. Only a hooded cloak defended him against the sky's assault. Splashing along the way, his feet finally led him back to Rinx's apartment. Before he could raise a hand to knock the door was yanked open.

"Sorry I'm late," Black apologized.

"It's late?" Rinx grumbled looking over his shoulder. She reached for the sky and let out a long yawn before pulling her own cloak from its hook and wrapping it around herself. "Let's go see what this bastard has to say," she shut the door behind herself with the sound of several bolts sliding into place.

"Lead the way," Black sighed.

They arrived at the prison. It was an enormous black stone building. At the front desk they were met by a guard bearing several scars on the right side of his face. One milky white eye stared into oblivion while the other inspected them with suspicion. "What's your business?" he inquired.

They both flashed their marks of the Guild.

"We are here to question a prisoner, Nictus Prothers," Black informed him.

"I brought him in yesterday," Rinx followed up.

"Both ya?" He clicked his tongue.

"Is that a problem?" Black returned his gaze.

"Nah, follow me." he made his way through a gate with the other two on his heels. "He's not far. Being kept in a special cell awaiting processing."

They followed the guard down a couple of corridors before descending some narrow stairs. The air smelled damp and they could hear the sound of trickling water in the distance. They came to a closed gate that the guard opened and ushered them through. They stepped into a short corridor with a single cell on the right. The door was wide open and the cell was bare. Outside the cell at the end of the corridor lay a sack.

"The prisoner isn't here," Black reported.

"What?" the guard cried and pushed his way past them. "Out of my way!"

He ran to the end of the hall, stopped at the bag and drew something from it. The guard seemed to be fitting something to his arm.

Black advanced closer to the guard passing the cell door only giving it a passing glance. Rinx remained near the gate, her eyes flitting around the room.

"What's going on here," Black demanded.

The guard rose and turned around. His mouth formed a sneer and he now brandished both a dagger and buckler. Black's right hand immediately went to the tattoo on his left forearm activating it. There was a blue glow as he drew a single edged sword with no cross guard seemingly from his arm. He recognized at once that the would-be assassin wore an Aegis. His magic would have no effect on it and likely the dagger would have the same ability. With the confined space of the corridor Rinx was in no position to aid Black.

The guard gave a cry and charged his foe. Black's sword connected with the man's shield. With his off hand he was able to grab the arm wielding the dagger by the wrist. The man was strong. Stronger than he should have been and in the closeness of the struggle Black could detect a sickly sweet smell on the guard's racing breath. With his totem's strength he was able to barely get the upper hand while grappling. Black delivered a powerful kick to the man's stomach knocking him back against the wall.

Rinx watched on looking for some way to assist. As the two men collided a shimmer caught her eye from the cell. For a moment Rinx thought it a trick of the eye but as she focused she made out the slightest distortion moving from within the cell towards the open door. The aberration moved towards Black's open back. Rinx filled her lungs as her partner kicked his opponent against the wall. She exhaled a cone of fiery death into the cell.

The guard regained his poise and charged again. Black felt the flash of heat and the corridor lit up accompanied by a painful scream. He could not afford to lose focus so he trusted that Rinx was handling the situation.

The scream filled her ears and as it died she heard the clattering of a blade falling to the cell's floor. She could see the outline of a figure aflame flailing at the open air before falling back into the cell in a motionless heap. The air was filled with the rancid stink of burnt flesh.

Black could see a glint of malice in the attacker's one good eye but also now the faint shimmer of desperation. The man propelled his blade toward Black's throat but he was again able to grab the attacking arm and pin it against the wall while countering with his own blade. However the guard deftly deflected it with the small shield and made his own counter with a headbutt stunning Black for a moment. The guard was unable to wrench his arm from the iron grasp. Black recovered quickly and delivered a straight kick to the assassin's knee summoning a cry of pain as he buckled to the ground. The man's arm remained held fast in Black's grip. The attacker raised his shield to block the downward stroke of his opponent's blade. Stayed by the shield Black followed up with a knee to the kneeling guard's chin. The shield dropped and the death blow slipped past and down the left side of his neck finding the heart.

Black withdrew his sword and the man's body slumped backwards. His eye remained open. Black knelt down and flicked the eye. Nothing. The man was dead. Black wiped the blood from his blade on the dead man's uniform. He activated the tattooed enchantment on his forearm and there was a blue glow as Black slid the sword back into his arm.

He turned to face Rinx and saw the smoldering body in the cell. "Are you alright?"

"Terrific," Rinx threw her hands up and smiled. "And nice trick." She pointed to the sanskrit style tattoo.

"Thanks, it took a long time to work out a pocket dimension enchantment. Now what the hell is going on here," Black questioned as they both surveyed the carnage.

Shortly after, they found themselves back at the front desk questioning the guard captain and his subordinate.

"Like I said, I didn't recognize a one of them but they had a writ from the Premiers themselves stating that the prisoner was to be placed under special guard," the young subordinate explained.

Black searched his face for the slightest hint of dishonesty. "And you're sure you saw three of them?"

"Without a doubt, sir," he nodded his head confidently.

"And now we have two bodies, one burned beyond recognition." Black brushed his hair back.

"Look," the captain pushed out his mustache and glanced at his subordinate. "It is an unusual situation but it's not the first time we've had an unusual request come down from the Premiers. The document they carried was legitimate and you can examine it yourself." he gestured to Rinx who already had it in her hand. "We just follow orders here." He patted the youthful guard on the shoulder.

"Very well. If there is nothing else to add then we'll be on our way then," Black looked back at Rinx and she gave a nod in return. "Alright then, I'll leave you to clean up this mess."

"Yes sir," the two gentlemen said in unison.

The young man started after them, "There is one more thing," he held his hands out for Black to see. "One of them had a bunch of scars on his hands like they'd been burned and cut all over."

The two gave a nod and then continued on their way.

Rinx and Black stepped out into the rain each of them pulling up their hoods as they did. There was the distant crack of thunder.

Black took a deep breath. "So I suppose it's safe to assume the man you cooked down there wasn't Prothers."

Rinx shook her head. "Seems unlikely."

"We have a guy that comes in dressed as a guard that can also turn invisible."

"Yep," Rinx replied. "Probably passed his uniform onto Prothers allowing him to slip out with our third mystery guy without attracting attention."

Black took another deep breath. "The one guy had an Aegis so I guess I know where to go next."

Now Rinx took a deep breath. "I'm coming with you."

"That's not necessary," He faced her and forced a smile. "Aren't you starting your vacation today? Going home to visit your mother? I can take care of this alone."

"Prothers was mine and he's out now. Plus," she argued and paused for a moment. "They left those two men for a reason. They were waiting for you."

"I can handle it," he countered.

"Let's go," she said dismissively and was on her way.

They made their way across the city and spoke very little. The rain had begun to break but the clouds still hung about the sky. With the rain letting up more people were in the streets going about their day. Running their errands. Rinx and Black passed through a large gate into a part of the city that was strikingly distinct. Unlike the typically mundane red brick buildings littered throughout the city these buildings looked to be made of white stone. The people too had changed. Several men and women wore brown and green uniforms typical with a short sword on their hip and a silver buckler on their arm. Others wore simple white linen and toiled about their daily routines.

Those in uniform regarded the two with a suspicious gaze as they passed. They approached a large mansion with several of the uniformed men stationed outside. As they neared the gate a broad shoulder man with a great bushy gray beard emerged from the front doors and descended the steps to meet them at the gate.

He remained on the other side of the gate. "Amadeus Black," he turned his dark gaze to Rinx and glared. "And Rinx Quint."

Rinx met his gaze and glared back but it was Black that spoke. "You were expecting us."

"Of course. I was informed of your approach as soon as you passed through the gate." He raised his chin. "What business do you have with the Order of Homme? Your Guild of Ravens has no jurisdiction here."

"Perhaps we are here to see an old friend," Black stated.

The man scoffed and looked again at Rinx with unfiltered disgust on his face. "You have no friends here."

"Then where is Damascus Mageese your master?" Black pressed him.

The man opened his mouth to speak but before the words could escape his mouth there was a call from one of the balconies above.

"You disgrace yourself Raija and more importantly, you disgrace me." The man standing on the balcony was shirtless and his bronze body was sinewy and muscular.

"Forgive me my lord. I only wished for you to not be interrupted during your morning exercises." Raija bowed.

"Send my friends up," Damascus commanded.

Raija gestured to the guards to open the gate and the two followed Raija up the steps and into the mansion. They entered into a large foyer with walls painted a deep forest green. The ceiling was high and a great chandelier hung down glowing with the light of many candles. On either side of the chandelier hung great green and brown banners adorned with the image of a mongoose holding a snake in its jaws. There were two stairs on each side of the room leading up to the second floor and from there another flight of stairs leading to the third floor. They followed Raija up the left flight to the second floor. They proceeded to the left, passing several paintings mounted on the wall with men and women in various states of combat. The most notable theme was of a warrior brandishing a sword and shield fighting some sorcerer. They entered the second door on the left to be greeted by Damascus.

He was dabbing sweat from his face and he now wore a white linen robe that hung open revealing his naked chest. His black curls hung down to his shoulders. He smiled, "Welcome my friends," and then "Raija, you may leave us."

Raija bowed and left the room, shutting the door behind him. The room was large with a padded floor and an assortment of armaments hung on the walls. Near one of the walls a table held a bowl of burning incense that filled the room with a sweet fragrance. A hazy cloud hung over the bowl and table.

Damascus untied a green string from around his wrist and used it to bind his hair back. "It has been a long time," he looked at Rinx. "Too long. I have missed you both."

"I feel the same," Black replied, reaching to shake the man's hand.

Rinx remained motionless with her arms folded across her chest.

Damascus gestured to a table and chairs in one corner. "Let us sit." After they were seated he asked, "So to what do I owe the pleasure? As much as I wish it, I don't imagine you have come for a social visit."

"Unfortunately not," Black admitted. "We are burdened by responsibility, all of us and it doesn't allow us enough time for those we care about."

"Seems like only one of us allows this burden to prevent them from being with the ones they care about," Rinx interjected. Her face took on the same shade as her hair when the two men looked at her. She turned away suddenly, more interested with the weapons hanging from the walls.

"It is as you suspect Damascus. We are here on business. Dirty business that we hoped you could shed some light on." Black continued.

"Of course," he raised a hand. "But first I must apologize-"

"Hah," Rinx blurted.

Damascus's expression seemed to drop for a moment but then he continued. "Here you are my oldest friends and I have been an unworthy host. I haven't offered you any refreshments."

"It's really not-" Black attempted to protest but was cut short.

"Nonsense," Damascus clapped his hands together and a servant entered the room in crisp white linen. "Bring us some tea and something sweet."

The woman bowed and then hurried away.

"I think this matter will require some discretion," Black informed him.

"Not a problem," he agreed. After a few moments the woman returned with an assistant. They wheeled in a cart with an assortment of dried fruit and biscuits. One of the servants set down a teapot and three cups. "Now we require privacy. Make sure we have it and are not disturbed." Damascus issued his orders and the servants bowed and were gone.

Damascus began pouring them each a cup of tea while Black waited a moment longer before he began again. "We have been on the trail of a sorcerer involved with making soul pacts and dealing with demons. He goes by the name of 'Mr. B.' Does that name sound familiar?"

Damascus rubbed his chin. "A rather vague name. I can't say it means anything to me."

Rinx helped herself to a biscuit while Black went on. He explained the connection to Nictus Prothers and the events at the prison. "So you see why we are here?"

Damascus sat back in his seat. "One of your assassins was carrying an Aegis. You believe he was a member of the Order of Homme."

"We're hoping you can identify him if you see him," Black explained.

"Oh no need," he rubbed a finger against his temple. "I know exactly who he was."

"Really?" Rinx finally joined the conversation.

"Of course," he shot her a smile. "You don't forget a face like that."

Rinx seemed to retreat again.

"So he was one of yours?" Black asked.

"Was, being the key word. Christopher Cussler. He was capable enough as I'm sure you can attest to but he was more interested in money. He left the order. Took whatever job filled his pocket. We try to keep tabs on those who leave. Last I heard he was doing some work for Premier Barnabas."

"We suspected they had someone on the inside but I didn't want to believe it could actually be a Premier," Black admitted. The incense was hanging heavy around them as if it was drawn to them.

Rinx slapped her hand to her head. "A Premier? What kind of shit have we gotten ourselves into?"

"They tried to kill you, my friend," Damascus said gravely to Black. Then turned toward Rinx. His knuckles went white as he gripped the arm of his chair. "They will likely know that you were involved as well. You're in danger now too and you don't know how long their reach is. You can not go home." His eyes darted between them. "Either of you."

"We'll be fine," Rinx said, chewing her lip.

Damascus leaned forward in his chair. "You should stay here. At least for the night until you can decide the next move." He kept his cool composure but Black knew him long enough to recognize when he was pleading.

Rinx opened her mouth to talk but was interrupted by Black as he put a hand on her arm. "Thank you. I think that would be our best move for now." He regarded Rinx. "At least for the night, as you said."

Rinx sighed and waved a hand in defeat.

"Excellent," Damascus exclaimed, pushing his chair back as he stood. "It is nearly time for lunch. I'll have my people make something for us and in the meantime someone will show you to the guest wing." He folded his arms behind his back and cleared the room to the door.

"Very generous of you," Black stood as well.

Damascus opened the door and called down the hallway. A moment later some footsteps could be heard rapidly approaching. "They will be staying with us for the night. Have them shown to the guest rooms and make space for them for lunch," he commanded. "And I will speak with Raija personally about increasing our security." He turned to his guests. "I will see you both at lunch. Make yourselves at home in my absence." And he was gone. A servant glided into the room and after a courteous bow was leading them to their rooms.

Chapter 5

Past

The next year and a half went by quickly. The children spent the bulk of that time learning. Mazurus would come and go. Sometimes he would be gone for a few weeks at a time always with a vague reason. When he was there he'd assist in their combat training. At the beginning he was physically involved. He would leap in to spar with them but as they improved he mostly opted to observe, coaching and pointing out flaws in their techniques. He continued to aid Black in his enchanting. Black could perform simple enchantments of the base elements competently. Water, fire, wind, earth. Earth being the most difficult for Black. The earth enchantments always felt slower and heavier than the others. Mazurus had begun to teach him the higher elements like lightning and ice but he had no real success with them. The old master explained that there are still other spells and enchantments even more complex that don't follow the elements. Some that could stop time or bend reality but it would be a long while before he could enchant those.

He once told Black, "There are some spells so unique that we could spend a hundred years and never cast one but then some kid comes along. Able to cast the spell as easily as walking." And then he smiled and added. "Like being born with a totem."

When they weren't with Mazurus they were usually with Rhiss. She continued to guide them in their spell mastery. Rinx had improved her fireballs, increasing both the size and distance she could effectively throw them. She could also recite the incantation in almost three seconds meaning she could perform the spell very quickly and in rapid succession. She would practice running and jumping while reciting the incantation and hurling the spell.

Black was not so impressive. He had improved his wind spell but despite his efforts he could do no more than whip the leaves and dust into the air.

One day while practicing Rinx began teasing him.

"You really have a lame elemental affinity don't you?" She sat lighting and extinguishing a log. "I just don't see how the academy will admit someone like you."

Black clenched his jaw.

"Oh I know," she lit the log and looked back at him smiling. "They probably need people to clean the classrooms at the end of the day." She laughed.

He raised his right hand and muttered the spell intending to extinguish her flame and maybe get some dirt blown up in her hair. However the wind had the opposite effect. It fed the flames, throwing them, spreading them, and toppling the log. The log rolled leaving fire in its wake. All of the flames raced towards the forest's edge, fanned by Black's dying spell. Rinx stood locked in a state of shock and Black clutched the air in vain searching for some way to prevent the approaching disaster.

As the children stood frozen Rhiss brushed past them. She calmly raised a hand and the flames responded, rising into a burning cyclone. She closed her hand in a fist and the blaze was gone.

Rhiss examined the two children for a moment. "There are two lessons to learn from this." She brushed some dust from her dress and her icy gaze fell on Rinx. "You must understand how one element affects another. How one spell can impact another. In this case, how the wind gave strength to the fire and pushed it forward. Also," She flicked her eyes between the two of them. "If you lose control of a spell a talented sorceress may exploit that and turn it against you." She turned and made her way back to the house.

They both felt a heavy weight from Rhiss's words and even though the fire was long dead they could each feel heat radiating from their cheeks stoked by shame.

When Black had some free time he would teach Mhimo fighting techniques and let the child throw some punches at him. He tried to repeat some of the lessons Rhiss had taught him for Mhimo's benefit but he felt too inept to trust his own advice. Despite this, he never failed to find time for the younger boy.

One summer day Rhiss set out on her own leaving the children in the care of Mazurus. They continued on with their studies as usual. There was nothing unusual about Rhiss disappearing into the forest for hours or sometimes days at a time. She returned back that evening with two beige folders. Later, after they had finished dinner and were sitting comfortably conversing. Rhiss rose and took the folders from the mantel, handing one to Black and then one to Rinx before she returned to her seat. Without a word she returned to enjoying a mug of tea she had been sipping on.

Black examined his folder and saw written across it in elegantly dark ink. 'Amadeus Black.' He looked to Rhiss who wore her usual expression of disinterest so he turned to Mazurus. The old man placed a hand to his mouth in a failed attempt to mask a smile while at the same time raising his eyebrows. This spurred Black on so he opened the envelope. At this point he heard a gasp from his left.

Rinx jumped out of her chair and with a sheet of paper in her hand she ran to Rhiss hugging her. "Yes! Finally! Thank you mother," she cried while Rhiss calmly kept her tea from spilling and patted the child on the back of the head.

Black removed the contents of the envelope and read. 'Tuatha Dé Academy' was presented in bold print across the top of the page. 'The Tuatha Dé Academy under the authority of the Guild of Ravens does hereby accept Amadeus Black for enrollment in the upcoming fall semester.' Black was on his feet now reading while Rinx was squealing and jumping up and down. 'The student is expected to be in attendance at the designated time and with required materials *see list below* for enrollment and orientation. Classes will be selected at this time and pending that all tuition is paid in full for the year the relevant books will be distributed along with any other necessary learning materials.'

Black looked again to the old man. "Congratulations my boy," Mazurus called. "And congratulations to you young lady."

Rinx grabbed Black by the hands and continued to jump up and down as they turned in circles. During the revelry Black caught a glimpse of Mhimo sliding out of his chair and quitting the room. Black's excitement died for a moment but was rekindled when Rinx spoke.

"There's a list of classes on the back for first year students," she held up her paper, slightly crumpled now. "We need to decide what classes we want to enroll in."

Mazurus laughed, "well there is time still for that. There will be representatives to explain each first year class and whether it's a good fit for you at the orientation if I'm not mistaken."

"But it's still a good idea to prepare early and know what you want," Rhiss countered.

"I suppose that's true," Mazurus conceded stroking his beard.

"I can't wait!" Rinx howled.

The rest of the summer the children were invigorated with fresh resolve. They put in more hours training than ever before. Black noticed that Mhimo was no longer interested in practicing with him and although he missed their time together the excitement of preparing for his first day of classes consumed him.

Soon that day was upon them and they woke early for breakfast.

"I've been awake for the past two hours," Rinx lamented, tapping her fingers in front of an empty bowl at the table. "I just couldn't sleep anymore."

"It took me ages to fall asleep last night," Black rubbed the crust from his eyes as he sat down to a steaming bowl of porridge.

Rhiss entered the room from the kitchen carrying her usual cup of tea. "I hope you are both well rested because you both have a big day ahead of you today." She sat down at the end of the table and took a sip. "We need to purchase some supplies before you arrive at the orientation, remember."

They had not forgotten, having just packed their things last minute the night before. A few change of clothes to wear outside of the academy, a few books for personal use, and whatever other private items they may want.

Rhiss continued, "According to the list of required supplies, we will need to purchase your uniforms from an academy sponsored shop called Ronald's Robes. With any luck we will be the only ones procrastinating until the last day. We will also require pens and notebooks. Should be easy enough to find those."

Mazurus enter from outside. "Well well well. Good morning you two. How are you feeling? Do you feel ready for the big day?" He tousled Black's hair as he passed and stood leaning on the back of the chair next to him.

"Of course we're ready," Rinx confirmed.

"Yeah, I have my things packed and ready to go." For the first time Black was suddenly hit with the realization that attending the academy meant he wouldn't be living with Rhiss, Mhimo, or Mazurus. For that matter, he would only be able to see them a handful of times a year.

Almost as if Rinx had read his mind she said, "but I am afraid I'll miss you all."

"And we'll miss you two as well. But don't forget that we'll see each other again for the holidays and I'm sure that with all the fun you'll be having they'll come around sooner than you think," Mazurus assured the children.

Rhiss nodded her head in agreement.

"That's probably true," Black found himself saying. He didn't know why but hearing Rinx's concerns actually made him feel better.

Soon they were preparing to leave. Black gathered up his things and met the others in the foyer.

"So you won't be joining us on the way to Tuatha Dé?" Black asked even though they'd already discussed the plan the night before.

"No, I'm sorry my boy but with this knee I'm afraid I couldn't keep up and it'd take too long walking at this old man's pace." He gave a pleading smile.

Black looked around the foyer and asked, "And where's Mhimo at? We need to say goodbye."

"I said my good bye last night," Rinx said. "He's been acting weird lately anyways."

Black hesitated for a moment then said, "no, I can't leave without saying goodbye."

He marched to Mhimo's room and flung the door open. Mhimo was sitting at the end of his bed. His eyes were wide and his face held an expression of surprise at the sudden intrusion. Black continued his march up to Mhimo wrapped his arms around him and hugged him tightly. After a moment he felt Mhimo's arms encircle him and squeeze with the same intensity.

"I'm going to miss you," Black said. "Keep practicing the things I taught you and hopefully when I'm back I can teach you some of the new things I learn."

Black could only feel Mhimo nod his head.

"Good bye," Black said and turned to join the others.

Rhiss and the children made their way to the treeline and stopped giving Rinx and Black a moment to turn and take one last look at their home. Mazurus stood in the entrance of the home waving. The two waved back. Black inhaled deeply appreciating the fresh air and observing the first signs of yellow staining the leaves then they were on their way. In totem form they must have looked peculiar with the smaller fox and wolf each of them sporting a backpack strapped to them. It felt like no time at all before they were walking down the streets of Tuatha Dé.

They found notebooks and pens easy enough. When they arrived at Ronald's Robes they discovered that they were not the only ones who had waited until the last day to get their attire. There were in fact several other students who had procrastinated as they'd done.

Rhiss surveyed the calamity within the store through the windows and then surveyed the street until she found a most suitable cafe terrace only two buildings down and across the street from Ronald's Robes.

"You two know what you need so I'll leave you two to it." She removed a number of gold coins from a pouch. "I'll be waiting for you over there. And try not to be too long." She strode away.

The two children entered the shop and soon realized that Ronald was the only employee and there were nearly a dozen parents all vying for his attention. He came running past them with a pile of robes draped across his arms.

"I'll be right with you," he said out of breath, never pausing to look at them.

"Excuuuse me!" A parent cried from across the room.

"Right with you!" He called back.

"Wow, this is a nightmare." Black said.

"No kidding," Rinx agreed.

A large woman with ginger colored hair had caught Ronald's attention and was yelling at him. "My sweet Gilbert can not be tripping over his robes!"

Gilbert stood not far from where his mother assaulted Ronald, his cheeks aflame. He wore an academy robe. It was dark blue with a crescent moon encircling a star, the mark of Tuatha Dé Academy embroidered on the left breast. The robe's sleeves were too long for his thick stubby arms. The bottom of the robe bunched up around his feet but was fitted quite comfortably around his rotund belly. Gilbert's build was quite obviously short and round. His blue eyes darted around the store as his cheeks grew more and more red in cadence to his mother berating the store's owner. Sweat was breaking out on his forehead just below his meticulously combed blond hair.

A couple of the boys near Rinx and Black snickered. "Damn there won't be enough fabric to make the rest of our robes," one laughed.

The other added, "fatass."

"Poor guy," Black whispered to Rinx.

"Yeah, so embarrassing," she cringed.

After an hour of running around the shop distributing robes, hemming, and collecting payment he finally made his way to Rinx and Black.

"Sorry for the wait," Ronald said but was quickly interrupted by another parent.

"Excuse me. I've been waiting for ten minutes-" the parent exclaimed.

Ronald held up a finger cutting off the impatient man. "I will be right with you, sir!"

Ronald was covered in perspiration. "Sorry for the wait," he began again. "Welcome to Ronald's Robes. I am Ronald. How may I robe you today?" He spouted in a single breath.

"We just need some academy robes," Rinx stated.

"Ah of course more first year students. Very good, very good." he examined the children with a hand on his chin. "Mmhm, mmhm," he said, nodding his head. "Right." He rushed out of the room and back again. "Try these on."

They both pulled them on.

"Mmhm, mmhm," he examined again. "Very good, very good. How do they feel?"

"It feels good to me," Black confirmed.

"Yeah, no problems here," Rinx agreed.

"Very good, very good," Ronald said again. He took the robes and bolted to the back room again. A moment later when he returned this time he had two bundles wrapped in brown paper and tied up in string. "This should cover you for the school year. Two and a quarter each, please," and he held out his hand.

Rinx paid the man and they were on their way.

As Rinx and Black exited Ronald's Robes they could hear Ronald shouting again over the chaos, "I'll be with you in a moment, sir!"

The two children found their way to the table Rhiss was seated at. Rhiss gestured for the two of them to take a seat.

"All sorted?" Rhiss asked.

"Yes mother," Rinx confirmed.

"We'll take our lunch here and then we can make our way to the Academy," Rhiss informed them as she signaled for the waiter.

They each took the special of the day, beef stew with an assortment of vegetables. Rinx and Black updated Rhiss about the interesting people and events they'd witnessed at Ronald's Robes while they ate. As they waited for Rhiss to settle the bill they observed the unique wizard and witches that passed by. People of all shapes and sizes dressed in all sorts of attire but mostly dressed in traditional robes or cloaks. Some appeared simple while others were finely embroidered in every such color the children could imagine.

After Rhiss paid the waiter they disembarked for the academy. They made their way to a part of the city that was scarcely populated. As they continued on their path a line appeared to creep above the skyline. The further they walked the higher it grew until they found themselves at a towering stone wall. In it was etched a large block three stories tall and next to it set a tiny shack. The shack had a dutch door with a decrepit old man peering at them from the top portion.

As they approached the door the old man scratched the stubble on his chin. "Well if it isn't the red witch herself. Rhiss Renard. It's been a long time." The old man spat some brown substance into some unseen destination at his feet.

"It has," Rhiss replied. "And it's Quint now. Has been for several years, Mr. Bayer."

"Ah so you married that Quint boy did you? He must have had a stronger constitution than he looked," he sneered.

Rhiss made no reply.

Mr. Bayer looked down his crooked hooked nose at the children. "These two come to enroll then?" He snorted and spat again.

A pigeon hopped across the top of the shack and eyeballed them.

"Of course," Rhiss replied dryly.

"Alright, let me see your letters of acceptance then." He reached out a dirty hand with long nails caked with black dirt and hooked fingers making his hand resemble a claw more than something belonging to a man.

The children passed their letters.

Mr. Bayer examined them closely, sounding out their names silently before saying them aloud. "Rinx Quint," he set one bloodshot eye on her then back to the next paper. "Ama-Amadeus Black," he struggled and gave Black a glare. Black returned his stare. "Hmpf. Fine, I'll let you in then."

He opened the bottom of the dutch door and taking a long walking stick from behind the wall began hobbling over to the enormous block on the wall. He slowly approached the stone and gently gave it a push. The whole block began to swing inward as if it weighed no more than a screen door caught in the wind.

Rhiss and the children each bid him good day and he merely grumbled in return. After they had passed through the gate he called out to them, both children turning their heads to listen. "Lesson one, children. I see everything on these grounds," he grimaced as a pigeon landed on his shoulder.

The grounds were enormous but the Academy was relatively close to the gate. A mere fifteen minute walk brought you to the main entrance of what resembled a fortress. The academy was situated on a hill and gently sloping down on the left and right were rolling hills and forests that stretched for miles.

"This is incredible," Black said, floored by the sheer size of it all.

"How is it possible for the academy to have so much space within the city?" Rinx questioned.

Rhiss responded. "Tuatha Dé Academy has long utilized spatial magic. From outside the walls it takes up much less space than what actually exists on the inside."

Both the children surveyed the area with their mouths agape and then continued up the several stairs to the large front doors propped open. Two older children dressed in the academy's dark blue robes greeted them.

"Welcome to Tuatha Dé Academy. I'm Sierra," the young woman shook their hands and gestured to her peer. "And this is Stanton."

Stanton shook their hands as well. "Welcome, welcome."

"My name's Amadeus," Black put a hand to his chest.

"And I'm Rinx and this is my mother."

"Rhiss Quint," Rhiss chimed in.

"A pleasure to meet you all and welcome again," Stanton said. "Please follow the green rugs." And he waved them inside.

They found upon entering that the stone walls were decorated in tapestries and ancient paintings. Several candles hung from the ceiling and spaced along the walls. A long rug stretched down the hallway and went around the corner to the left. They followed the rug down one corridor and then another, passing some students and the occasional adult along the way until they finally entered a large hall.

The hall had several tables and comfortable chairs. It was so large that it had four enormous fireplaces, two on either wall with metal grates to bar anyone from falling into them. There were several students sitting around casually. To the left just as they entered the room was a desk and a banner hanging from the front that read 'Check In.'

A young man sat behind the desk, his head nodding and his eyes shut. As they approached him he jerked his head up. He blinked at them several times and began to talk but was halted by a yawn.

"Welcome to check in," he said, taking a pen. "Can I have your names please?"

"Rinx Quint," she said.

"Amadeus Black," he added.

"Black and Quint," the young man repeated to himself. "OK, you both have officially been checked in and your tuition was previously paid upon the submission of your applications so," he turned and snapped his fingers at a group of students sitting around one of the fireplaces chatting. An older girl and older boy broke away from the group and joined them. "So, Rinx, Jenny will show you to the girl's dormitory and Tom will show you , Amadeus, to the boy's dormitory. Welcome."

Both the children turned to Rhiss.

"This is where I leave you." Rhiss said.

"I will miss you mother," Rinx wrapped her arms around her.

"I will miss you too," Rhiss admitted.

Rinx released her mother. Rhiss put a hand up to Rinx's cheek and managed a smile. "Work hard," Rhiss glanced from Rinx to Black. "Both of you."

"We will," they both said in unison. Then they both left her to follow their guides.

They all walked together down the first hall.

"So you are brother and sister," Jenny asked.

"No," they both said at the same time and they all laughed.

"No," Rinx repeated. "Deus has just been staying with us for the past couple of years learning magic."

Black nodded his head.

They reached the end of the hallway and split in two different directions.

"Well the boy's dorm is this way, the girl's dorm is that way so we will be parting ways here." Tom said, looking at Black.

"But you can both meet back up in the lounge we just came from after," Jenny added.

Rinx looked at Black. "Ok let's do that."

"Sounds good to me," Black agreed. "See you then."

And the two parted ways. Black followed Tom through the winding corridors past several different rooms at one point climbing two flights of old creaking stairs. They talked as they walked.

"So what do you think of the academy so far?" Tom asked.

"Well it seems impressive. Especially all the countryside that surrounds it." Black responded.

"Tuatha Dé Academy is the best of all the magic schools," Tom said. "But it should be. It's the only one directly funded by the Guild of Ravens. But I suppose that makes sense, since they snatch up a lot of their recruits from here."

Black nodded his head feigning like none of this was new to him.

"So I know it's your first year but are you any good at magic yet?" A few kids Black's age ran past them on the stairs.

Black shrugged in response. "Not really but I know how to enchant a bit."

Tom seemed to deflate. "Oh, that's too bad."

And then Black added, "But I'm not bad at the martial arts."

"Really?" Tom seemed to regain his vigor. "Have you thought about joining the Combat Tournament Club?"

"No, I don't even know what that is," Black admitted.

They made their way past several portraits of distinguished looking gentlemen and ladies of years past.

"What?!" he exclaimed. "Well I guess I shouldn't be too surprised. So few students join. I'm the captain of the Tuatha Dé teams now and I could use some more members. We compete against other schools to see who has the best mages. It's not all about who can cast the strongest spell though. You can use martial arts too." He gave Black a slap on the shoulder.

"I'll think about it," Black promised.

"Well don't think too long. Tomorrow they'll have the booths on display and representatives for each of the classes and extracurricular activities available for first years to learn about. You then have until the end of the week to select which to sign up for. We'll have a booth there too." They'd stopped in front of a red door with a gold handle. "You should stop by and sign up. It's the best way to learn how to use combat magic in real combat scenarios. Well, we're here."

Tom opened the door and said, "The door is enchanted so that it only opens for boys and faculty so no chance of any girls sneaking in." He sighed. "Unfortunately."

They entered the room which was like a smaller version of the lounge they had come from. There was a fireplace on the far wall with several chairs, tables, and even a long couch scattered about. A few were filled by students. On either side of the room were several doors. One on the far left read 'Bathroom' while the other doors had a pair of names fixed to them.

"This is the dorm for first years so you will only be with other kids your age. You just need to look for the door with your name on it and that's who you'll be sharing the room with." Tom put his hands on his hips and looked around. "So do you have any questions?"

"No, I don't think so," Black shrugged.

"Great," he smiled and reached out his hand. "I suggest you just stick to the dorm and the lounge for now. It's easy to get lost. See you around." They shook hands and he took a step to walk away but then turned back. "Oh and they start serving dinner at 6:30." And then he was gone through the red door.

Black searched the doors for his name. From the sound of it some were already occupied by students. Finally he discovered the room he'd be sleeping in every night for nearly a year. It was the third door on the right side of the room. As he read his name to himself a voice came from behind.

"It seems we will be sharing a room together," the voice said.

Black turned to see the same boy he and Rinx met in front of Sharla's stall nearly a year and a half ago.

"Damascus?" Black asked, struggling to remember.

"You remember. It seems providence has brought us together again." He stood smiling with both arms tucked behind his back before then extended a hand. "Amadeus, I believe." They shook hands.

***

Present

Rinx and Black were each given their own rooms across from one another on the top floor. The rooms were nearly as large as Rinx's whole apartment and were equipped with their own large bath, a wardrobe, desk, dresser with attached mirror, and a four post bed. The walls were decorated with several small landscape paintings and floral patterned wallpaper of red and gold.

Black took a seat at the desk and was considering the events and the revelation that a Premier could be involved. This complicated things. It was within their right to move against a Premier if evidence alleged of crimes as serious as these. Black leaned back in his chair, closing his eyes meditatively. The musk of the incense still clung to his clothes.

If Premier Barnabas is involved in all this, what could possibly be his motive, he thought to himself.

He was interrupted by a servant knocking at his door.

"Lunch is being served, sir," the servant informed him and held the door open for him to follow.

"Thank you," Black stepped into the corridor and the servant proceeded to lead him down the hall. Black stopped her halfway down the hall. "Should we not grab Rinx as well?"

"Ms. Quint is already with the master in the dining hall," she replied.

Black nodded his head and proceeded to follow the servant to their destination. The dining hall was situated on the ground floor complete with a long wooden table and a fireplace that sat empty. Damascus was seated at the head of the table and Rinx two chairs down from him. The sun occasionally broke through the clouds, shining through the tall windows that nearly went to the floor filling the room with daylight. Damascus stood as Black entered the room.

Black took the seat nearest to Damascus across from Rinx and his host sat back down. "It seems the storm has passed," Black motioned to the windows. A servant hurried to place cutlery on the table in front him. They followed with two glasses, one filled with water.

"For the time being. I'm afraid we can expect its fury to return tonight." Damascus mused.

Servants emerged from the kitchen preceded by a strong aroma. They placed a plate of brown rice and fish drizzled in lemon sauce accompanied by a glass of white wine.

Once everyone was served Damascus exclaimed, "Enjoy," and they commenced with lunch.

"Where is your father?" Black inquired.

"He is away on business in Tristandale. He will likely not be back for some time." His glance quickly jumped to Rinx and then back to Black.

"He has always been a busy man, your father." Black tore into the fish as he spoke.

"His position in the Order of Homme keeps him quite busy," Damascus said as he took a healthy drink of wine.

Black did the same. "And when do you think his son will take over as head of the Order." Black flashed a playful smile.

Damascus stared at his food as he replied, "It is hard to know what my father intends but I know there are some burdens of the Order that are made ever more complicated in such a prominent position."

Rinx downed the last of her wine and held the glass up for more.

"So Black," Damascus said after a long draught in the conversation. "Tell me where have you been busying yourself lately?"

"My work has mostly been taking me to the Earthen Realm. No shortage of parasites to feed on those unfamiliar with our world. And too few of us to police them. I spend a lot of time in the major cities, London, New York, Paris. I've been to Tokyo a couple of times. Occasionally something will draw me to the small towns and villages that are scattered across too many countrysides."

"Well I suppose that's the advantage of being on freelance status. You go wherever you please." Damascus said.

"Speaking of which," Black turned his attention to Rinx. "I'm not the only one on freelance status here. Rinx just received her status yesterday."

Rinx jumped at the mention of her own name and the attention that was directed to her.

Damascus turned towards her. "Well congratulations," he said as he raised his glass of wine.

"Thanks," she replied simply as the servants were replacing her empty plate with a desert. A spongy cake with strawberry sauce.

Damascus waved the desert away and Black did the same thing. Rinx dug in unabashedly. The rest of the meal went on with the occasional small talk. Damascus excused himself at the end of the meal and was absent for most of the day.

The two mostly lounged about for the day debating on their next move. It seemed like the obvious choice would be to confront and question Barnabas but they were uncertain if whether they would be acting prematurely considering his status as a Premier.

The evening rolled around and the servants brought them clean beige linen attire for the evening and prepared a bath in each of their rooms. The servants took their dirty clothes to be cleaned for the next day.

As Black came down the stairs dressed in the clean linen trousers and tunic for dinner he could detect the distant rumbling of thunder. He entered the dining hall to find Rinx waiting by the window. She had the curtain pulled back peering out into the night. Damascus loomed near the fireplace which was now ablaze.

"It seems you were right," Black called to his old friend.

Damascus looked up from the flames with a face of questioning.

"It seems the storm is upon us again," a flash of lightning came through the window Rinx was peering out of. Its brief presentation had cast harsh shadows throughout the room. Damascus's face combined with the light from the fire particularly resembled that of a skull.

"Ah yes," he smiled. "It sounds like it will be quite formidable too."

The dinner went on quite the same as their lunch. This time they dined on pheasant preceded by a salad and accompanied with vegetables. At the end of the meal the servants came around to pour them each a brandy.

Damascus placed his hand over his glass and shook his. "Not tonight I think."

The others helped themselves to one glass each. The little sleep they'd had the previous night was catching up to them and the beds in the rooms above called to them. After their drinks they said their goodnights and went on their way.

Black entered his room and blew out the candles. He pulled off the tunic and slipped between the crisp sheets of the bed. He laid awake for some time still contemplating how they should proceed but eventually his thoughts became more dreamlike and he was lost in sleep.

Black awoke a few hours later. His heart was pounding in his chest. What had chased his sleep away? He didn't know. He immediately strained his eyes checking the door. It was still shut or was it just closed. His eyes continued to penetrate the inky darkness searching for the source causing the sweat to bead on his forehead and his anxiety.

He caught the slightest movement at the end of his bed and something stood up. He could make out the shape of a woman. The details were becoming clearer now. Her hair fell down around her shoulders and bunched up just above her breasts. She was naked. Black couldn't be certain if she knew he was awake. Could she see his eyes in the darkness? She hunched forward and there was a popping sound. Black was transfixed, his blood pumping hard in his ears. She was erect again but she looked darker now and taller maybe. Again she hunched forward and again definite cracking sounds. A stifled moan and heavy breathing.

Black detected a familiar odor and the image of what was happening in front of him started to take shape in his mind. Again she stood erect but undeniably taller now and broader too. Black realized what he was seeing just as the beast leaped onto the bed. He narrowly rolled out of its path as it caught his pillow in its enormous maw and shredded the bed with its claws. Black heard a crash from across the hall and shouting in another room.

The beast came at him again leaving the bed collapsing to the floor in its wake. It cleared the distance so fast that he had no time to react. He managed to raise his arms in a meager defense. Black grabbed one of its claws while the other dug into his shoulder, evoking a cry of pain from his throat. The monster's maw lunged at his head missing only barely. Its long fangs pierced into his already aching shoulder. Black's own bestial blood was fueling his strength on pure instinct but with the brute's teeth buried in the same shoulder it clung to, pain was overcoming his might.

With his one free hand he desperately clawed at the monster's face until he found the warm wet eye. He buried his thumb up to the knuckle. The monster wrenched backwards roaring as it released its grasp. Black stole the opportunity to activate the runes tattooed down his spine, further enhancing his strength for a kick into the beast's exposed belly. This blow sent it hurdling back against the far wall. The wolf inside Black could be held back no longer. Fenrir screamed through Black's veins and a giant white wolf was now squaring off with the werewolf.

Black met his adversary's next charge and the two danced around the room. A whirlwind of tooth and nail and fur and blood. Furniture shattered as their bodies collided with the environment. It was a dance of death to the tempo of snarling and tearing.

The door to Black's room was flung open slamming into the wall with a powerful thud. Damascus stood in the doorway holding a bloody short sword in his hand. His sinewy upper body was naked and covered in perspiration and streaked with more blood. Black eyed him as he bared down on the werewolf's neck, shaking the last bit of life from it and claiming his victory over the monster. His white fur was caked with blood. His keen sight caught a glimpse of movement behind Damascus. It was Rinx.

"Black, are you safe?!" She cried out, crowding in beside Damascus.

Black let the lifeless monster slip from his fangs to the floor. He heard the pounding of several feet coming down the hall.

Damascus stepped past Rinx and shouted into the hall, "Bring us a doctor and something to treat these wounds now!"

Black began to relax and let his senses return to him. A whimper escaped him as he moved forward and forced his body to take the shape of a man again. He sat down on what remained of the bed.

"Help is on the way," Damascus assured him.

"You two alright?" he winced as he spoke.

"We're ok," Rinx confirmed. "Someone snuck into my room, too but Damascus came rushing in and woke me up before they could attack. Another werewolf."

They all turned to the bloody mess on the floor. It was looking more and more like a human again.

"Bloody werewolves," Damascus exclaimed and then said more to himself. "In my house."

"I suppose we should count ourselves lucky it wasn't a full moon," Black winced in pain. "Three nights from now and they would have been at full strength."

Three guards had posted up on the door awaiting orders including Raija. A man in long baggy white robes stepped into the room.

Raija spoke, "The doctor is here, master."

"Then see to my friend immediately," he gestured to Black and the doctor hurried to him followed by a much younger man carrying a bag of tools.

The doctor cleaned Black's many wounds and commenced sewing the several deep gashes shut and wrapping them in bandages. Damascus disappeared for part of the procedure and returned with a small bottle.

"I know you heal fast but take this potion," he said kneeling beside Black. "It will speed things along much quicker."

Black uncorked the glass bottle and grimaced as he swallowed the thick acrid solution. His throat resisted the liquid but he was able to force it down. When it hit his stomach it was like magma cooling into heavy stone. Every inch of his body ached or stung from the antiseptics applied by the doctor. His leg was sore from the strain of using his strength runes and he could feel the oozing of some of his more severe cuts.

Raija surveyed the room and the destruction that was wrought. Blood was spattered across the walls and what paintings remained in place had an addition of crimson paint. His eyes settled on the monster lying in a lake of blood now completely human again.

"It's one of the servants," he said flatly. "We've been infiltrated."

Damascus addressed him calmly, "How did this come to be in my house?" He rubbed the temples of his head.

"They must have been compromised after being cleared for ser-" Raija was cut short.

"IN MY HOUSE!" Damascus raged. He closed the gap to Raija coming face to face. "In my father's house." Damascus had regained his composure. "This is a disgrace on the Order of Homme, a disgrace on the Mageese house, and a disgrace on you, Raija. As our chief of security and my father's right hand."

Raija struggled to meet Damascus's eyes. "My apologies master." His bearded face was a mix of shame and anger. "I-"

"You will round up the remaining servants. They will be tested for lycanthropy and thoroughly investigated before they are released back into service. During the remainder of our guests' stay," he glanced back at Black who appeared pallid and near to fall over. "Which will likely be extended, you will only deploy the most loyal of guards at your disposal."

"Sir, it will be done," Raija snapped to attention.

"And have someone clean this mess up," he added. "You may go, Raija."

He turned back to Black who was now propped up against Rinx. "Let's get him into a clean bed."

Rinx nodded and they both heaved Black up and assisted him to a larger room that had twin beds. Black eased into one them with their help. He was beginning to feel the effects of the potion. His body was becoming numb as the pain seemed to melt away.

"There's one more thing. Stay with him and I'll return," Damascus told Rinx.

He rushed out of the room and returned a short time later with two more small glass bottles. "He runs the risk of catching lycanthropy." Damascus turned to Black whose eyes could barely remain open. "Drink this before you sleep. This will clear it from your system as long as it's taken in the first forty-eight hours."

"Great," Black croaked. "This one going to taste like demon piss too?" He didn't wait for an answer and just swallowed the concoction and coughed hard in the aftermath.

Damascus turned to Rinx and handed her the second bottle. "You too. You were in contact with the other one. Just to be safe. I already took mine."

"Thanks," she placed a hand on Damascus's shoulder, raised the bottle and choked down the contents. "Just awful. Demon piss would be an improvement." The two exchanged smiles as Black slipped into sleep.

Black was in and out of sleep for almost twenty-four hours. Rinx spent the rest of the night sleeping in the other bed while Damascus watched over them. After that they alternated keeping watch over Black. Damascus refused to leave Rinx's side until Black had regained consciousness. By the second day Black was back on his feet having had another dose of the healing potion Damascus concocted. He was able to move around quite easily and they were all confident that he would be fully recovered by the next day.

The three of them sat around the room discussing the situation. Black delicately rotated his injured shoulder, testing its mobility.

"Whoever is behind this is very well connected," Rinx said.

"Indeed, to have sleeper agents embedded in my own house," Damascus winced at the thought.

"We need to be very careful with our next move," Black added.

"Yes, but it was a desperate move attacking you both here," Damascus folded his arms across his chest and sat back in his seat. "They must have known there was no chance of their agents making it out of here alive even if they were successful in killing you two. They lost some valuable spies in that play."

There came a knock at the door and Raija entered. "Sir, there is a report that just came in that I think you will find important."

"Thank you Raija," Damascus turned to the others. "One moment please," and he stepped into the hallway with Raija closing the door behind him.

A few moments later he returned and regarded them a moment before speaking. "We just received a report that both Premier Roth and Premier Valen have been discovered in their homes dead."

Rinx put her hand to her mouth. "Premier Valen?"

"How?" Black inquired.

"It's unclear. It seems as if they were both discovered just this morning. There are no other details." Damascus said.

There was a moment of silence and then Black stood up.

Damascus nodded to Black.

"What are you doing?" Rinx said more rhetorically than with the expectation of receiving an answer.

"I've rested long enough. I need to get back to work," he responded.

Rinx stood up too. "I want to investigate Premier Valen's death myself." She sighed. "I need to see it. We should move quickly before they-" she swallowed but it seemed to catch in her throat. "before they take the body away."

"I understand. We stay together for this," Black said reluctantly. "We'll visit Valen's house together."

Rinx and Black each changed into their own clothes while Damascus dismissed himself, returning just before they were about to leave.

"How are you feeling my friend," he asked Black.

"Well enough," Black responded.

Damascus was standing with his arms crossed behind his back at that moment before extending a hand with another glass vial. "Your body may be nearly healed but it must still be exhausted from the effort. Take this." He placed the bottle in Black's hand. "It will invigorate you. I made it just for you. Weaker than the kind we normally consume but potent enough for someone unaccustomed with its effects."

Black slapped Damascus on the shoulder and threw back the tonic. It was much sweeter than he had expected. A far cry from the vile medicine he had experienced earlier. It took effect moments later. His heart began to race and then leveled off to a steady beat. His mouth was dry but his senses were sharp and he felt hyper alert. His muscles felt poised and ready to spring into action at any moment but his hands were steady and without jitters. *This was supposed to be a weak dose?* he thought.

"I'm sorry I can not join you two," he looked quickly at Rinx. "But you are both always welcome in my house. My duty binds me however and in light of these recent events there will be much work for me to do here."

"I understand," Black responded while Rinx let out a small grunt. "Thank you for your hospitality."

Rinx seemed to concede to some battle in her own head and said, "yes, thank you for what you've done."

She hugged him, Black shook his hand, and they departed.

They wasted no time rushing across town to Premier Valen's home. It was relatively modest considering his station. Behind a tall wrought iron gate stood a red two story home with black shutters. As they approached the house they were passed by several other members of the Guild of Ravens and the city guards. They flashed their emblems as they passed. Some of the guild members were collecting shards of glass from the front yard.

"Do you smell that?" Black asked.

"Yeah it smells like something was burning," Rinx clenched her jaw as the words left her mouth.

Black quickly scanned the outside of the house before they let themselves in the front door. They paused just long enough to ask someone where the crime was committed and they were directed to the study up the stairs. Black was leading the way but stopped just in front of the doorway to the room. He turned toward Rinx but as he opened his mouth to speak she pushed past him to the study.

She froze trying to make sense of the carnage before her. Black followed behind her and gently placed a hand on her shoulder as he continued on to examine the scene.

Valen was unrecognizable. Parts of him were scattered about the room. Black could make out obvious bits of bone embedded in the floor and in one of the walls. That same wall had some teeth laying at the base of it and a hand was in the middle of the floor. Most of the parts though, just looked like smoldering chunks of meat.

One of the guild members approached Black and he quickly flashed his emblem again.

"What the hell is going on here?" the woman asked him motioning to the bloody mess behind her.

"I was hoping you could fill me in," Black responded and pointed to the notebook she was carrying in her hand. "What do you have?"

"Well not a lot yet. A couple of people in the area reported to a city guard of hearing a loud noise coming from the house.

The CG found the gate ajar so entered noticed glass in the yard and a window blown out on the second floor so when no one answered the door he forced it and found this nightmare up here."

"And what have you found?" Black turned back to see Rinx had joined him.

"It's a bit unusual." The guild member turned towards the scene. "There is a lot of damage to the body and to the nearby furniture indicating that it was quite a powerful spell that was cast on the victim based off the, uh, debris we can tell that it was fired in this direction." She indicated a corner of the room.

"It didn't do much damage to the wall, though," Black said. "But it was able to blow out the windows in the line of fire."

"Yes," the woman confirmed. "And there's something else."

"There's hardly any burn marks," Rinx chimed in.

"Exactly," the guild member exclaimed. "So what we have is a spell that does massive amounts of damage in a concentrated area with only minor burning and has a concussive force that can blow out the windows being heard from down the street."

"It's like a bomb," Black said. "Anything else?"

"Not yet but we are scouring the place."

"Alright, thank you," Black said as she went back to her work. He turned again to Rinx. "What could this be all about? Some kind of power grab?"

He searched her face.

She met his gaze with steely resolve, "It's time we pay Barnabas a visit."

"I'll go ahead and you return the Order of Homme," he replied.

Rinx's eyes burned with fire. "I'm coming with you. Period."

Black conceded with a sigh and a nod.

Chapter 6

Past

Damascus entered the room and Black followed. The room was simple. Two beds with trunks at the end of each, a pair of desks, dressers, and wardrobes. The room smelled of dust, like it had been sealed for a hundred years.

There was a tidy stack of folded sheets and a blanket on one of the beds while the other was made up.

Damascus pointed to the made bed. "Sorry I already selected my bed."

"That's fine. Neither one looks all that comfortable," Black responded.

"You're right about that," Damascus laughed.

Black noted that Damascus was dressed in his academy robes. "I guess I should start wearing my robe too." He removed one from the bag he was carrying and pulled it over his head.

"As drafty as this old place is, we'll need another layer of clothes to keep from catching a cold," Damascus said.

Both the boys laughed as Black hung the rest of his robes in the wardrobe along with his cloak. After he had finished putting the rest of his things away they both walked back into the common area.

There were several kids in the common room. Black recognized one right way, the round bulk of the boy they'd seen earlier that day at Ronald's Robes. He sat stuffed into one of the many cushioned chairs reading a book. Two other boys that Black also recognized from the shop made their way towards him. One of the boys was tall with short black hair while the other was of an average build with long brown hair parted down the middle. The tall boy leaned over and yanked the book free from Gilbert's hands and tossed it to his friend.

"What are you readin'?" the smaller boy asked flipping through the pages.

Gilbert reached for the book but the boy yanked it further from his reach. "It's just a history of Tuatha Dé between the 1500's and the 1800's," Gilbert pleaded with his hands.

"Boring! Nobody cares," the tall boy responded.

"Whatdaya think Newt?" the smaller boy said to the taller. "How many robes do you think they had to sew together before they had one big enough to fit his fatass in?"

The taller boy laughed and a few of the other kids watching struggled to hide their amusement at the question as well.

Damascus was studying Black's face as he watched the events unfold.

"Just give me my book back," Gilbert whined.

The boys were now tossing it back and forth taunting the chubby boy. Black took a step forward but stopped when Damascus caught his eye.

"This is not our business," Damascus advised him. "We should not get involved in this."

Black considered his words for a moment. He didn't know this kid but something chewed at him from within.

"Give him his book back," Black called out.

The two boys stopped tossing the book back and forth and turned their attention on Black.

"And who the hell are you?" The tall boy asked him.

"My name's Amadeus," the boys approached him.

The boy with brown hair spoke, "I'm Darius and that's Newt." Darius looked Black up and down.

While he did this Black realized that at some point Damascus had moved around behind the boys without ever making a sound.

After Darius had finished his inspection he said, "Sure. Fat-ass can have his book back." Darius flung the book at Gilbert.

Gilbert tried to catch the book but it fumbled in his hands and fell to the floor.

The two boys shoved past Black. "Just watch yourself," Darius said as both the boys left the dormitory.

Gilbert retrieved his book from the floor. "Thank you."

"It's not a big deal," Black replied. "But you shouldn't let people push you around like that."

"I'm not good with confrontation," Gilbert said, refusing to meet Black's gaze.

"Obviously," Damascus chuckled.

Gilbert's face was turning red and he was shuffling his feet.

Black let out a sigh. "Forget it.," and he extended a hand. "I'm Amadeus."

"I heard. My name's Gilbert," he said, taking Black's hand.

"Well if introductions are going around I'll join in. Damascus." He did a short bow and then shook Gilbert's hand as well.

"I need to meet my friend downstairs in the lounge if you two want to join." Black said.

Gilbert looked nervously at Damascus.

"Is your friend the same one that was with you when we met before? What was her name? Rinx I believe," Damascus inquired.

"Yes, that's right," Black confirmed.

"Sure I'll come with you," Damascus decided.

"Are you sure you guys don't mind me going with you?" Gilbert asked as he turned his book over in his hands.

Both the boys assured Gilbert that it was fine. They proceeded back to the lounge. It was fortunate that Gilbert had accompanied them because neither of the other two boys remembered the way back to the lounge. When they arrived Rinx was already waiting for them.

"Took you longer than I expected," Rinx greeted him.

"I got carried away making friends," he pointed a thumb back at the other two boys.

"I see," she replied.

"And enemies, I'm afraid," Damascus smiled.

Rinx looked at Black confused. "It's nothing," Black assured her. "You remember Damascus?"

"I do," she said smiling while she performed a parity of a bow.

Damascus laughed and bowed back.

"He's going to be my roommate," Black patted Gilbert on the shoulder. "And this is Gilbert."

She gave Black a quick smile. "Nice to meet you, Gilbert. My name is Rinx."

"It's nice to meet you, too," Gilbert said as his face took on the shade of a giant tomato.

"So," Rinx leaned in with a big smile. "What is your magical affinity Gilbert?"

"Nothing all that exciting, I'm afraid," Gilbert replied as he picked some fuzz from his robe. "Earth." He looked around the group. "What about you all?"

Rinx spoke first. "Fire." she said proudly with her hands on her hips.

"That's a good one. I wish I had something like that but isn't it a bit-" Gilbert struggled to wrap his arms around his wide body. "Dangerous?"

"That's part of the fun," Rinx laughed.

"And you?" Damascus cut in asking Black.

"Wind," Black replied.

Gilbert winced and Damascus gave Black a sympathetic look.

"Well it could be worse I suppose," Damascus said, shrugging.

"What could be worse?" Gilbert blurted out.

Damascus just smiled and shrugged again.

Gilbert's face turned that familiar red color again. "I mean, at least it's unique."

"So earth doesn't seem so bad now, huh?" Damascus nudged Gilbert.

"Yeah it hasn't been very easy to use but I didn't realize it was considered bad," Black admitted. "I just thought I wasn't very good at magic."

"Well, maybe it's a bit of both," Rinx said and they all started laughing.

Gilbert spoke up again, speaking very carefully. "I just think some people don't find it very practical or useful."

Black looked at his hands and grimaced before turning his head to Damascus. "And what about you?"

Damascus smiled and rubbed the back of his head. "I don't have any magic."

The other three children stood mouths agape for a moment before Rinx spoke.

"I guess that's worse than wind magic," she said, slapping Black on the back. "But what are you doing here at the Academy then?"

"I admit," Damascus said. "That my family was a bit reluctant allowing me to attend but there is still a lot to learn even without magic." Damascus waved his hands about. "There's lot's of value in studying the different types of magic, history, and potions of course." He crossed his hands behind his back. "My family are experts at brewing various potions," he said, raising his chin.

Gilbert nodded his head.

"I suppose that could be useful," Rinx rubbed her chin. "My mother makes potions sometimes but she hasn't taught me too much, but you must be the only student here that doesn't have any magic."

"Probably," Damascus admitted. "We normally have our own schools."

The children chatted for a while longer until eventually an older student appeared in the doorway to announce that dinner would be served soon and they could all follow him to the dining hall. The students filed down the hallways until they passed through two enormous wooden doors into the dining hall. There were several long tables but they were all instructed to take a seat at the same one. The rest remained empty.

A woman in a white robe with raven coloured hair waited for them all to be seated. She had her hair in a single long braid that hung down her back. Once they were seated she raised a single hand.

"Good evening and welcome to your first day as Tuatha Dé Academy Students," she said, holding her hands in her lap. "I am Maitresse Brunel. Unfortunately your class warden is not here to greet you because he is an irresponsible layabout and I pity any class that has the misfortune of being placed under his guidance."

"Thank you my dear sister Abigail for the lovely introduction," called a man strolling into the hall with a bit of sweat beading on his forehead. He wore a pale blue robe and his black hair was pulled back in a short ponytail. "Forgive me class. I lost track of the days. I am your class warden Maitre Brunel.

Abigail glared at her brother for a moment and then turned to address the class again. "Good luck," she said and then marched out of the dining hall.

Maitre Brunel watched her stomp out and then he continued speaking to the class. "Right, so uh, I am your class warden so I am responsible for you all while you are attending the academy." He clapped his hands together. "So if you have any questions, concerns, grievous wounds, just let me know and I'll try to help you out."

All the students exchanged nervous looks.

"Now, as you can see, you are the only class present this week. Except for the class assistants, all the other students only arrive the weekend before classes start."

Black was becoming aware of the delicious scent wafting into the hall from some unseen kitchen. That's when he heard a sound like gravel grinding together. Maitre Brunel paused for a moment.

"Wow fatty," someone from the crowd said. The whole room burst into laughter.

Black could guess at who said it. He looked at Gilbert sitting across the table with Rinx. His face was glowing red and even Rinx looked embarrassed to be next to him.

Gilbert looked from Rinx to Black and then to the Maitre. "S-sorry. I'm just a little hungry I guess."

The students continued to laugh. Maitre Brunel raised his hands to silence the class. "It's alright, I'm a bit hungry myself so I'll try to wrap things up quickly so they can bring us dinner." The last few giggles died out. "Where was I? Uh-yes. This week is just for the first year students to meet one another, become a bit familiar with their new home, and of course decide on which classes to commence their academic career." He smoothed his hair back. "I probably should tell you which class I teach. I am the Maitre for all elemental magic classes." He gave the class a wolfish grin. "And since Introduction to Elements is mandatory for all first year students." He held his arms out. "You will all be in my class. Oh and one more thing before I forget. All first year students need to be in their dorm by nine o'clock every week night and ten o'clock on the weekend." He shook his head. "I know it's a real drag but there will be nightly patrols and you don't want to get caught by them, believe me."

"Ok so does anyone have any questions?" He asked.

A blond haired boy raised his hand. Maitre Brunel waved the boy's hand down.

"I'm sure you can figure it out," he said to the blond boy as he scratched the stubble on his chin. The boy reluctantly lowered his hand. "Alright so no questions. Let's eat then." He waved to an old woman standing in the doorway to the kitchen and dinner was served.

Maitre Brunel caught one of the kitchen workers. "I'll take mine to go please."

And without even a farewell their class warden took his food and left them.

The students ate their dinner and chatted with their new classmates.

"I don't know about that Maitre Brunel," Gilbert said to the others.

"Seems a bit flaky to me," Rinx said.

"Not very disciplined if you take his sister at her word," Damascus added. "And he didn't really inspire a different impression."

Julius, the blond boy who had raised his hand, introduced himself to the other students around him before he called down to Black and the others. "I heard this is his first year as a Maitre."

"Not a good start," Black stated.

"Him and his sister are total opposites they say and his sister is widely known as a genius. So I guess we know what that makes him," Julius told them. They all erupted in laughter.

"How'd he get a job here?" Gilbert asked.

Julius shrugged his shoulders. "Guess the old Maitre croaked and maybe his sister put in a good word for him."

"I doubt that," Black added and they all laughed again.

They eventually finished their meals but continued to talk until Gilbert reminded them of the hour.

"We have to be back before nine," he said with a slight quiver in his voice.

They agreed that it was probably time to head back and so their little group stood to leave. Some of the other kids had already left and the ones that still remained took their standing as a sign to leave as well.

Black overheard Rinx whisper to Gilbert, "Thank you for taking the fall."

"It was nothing, really," He replied.

They walked back until Rinx needed to part from them and make her way to the girls dorm. The boys continued to their own dorm where they, after a bit more chatting in the common space, decided it was time to brush their teeth and be off to bed.

Black and Damascus settled into their beds without having much to say and soon they were asleep.

The next day they were awakened by a bang at their door. Black set up in bed just in time to see Damascus spring from his bed to his feet. The banging continued but further away. Then they heard a shout.

"Everybody wake up, you're going to be late for the class orientation!"

Black and Damascus exchanged looks before Black climbed out of bed and made his way to open their door. They found other students stepping out into the common space. Several of them were still rubbing the sleep from their eyes. In the middle of the room stood Maitre Brunel. His robe looked crumpled and some of his hair had come untied and was falling down his unshaven face.

"Have you all forgotten?" he said, trying to push some of the hair back out of his eyes. "You have thirty minutes to be in the student lounge."

"We can forget if you don't tell us," Julius grumbled.

"I guess the girls will be wondering where we are," another student said.

Maitre Brunel spun around towards the student. "The girls!?" He shouted as he ran from the boys dormitory.

"This guy," Damascus laughed.

They both hurried to get ready and then made their way down to the student's lounge. The lounge was transformed. Most of the furniture had been moved out to make way for the several tables and booths meant to showcase the various clubs and classes available to the first years. Several of the booths had banners displaying the class or club names.

Damascus and Black weren't the first to arrive. Others were already speaking with some of the class representatives. Black spotted Gilbert chatting with the rep for the chess club.

"Take a look," Damascus pointed to Abigail.

She was sitting at her booth labeled 'Intro to Medical Magic' scowling and tapping her finger on the table. She glanced to the empty booth next to her with a banner reading 'Intro to Elements' printed across it.

"She's not going to attract any students with a scary face like that," Black said and they both laughed.

Damascus and Black approached a booth with a banner reading, 'Body Fortitude.' The booth was headed by a burly man with bushy brown hair and an even bushier beard. His robe lacked sleeves and his brawny arms were folded across his chest which had a healthy amount of dark curly hair spilling over the collar.

"What is this class about," Black asked the man.

The man narrowed his shaggy brow at him before saying, "It's about not being a noodly-armed whelp of a wizard is what it's about." He jutted his hairy chin at the boys. "It's about not running out of breath when you need to spit out some incantations is what it's about." He raised his enormous fist to eye level. "It's about breaking a mage's jaw before he can spit his incantation at you is what it's about." The boys stood stunned. "Now lads, what are you about?"

"I'm about to join this class," Damascus stated and Black nodded in agreement.

"Good lads," The man handed them a card with 'Body Fortitude' written on it. "Take that for your enrollment."

Black and Damascus stepped away feeling energized. Damascus spotted the booth for 'Intro to Potions' and decided to investigate while Black continued to peruse around. He was examining a banner with the words, 'Mysteries of Nature' when he felt a tap on his shoulder.

Black turned to find Darius and Newton.

"Newt and I were thinking last night," Darius said.

"You must be exhausted," Black sighed.

"That's funny," Darius replied. "Don't you think that's funny Newt?"

"Hilarious," Newt said dryly.

Darius continued, "So we were thinking that we don't like you very much and we don't care for how you spoke to us while we were having some fun with the fat-ass."

"I don't care if you like me or not Darius," Black informed him.

"You should," Darius slapped Newt on the back.

The boys attacked. Newt tried to grab hold of Black. Black instinctively stepped into Newt's body, dropped his hips, and with his lower center of gravity was able to easily toss the taller kid over his shoulder and to the ground.

Darius took a swing at Black's face but he ducked under, placing a foot behind Darius's heel and toppling him hard to the floor with a shoulder to the chest. Black heard Newt scrambling back to his feet from behind beginning an incantation. He spun around and planted a straight jab to the kid's face, knocking him back on his butt with a bloody nose. Black turned back on Darius who was still on the floor, his face red with rage.

Directly behind Darius still standing at his booth was the burly man from 'Body Fortitude' nodding to him and presenting a 'thumbs up.'

"Deus!"

Black turned to see Rinx standing next to Maitre Brunel. Brunel let out a loud laugh and then as if startled by his own voice went very serious.

"Ok break it up you three," he said.

"I think my nose is broken," Newt said, still sitting on the floor holding his head back while little trickles of blood slowly slid down his cheeks.

"Yeah, yeah. You're fine, you're fine," Maitre Brunel waived his hands at him. Abigail was still sitting nearby giving her brother a look of pure contempt. "My lovely big sister, could you give this kid some of your medical expertise?"

She let out a sigh and pulled a silver tin from the folds of her robe. From the tin she produced a small red berry. "Eat this and you'll be fine in an hour," she said, still glaring at Maitre Brunel.

"And you," Maitre Brunel looked at Black. "Come with me."

As they walked away Rinx gave him a look of concern and followed him while Darius, now standing, smiled with pleasure. The Maitre led them to another booth manned by Tom, the boy they'd met the night before.

"I saw the whole thing," Tom said, shaking his head with a big grin on his face.

Maitre Brunel held Black by the shoulder. "Where did you learn to fight like that?"

Black shrugged, "my master taught me how to fight and I trained with her for a while too." He gestured to Rinx.

Brunel looked back at her. "You know how to fight like that too?"

"Of course," she said with a puzzled look on her face.

"Look kid," the Maitre said, speaking to Black again. "I should probably expel you for that but since it's your first day I'll make a deal with you. You join the Combat Tournament club with your friend," he said, nodding to Rinx. "Then we just forget any of this happened." He paused waiting for an answer.

Black and Rinx looked at each and spoke at the same time, "Sure."

A voice came from behind them, "count me in too." It was Damascus.

Maitre Brunel stood up straight and turned, smiling at Tom. "Three new members this year. That's a full team."

Tom nodded. "And we know at least one of them can fight a bit."

Each of the students introduced themselves to the Maitre and then he left them with Tom to go man his vacant stand.

The rest of the orientation went on without incident but Black made sure to stay clear of Darius and Newt for the remainder of the event. He caught them occasionally shooting him some dirty looks.

Black had a fairly good idea which classes he would choose but he still had until Friday before the final decision would be made. He needed seven total. Four classes Monday, Wednesday, and Friday and three longer classes Tuesday and Thursday. He discovered the class 'Beginner's Enchantments' so that was definitely on the list. 'Intro to Elements,' 'Magical History,' and 'Magical Ethics' were all mandatory first year classes so it left him with three more slots to fill. 'Body Fortitude' was a good fit. He decided the last two would be 'Beginner's Beastology' and 'Mysteries of Nature.'

The children spent most of their time leading up to their first day of classes chattering about their expectations for the year. All of the older students began arriving over the weekend. Black found it interesting examining the kids that had once been in the first year students' shoes. They had all at one point arrived at the academy without knowing what to expect or what excitement was in store for them.

When the first day was finally upon them Black, Rinx, and Damascus got up early to meet for breakfast. They were joined by Gilbert. They all had the first class together so they finished their breakfast and strolled to 'Intro to Elements.'

When they arrived the Maitre was nowhere to be found so they took their seats. The room was large with several desks for the students and a podium for the Maitre. Behind the podium was a large empty space with a dirt floor. Across the empty space on the back stone wall were several spots of dark soot.

Twelve minutes after the class was meant to begin Maitre Brunel rushed into the room.

"Forgive me class I was-" he surveyed the room and threw his hands up. "busy."

Damascus shook his head and whispered to Black, "this guy."

"Alright," Brunel continued. "I'm going to do a quick roll call, I guess." He took a parchment from the podium and commenced to read off the names. He got to one name and hesitated before continuing. "Gilbertson?"

Gilbert responded in the affirmative. There were a couple of mutters and Black furrowed his brow before turning to the seat on the other side of Damascus.

"Is your name Gilbert Gilbertson?" Black asked him as he winced.

Gilbert nodded and Black had to fight the urge to shake his own head. Black shamefully thought that this kid was born to be a victim.

Brunel continued on the list until he tripped up on another name. He looked from the paper around the room and said "Mageese?"

Damascus responded, "Present."

"You're the son of Constantine Mageese?" Brunel asked and Damascus nodded his head. "What the hell is a member of the Order of Homme doing here and specifically what are you doing in my class?"

Damascus glanced around the class. "I thought it would be a good learning experience and this class was mandatory anyways. Remember?"

Brunel rubbed his bristly face. "Know thy enemy." Brunel flashed a smile. "And I guess I won't be able to grade you on participation either?"

Damascus shook his head. "No sir."

Both Black and Rinx gave Damascus a suspicious look while Gilbert and several of the other kids seemed awe struck.

Brunel exhaled hard and then completed the list. "Okay," he gripped the sides of the podium as he spoke. "So the reason this class is mandatory is because each of you should have a basic understanding of how to perform a spell. Now I assume you've all had some instruction or at least some experimentation with casting some simple spells. So the first thing you all should know is the common elements; earth,fire,water, and wind. Most spells are some version of these and even the higher elements are either a variation or combination of these spells."

He scanned the students. "I see a few confused faces out there so let me elaborate. Take lava for example. Lava is a combination of fire and earth. How most sorcerers harness the power of lava is usually by having an affinity for one of the two basic elements that make it up and then working on strengthening the other until they can combine them to create lava. Understand?"

Julius raised his hand, "that explains a combination but what is a variation?"

"A variation is like taking a base element to its more complex next level. For example making water into ice. Both combination and variation higher elements can be attained one of two ways. Either by perfecting and advancing the necessary base elements through rigorous hard work or the easy way which is being lucky enough to be born with a rare affinity for them. Although with the latter you miss out on developing your skills with the base element."

"There are of course exceptions to all the rules so keep that in mind," he added.

After he was done with the basics he clapped his hands together. "Alright, I guess I should see what I have to work with." He pointed to the aisle that ran down the middle of the room and divided the desks. "I want all of you to line up in a single file line there. We're going to see what you can do. I assume everyone already knows their affinity?" Everyone either nodded or muttered in the affirmative.

With everyone lined up Brunel called Damascus to his side. "You can watch with me." Brunel addressed the rest of the class. "Okay, so I want each of you to impress me with your best spell." He held his chin considering for a moment. "But tell me what it is first. Oh and-" He grabbed a short steel target sitting to the side and wheeled it to the far wall. After it was in place he returned to his post standing on the edge of the dirt floor.

"Ok, who's up first?" Brunel found the girl standing at the front of the line. "So?"

The girl spoke confidently, "this is my 'water bomb' spell."

"Oh? Sounds exciting." Brunel raised his hands up in feigned fear. "Don't get us all wet," he laughed.

Placing both her hands palms facing one another she began her incantation as she slowly raised her arms over her head. A grapefruit size ball of water was swirling in her cupped hands and with a grunt she heaved it at the target. The ball fell quite short of the target with a splosh.

Brunel stood in silence for a moment with his jaw hanging open before asking, "That's it?" There was some snickering from some of the other students.

"Alright next person, whadda ya got?" He pointed to the next student in line.

The next student, a boy, stepped up. "This is 'stone bullet,'" he said nervously.

Brunel glanced at Damascus, "Well it sounds interesting. Let's see it."

The boy reached to the dirt floor and grabbed a handful of soil. He held his clenched fist close to his face as he recited his incantation into it. He wound up and launched a projectile at the target hitting it with a PING.

Brunel rubbed his eyes. "So you turn the soil in your hand into a rock and throw it?" The kid nodded his head. Brunel looked to Damascus again, "Well you're going to have your work cut out for you with this new generation," he moaned.

Then he said to Damascus, "go grab some parchment and write each kid's name, the spell they are using, and a description."

Damascus obeyed while Brunel continued. Some of the students performed better than others. Newt managed to produce a 'water dragon' that resembled more a snake of water than a dragon but nonetheless slipped its way through the air colliding with the target with some force.

"Has potential," Brunel declared. This was likely the first genuinely positive praise he'd given.

Darius followed Newt and they gave each other a high five as they passed one another.

"Glacier lance," Darius said as he walked to within a few feet of the target. He spoke the words of power and with a hard stomp on the earth a large icicle shot from the ground. It's point breaking off as it connected with the target.

"Okay, here we go," Brunel said, smacking Damascus on the shoulder. "And ice, a higher element. Nice to see someone able to use something other than the basic four."

Up next was a short boy with robes that looked two sizes too big. He also wore a large witch's hat that looked many sizes too big for his small frame. The hat was pulled down so that his face was almost completely hidden with white hair spilling out.

Black turned to Gilbert standing behind him in the line. "Isn't that your roommate?"

"Yes, Moral," Gilbert said and then in a hushed voice, "but he's kind of peculiar."

Black turned back to watch the boy.

Moral didn't say anything but went directly into his chant and when it was complete he bent over and tapped the ground. Instantly a few mushrooms popped up through the earth. The heads of them were violet and the light seemed to reflect off little flecks sprinkled upon them.

Brunel rubbed his chin in thought. "Chanterelle, was it? I see you inherited your family's Deviant." He looked at the students. "A Deviant for those of you who don't know, is a magical affinity that falls outside the established elements. Typically only certain families possess them and they are passed on through the blood lines." He eyed the handful of mushrooms. "But it was a bit underwhelming. Oh well, next."

Moral walked back to his desk and the next kid stepped up. The kid kicked the mushrooms away as he walked up and began to name his spell but was interrupted. His speech became slurred before his jaw went slack. A moment later the kid's legs buckled and he was face first in the dirt.

"Oh bravo," Brunel clapped his hands. "Well done Chanterelle. And let that be a lesson to you all. Magic doesn't have to be obvious and flashy to be effective."

The kid wasn't unconscious for but a minute before he was climbing back to his feet with a confused look on his face.

"Just go to the end of the line and take the time to wake up," Brunel advised the groggy child.

Next up was Rinx. "I'm going to cast a fireball," she said.

"A classic," Brunel commented.

Rinx spoke the words she'd spent endless hours rehearsing and a ball of flame ignited in her hand. She flung it at the target sending a shower of flame and sparks into the air as the ball rocked the target back on its wheels. The target fell back into place with a loud thud.

"Very good," Brunel said to Damascus. "Maybe I was wrong about this batch."

Finally it was Black's turn. He took his place and looked at his hands before regarding Brunel. "My spell is-" he swallowed hard and it felt like a lump caught in his throat. "gust," he finished.

He recited the rites and sent forth a strong wind that did nothing more than kick up some dirt.

"Wind magic," Brunel said. "Tough break. Not a very practical element." He shook his head.

Black feeling discouraged made his way back to his desk. He could see Darius and Newt in the corner of his eye laughing at him. Rinx leaned close to him.

"Don't worry about it," she said. "We're here to get better anyways."

Black slid down into his chair and watched Gilbert wobble into position. The round boy stammered through his words. He was sweating profusely and his beady eyes were darting around the room.

"It's stone skin," Gilbert blurted. He placed his hand to the ground and as he recited the spell his hand slowly sank into the earth up to his wrist. When he pulled it out there was a layer of rocks clinging to his skin. As he moved his fingers and bent his wrist the rocks could be heard slipping and grinding against each other to accommodate the motion.

"Simple but effective," Brunel nodded. "Yeah there's some potential here."

A couple more students later and Julius stepped into place. He brushed his blonde locks from out of his azure eyes.

Brunel raised an eyebrow. "You must be the Licht kid?"

"I am Julius Licht, ja," he answered with his hands on his hips.

"Your family is well known for their skill with the higher element of light," Brunel smiled and looked to the rest of the students excitedly while he rubbed his hands together.

Julius gave a nod and said, "This spell is called Daybreak." he stretched his right hand high over his head. As he neared the end of his incantation Brunel quickly brought his forearm up to shield his eyes just in time for a sudden burst of yellow light to engulf the room. The students were stunned.

Black rubbed his eyes in vain as he attempted to restore his sight. It was a solid two minutes before he could see clearly again. He listened as Brunel congratulated Julius and commented on the utility of such a spell.

The rest of the students went on demonstrating their techniques while Black sunk into a state of morose, feeling he'd been dealt a bad hand. He envied the magic of his peers, even the ones that performed terribly. The feeling of being left behind stung all the more when he'd concluded he was the only student with a wind affinity.

***

Present

Rinx and Black raced across the city until they were standing before the residence of Barnabas. Another storm was building overhead and the first few raindrops were beginning to fall on their heads. The mansion loomed before the expansive garden that encircled the tired old building, unkempt and overgrown. The first floor was encased in a row of pillars. They resembled teeth giving the appearance of a multi-eyed giant's skull ready to devour them as they approached. They inched slowly along as they crossed the savage grass. When no one came to the door they forced their way in, swallowed by the giant's skull.

Inside the building there was a strong smell of mildew. The only sounds that could be heard were the occasional creaking of the foundation and a persistent whistling through the rafters. Black couldn't shake the feeling that it felt less like a house and more like a crypt. The rain had begun to pick up outside and a faint trickle could be heard commencing somewhere deep within the bones of the structure. They silently moved from room to room with no evidence that anyone living had occupied the home in quite some time.

They stole their way into a large library. Some of the shelves were barren or sparsely filled while sheets of torn papers scattered the floors. The stillness closed in around them, smothering them. Black could hear his heart thumping in his ears and hammering against his chest. The hairs were rising from the back of his neck. The beast inside him was rising to the surface in response to some unseen threat. He turned to meet Rinx's gaze and could see the wordless message in her eyes; we're not alone, it said.

Both of them surrendered to the will of the totem letting it enhance their body and their senses. As they changed, a new scent filled their nostrils. It was the growing smell of smoke like a smoldering campfire. It rose into the pungent aroma of burnt leaves and a haze was beginning to spread throughout the room. They followed the now darkening clouds of smoke back to its source in the corner of the room. A distant crash of thunder sounded outside and as the day darkened from the growing storm outside, so did the smoke continue to darken the room.

Black drew the sword from the dimensional enchantment on his forearm as Rinx raised her gloved fists. There was the sound of a mechanical ticking and then an explosion of smoke as a trap door was thrown open on the floor. As a heavy draught of dark smoke billowed from the trap door two black masses leaped into the room followed by a third that seemed to be completely cloaked in the miasma. The room quickly was overcome by the haze and the figures were soon entirely obscured.

Black and Rinx stood side by side. The smoke was beginning to sting their eyes and Black could feel an acidic sensation creeping from his nose down the back of his throat. Suddenly a cerulean point pierced through the dark haze aimed at Black's throat. He managed to deflect the icy spear with his sword at the last moment. Rinx took a step to the side giving Black more freedom of movement but at the same time a long black tendril almost invisible in the smoke whipped through the air and slammed into her body like a heavy wet rope. The impact took her clean off her feet and propelled her into the haze. Rinx was now out of sight but Black had no time to provide aid as the other end of the spear rushed towards his head carried by the momentum of his deflection. He ducked under and countered with a slash that caught nothing but air. He retreated back a few steps trying to buy himself time to think. He could hear a crash in the direction that Rinx had been thrown.

Rinx had slammed against the wall with a muddy residue streaked across her chest. The wind nearly cleared from her lungs, she rebounded back to her feet. Two more muddy tendrils closed in on her. The first she ducked under while the second swung at her legs. She cleared it in a single bound backwards inhaling in preparation for her 'Dragon's Breath' spell but the smoke gagged her. She could only muster a painful cough. Quickly she raised a hand as the sparks of a fireball began to manifest but her arm was swatted down disrupting the spell. The second tendril was in quick succession flinging her back. The points of impact cried out in pain as her unseen assailant pressed the attack.

Black's lungs burned as he was choked by the smoke. All his senses felt disrupted. His eyes were obstructed both by smoke and the stinging tears. His nostrils were filled with an acrid burning and the growing storm outside hid the faint sounds movement from his enemies. The spear lunged again at him as he defended and countered, still hitting nothing. He caught the glint of something flashing from his left and he dodged back as a shiny blade narrowly slipped past his face. He found himself defending against two attackers now. Rinx was mixed somewhere in the fray and he feared that any inaccurate attack could result in friendly fire but a plan began to take shape in his head.

Another dodge of the spear followed by another parry of the blade. He retreated back further, buying himself some time and slammed himself back against the wall. He cut off any chance of further retreat but had already completed the incantation he was reciting during the last assault. A gust of wind tore through the whole house and blew the windows out in the library they'd been fighting in. The smoke was cleared and the attackers were revealed, knocked off balance by the force of the gale.

In front of Black stood two men both in long black robes. One was tall and bald with skin so white you could see the blue veins beneath it. He held a spear made of ice in both hands. The other was a bit short with a slighter build. He had black shaggy hair and there was still smoke pouring out from under his robe that was being carried away on the wind. He had a broad blade that extended from one of his hanging sleeves. Rinx stood off to his right and before her was a broad shouldered man with dark skin and dreadlocks. He had the same kind of dark robe minus the sleeves. The bottom half of his arms were caked in what looked like mud that extended down into coiled tentacles around his feet.

The rain was blowing in through the windows wetting the floor and Rinx's hair. Her opponent had regained his balance and stared at her with a blank expression as his whips transformed themselves into a hammer and shield. He took a step forward to rush her but was stopped in his tracks by one of Rinx's fireballs. The man had blocked it with his shield and the remnants of the flames sizzled as they landed in the gathering puddles on the floor.

The tall man charged Black with another lunge of his spear. Black side stepped as he blocked with his sword and delivered a crippling kick to the man's knee dropping him to a kneeling position. If the man felt any pain he gave no indication of it. His glossy eyes remained locked on Black even as he took a kick directly to the face. The man was sent somersaulting backwards by the impact. The second man was on Black in an instant and submitted him to a barrage of attacks. Black defended before spotting an opening to counterattack but as he was delivering the killing blow the enemy pulled back spitting a plume of miasma in Black's face. Black coughed and swung wildly as he struggled to keep his burning eyes open. Having exchanged places with his opponents he could now see the flashes of fire to his left as Rinx bombarded her target.

The man with dreadlocks blocked each fire ball either with his shield or by swatting it out of the air with his oozing hammer. Rinx could clearly see the hatch they had sprung out of and made out stairs leading down. At the same time she saw Black wheezing and swiping at the air.

"To the stairs behind you!" Rinx shouted to him. Black began retreating back as the smoking man closed in and the tall man slowly climbed back to his feet with blood streaming down his face. Rinx intensified her assault on the mud manipulating man before channeling a stream of magic into her enchanted shoes. She abruptly blurred past the enemy meeting Black at the stairs. Both of them seeing that the stairs cut deep into the earth simultaneously decided to take their chances in the abyss. Black slipped down first leaving Rinx to cover their retreat with a volley of dragon's breath.

The strategy bought them enough time to hit the bottom of the stairs in a dead sprint only then turning to face any pursuers. However the opponents could not yet be seen. They waited like coiled snakes ready to strike but their prey did not emerge.

"They know we're waiting," Black said, clearing the last plumes of smoke from his lungs.

"They're strong, these guys," Rinx added.

"Too strong. And there's something strange about them," Black admitted.

After a moment longer Rinx illuminated a flame in her hand and used it to light their surroundings. A dark corridor led to another set of stairs cutting further down. They proceeded on with Rinx leading the way while Black followed watching the rear. Black couldn't detect any trace of the enemy but he had the feeling that they were close, just at the edges of his vision in the darkness. They continued deeper into the musty earth until they found themselves in a large man-made stone chamber. There was the faint hum of machinery and the walls had several electrical lights leading the way to a simple steel door set into the far wall.

Rinx extinguished her light as they cautiously moved toward the door. There was a faint shuffle from behind that provoked the two to spin around. They beheld the tall man creeping unsteadily on his wounded leg down the last step. He leveled his icy lance at them as the other two assailants moved to flank them on either side. The spear was launched at Rinx and Black with incredible speed despite the man's obvious difficulty to remain upright in the aftermath of the act. Rinx and Black separated to avoid the projectile only to be met by the tall man's accomplices.

Black was barreling head long into the smaller man with the broadsword protruding from his right sleeve. Black leaned in as he closed the gap, raising his sword to attack. At the same time the smaller man raised his left arm and blanketed his path in thick smoke. With no time to change course he plummeted headlong into the cloud slashing before emerging on the other side with his eyes burning. He realized too late that the man had sailed over his head landing behind him in the smoke. As Black turned around his enemy's blade was piercing the smokey veil on a direct course for his chest. Black barely managed to side step suffering a deep cut to his upper arm as a result.

Meanwhile Rinx stood before her opponent mustering her dragon's breath for another attack when she caught a blue glint from the corner of her eye. She swallowed her spell and dodged backwards avoiding another icy projectile. This time the tall man fell forward from the momentum of his attack. Rinx hit the ground and rolled back onto her feet fluidly but was forced to dodge again as the dark skinned man brought down his muddy hammer on her position.

The smaller man pressed his attack on Black slashing away as Black back peddled defending blow for blow. Black could feel the blood painting his left arm from his open wound. The smaller man suddenly dropped low as another spear whipped over his head directed at Black's chest. Black used his enchants to temporarily boost his speed. He blurred to the left avoiding the attack and witnessing the tall man again stumble before beginning to reform another spear in his hand. Black knew it was just a matter of time before the tall man landed a blow.

Black leveled his left hand at the tall man after quickly gauging that Rinx was safely far enough away. The rune on the palm illuminated with a tiny spark of electricity before a bolt of white hot lightning snapped through the air. Smaller strands arched from the main body of the bolt as it first connected to the spear in the tall man's hand exploding it into shimmering particles. The bolt then jumped to the man's chest with branches leaping to his extremities. The smaller man tumbled away to avoid being caught up in the storm. When the spell ended Black wasted no time in pursuing the smaller man that was already reeling back on his heels. For the first time Black could see the man's eyes clearly. They were glossy and seemed to carry no fear or emotion of any kind.

As Black's lightning spell tore through the cavern Rinx too managed to spew out her spell. The flames billowed from her lips in a tight cone but as it rushed towards her victim he slammed his hammer to the ground causing a muddy wall to wretch up from the earth creating a wall that separated him from the fire. The muddy barrier sizzled and boiled under the intense heat of Rinx's spell until it was hardened into a stony blockade. A muddy tentacle suddenly lashed out from behind the wall. Rinx redirected her magical flow into her enchanted gloves. With her strength reinforced she caught the tentacle, dug her heels in, and yanked the broad man from his fortified position. Rinx allowed the momentum to fling her enemy into the steel door, busting it off of its hinges.

Black bombarded his prey with ruthless attack after attack until finally his sword slipped past his opponent's blade severing his arm at the elbow. The man gave no hint of pain as his arm clattered to the ground. Instead he issued a cloud of black smoke from his mouth as he retreated back.

There was finally a lull in the battle giving time for all to take stock of their surroundings. Black could see the smaller man poised to continue the fight. His arm was lying on the ground not clutching a sword, no, Black could now make out that the blade was an extension of his arm. The tall man was propped against the stairs with a smoldering hole in his chest and several jagged scorch marks peppered his body and the ground around him. There was the hint of shiny metal in the tall man's exposed chest and in the dim electric light Black could now make out gears and metal parts about the dead man's feet.

Rinx's opponent was lying on the twisted door. He set up with his dreadlocks a bloody mess and his head at an unnatural angle. The man's head tried to right itself but with a click fell back into its grotesque position. Again and again it did this. Rinx surveyed the room he came to rest in. It was illuminated by electric light and had a noticeable hum. There were several glass jars and vials sitting on many rows of tables. Some were filled with various colors of liquids. From out of view stepped a tall man cloaked in white. He wore a bronze mask with a khaki rubber hood tightly wrapped around his head. The mask had a round canister protruding from the mouth giving the appearance of some kind of giant insect. His left hand was gloved but his right was the same bronze metal of his mask.

Hatred seethed deep from within Rinx as she hissed through her teeth, "Barnabas." She recognized his masked face from the few times he'd projected himself for Guild meetings.

Black cast a backwards glance at the sound of Rinx's voice, still keeping one eye on his enemy.

Rinx balled her fists and ground her teeth as she took a step toward the lab. The attacker with the broken neck started to awkwardly raise himself from the ground.

Simultaneously Barnabas raised a hand and the broken man fell back down into a seated position as someone else called from the darkness of the stairs.

"Enough!" the voice commanded.

The voice was familiar to their ears. Black peered into the gloom as Rinx held her blistering gaze fixed upon Barnabas. A figure emerged from the shadows and delicately stepped around the still body at the bottom of the stairs. Her gloved hands lifted her dress keeping it from coming in contact with the lifeless heap as she descended. Black noticed that the one-armed man was now quite relaxed. The woman made her way towards the laboratory past Black. The electric light reflected off her mask and her green dress flowed behind her.

Rinx finally swiveled her head to examine the approaching woman. Her anger evaporated and was replaced with confusion. "Premier Morgu?" she mumbled to herself.

Morgu pursed her lips as she regarded Rinx behind the tinted lenses of her mask. "You've both been misled."

"Good, Margret," came a gravelly voice from the lab. "Could you explain this intrusion?"

Morgu turned towards Barnabas. "Someone has murdered two Premiers and these Battlemages believe the evidence points to you."

"Preposterous," Barnabas growled. His breath wheezed through the canister attached to his mask.

"Of course," Morgu replied.

"Who were the Premiers that got themselves murdered," demanded Barnabas.

"Premier Roth and-" Morgu began.

"And Premier Valen," Rinx blurted. The vein at her temple was pulsing and her eyes darted from Barnabas to Morgu. "What do you mean we've been 'misled'?"

Black had relaxed a bit and the bleeding on his arm had stopped but his sword remained tightly gripped in his fist and his muscles ready to react at a moment's notice. "Yes, please explain," he backed up Rinx.

The lights played across the jewels embedded in Morgu's mask. Several little emeralds glittered like a spider's eyes and it was difficult to read her expression as she addressed them. The ends of peacock feathers framed the edge of the mask and laid against her perfectly smooth, long, raven-black hair.

"As you likely don't know," she told them with a heavy emphasis on the 'don't.' "I have several individuals I retain in my private employment that keep me well informed." She smoothed out her dress as she spoke. "Several soul pacts have been cropping up. A potential accomplice with a wealthy benefactor."

"Prothers," Black stated.

Morgu nodded and turned her obscured face back to Rinx. "So I issued the order to apprehend the suspected accomplice. I was then made aware of some commotion at the prison and later of an incident involving the Order of Homme." She turned back to Black. "I of course knew of your involvement in the hunt for who now was likely either a Premier or close to one. Then two Premiers were brutally murdered." The last two words she spat out more than spoke. "Our rat has slipped from our grasp and the only thing we have left is the name 'Mr. B'."

Barnabas scoffed from behind his mask. "Don't tell me," he said as his beady yellow eyes rolled in his mask. "You foolishly thought that a 'Mr. B' must be me?" A long wheeze issued from his mask which may have been an attempt at a laugh. "You believe me to be so infantile in my ability to both conceal my identity and create a pseudonym while skulking around stealing peoples souls and killing Premiers?"

Black suddenly felt stupid and winced at the accusation. He couldn't help but admit that it all seemed suddenly too obvious.

"Well, to be honest," Morgu stated. "Your reclusive nature does naturally inspire some suspicion."

Barnabas only shrugged.

Rinx fists loosened a bit but the vein still pulsed at her temple. "Maybe, but how can you be certain that he wasn't involved," she asked Morgu.

Morgu threw her hands up, "Because I know him and I know the only thing that motivates him is knowledge." An ever so slight smile massaged her green lips as she added looking at Barnabas, "And not a day goes by that I don't have someone watching this house."

As if detecting the threat had passed the one armed man casually and silently collected his limb from the ground and proceeded to drag his fallen comrade to the laboratory.

There was a low whorling sound as Barnabas folded his arms across his chest.

Rinx halfheartedly demanded, "Then why did you attack us if you have nothing to hide?"

Barnabas waved her away. "You mean after you invaded my home," he asked, not pausing for an answer. "My security system is set to respond if there is a risk of breaching my lab," he gestured to the three broken men that now shuffled past him. They proceeded to place the dead man on a steel slab before coming to rest on their own tables. "So for all the destruction you've delivered on my property and the disruption of my work, what did you gain?"

Black hung his head in something akin to defeat as he returned his sword to the pocket dimension printed on his arm. The old man was right; what had they gained? Black still felt a duty to ask, "And what is all of this," he gestured to the damaged men. "Necromancy is a forbidden magic and crime."

"Please," Barnabas scoffed. "Do not confuse my work with those dark arts." He placed his hands firmly on his hips. "These loyal servants to the Guild agreed to donate their bodies upon death," he raised a finger on the last part. "To science. That is what this is. And you've mutilated them."

Black was uncertain if there was really any distinction but decided that given the circumstance and the Premier's status that he should let the technicality stand. Barnabas without a word moved to the dead man lying on the cold steel table and began to examine him.

Morgu turned away from Rinx and Black. She entered the lab while calling to the pair, "come. You are injured. Let's get you patched up."

They followed Morgu into the lab and reverted back to their human forms as they did. Now inside they could see several large glass vats lining one wall filled with a blue liquid, some holding various unfamiliar creatures. They were not all fully intact. There were many mysterious machines and a strong odor. It was a mix of sterilizing chemicals, mildew, and something sickly sweet. Black's stomach squirmed.

Without looking up Barnabas spoke, "I assume you remember where the supplies are?"

"Of course," Morgu answered.

She pulled a bottle of solution, a rag, and a roll of gauze from a dusty cabinet. Black pulled his sleeve up as Morgu soaked the rag in the solution.

Morgu pressed close as she examined the wound. Black could detect a floral fragrance that cut through the musk of the lab setting his stomach still again. "Your wound has stopped bleeding and is already showing signs of closing," Morgu mused. "A benefit of your totem no doubt."

Barnabas cast a curious yellow eye back at Black and then continued to survey another puppet. Morgu then slapped the damp cloth on the cut. A white hot fire rushed down his arm, summoning a hiss from Black's lips and then followed by a numbing sensation.

Black thought he caught a quick smile on Morgu's face as he relinquished the sound followed by, "I thought Amadeus Black was made of tougher stuff." She continued to wrap the gauze around his arm. "It's finished." She stepped back to better take in the two Battlemages. "There's something else that's occurred. There were some small disturbances detected by our Clairvoyant division. A tear in the barrier that separates our world from Hell."

"A small disturbance!" Rinx shouted.

Black's eyes grew wide and Morgu waved her hands dismissively.

"Nothing came through that we are aware of. It was nothing like the Great Calamity," she assured them.

Black and Rinx exchanged painful looks.

"How is this connected?" Black asked.

"It's a thin thread," Morgu admitted. "I'm not sure if you knew this about Premier Valen but he had a personal vendetta against demon-kind."

Barnabas wheezed, "I'd call it an obsession. I recall he proposed going to war. Could you imagine marching into their domain? Utterly foolish."

Black chimed in, "It would be a slaughter."

"Of course," Barnabas proclaimed. "Even the weakest demon would be formidable in their own domain. Thankfully Roth stoutly opposed any notion of the idea. One of the few competent things he did." He rooted around in the dead man's gaping wound. "Utterly foolish," he repeated.

"Foolish, yes, but I understand how he felt," Rinx said softly as she stared at the floor.

"I'm sure you do," Morgu agreed. "I'm sure you both do."

Black hung his head and felt the pang of old wounds that never fully healed. "So there could be a link between Valen's murderer and these rifts opening up?"

"Or it could be a coincidence," Rinx stated.

Barnabas let out a short wheezing laugh and Morgu retorted, "coincidences are rarer than unicorns in our world." She set her cold gaze on Rinx. "A Battlemage of your status should have learned that long ago."

Morgu proceeded to explain that the last rift detected was in the Earthen Realm. "The city of London," she stated. "We couldn't narrow it down more than that. There was some disturbance."

"Well I know just who to ask," Black said as he adjusted the bandage on his arm. "One of my old contacts for Earthen occult goings-on, Jackie. And if we leave now we should catch him just in time for the opening act." Black momentarily fell into deep contemplation. "There is something about this that still doesn't sit right with me." Black rubbed his chin. "Premier Morgu, can you send one of your agents to question Premier Roth's assistant?"

"It will be done but what exactly should they be asking?" Morgu questioned as she cocked her head to the side.

"This demon connection. What does it have to do with Premier Roth?" Black asked. "I want to know if Valan was planning something with Roth placing them both in the crosshairs of our unknown assassin."

Chapter 7

Past

Black's first day had been off to a rough start. After his 'Intro to Elements' class he proceeded to the next course with the rest of the students. It was another compulsory class for first years, 'Magical History 101.' They strolled into a lecture hall style room with a descending floor leading to the teaching platform. Several full book shelves lined the walls around the platform. Black, Rinx, and Damascus with Gilbert tagging along took their seats in a middle row. Each desk had an enormous and well used book sitting on it. Clearly this was to be their text book for the class.

The spectacle wearing Maitre was there when they arrived tapping his finger on the podium as the students funneled in. He was adorned in crimson red robes that hung loosely and he had a matching skull cap. His stringy gray hairs poked out from under his cap and with his large hooked nose he very much resembled a vulture. He eyed every student as they entered until finally the bell rang.

As soon as the bell had sounded he slammed his fist on the podium and proclaimed, "Any student not in a seat is tardy!"

Several students had been still in the process of finding a seat including Newt and Darius who now stared at the Maitre with pure contempt. Darius in particular gritted his teeth as he shuffled quickly into an empty seat.

The Maitre wagged his finger at the class and one eye was opened wide while the other squinted. "This will be your only warning," he advised. "I will not tolerate any tardiness in my class. Transgressors will be punished."

Black exchanged looks with his friends and noted a particularly terrified look on Gilbert's face.

"Allow me to introduce myself," The Maitre proceeded to scribble his name across a blackboard. "You will address me as Maitre Karrion."

Karrion took the student role call. When he arrived at Damascus's name his eyes bugged out of his head.

"Mageese?" He cried. "Of house Mageese? The head family of the Order of Homme, Mageese?"

Damascus for the first time in the short while Black had known him began to shift in his seat with obvious embarrassment. Karrion forgetting about the rest of the students on his list dove into a lengthy lecture of the Order of Homme. He described their humble start as a safe haven for those lacking magic. How they developed techniques and weapons for defending against what they considered tyrannical rule by the magical elite. How they went to war against the precursor to the Guild of Ravens ages ago. How despite their fewer numbers and eventual defeat managed to negotiate a semi-autonomous state within the very walls of Tuatha Dé. And of course, their expertise at potions, magic nullifying aegis shields, and their steadfast disdain for magic.

Black hadn't realized that Damascus was such an important person, or rather, his family was. Normally he wasn't concerned with such things but being in such close proximity to a semi-celebrity after his experience in his previous class left his self-worth at an all time low. He felt eclipsed by his peers and a creeping fear was beginning to rise in him. Maybe he didn't belong here.

The next class on Black's agenda he again had with his friends; Damascus, Rinx, and Gilbert. They strolled into a large gymnasium for 'Body Fortitude' class. Though none of them said it out loud, they were all surprised to see Gilbert in attendance. The boy appeared to begin sweating the moment he set foot in the gym and fidgeted uncomfortably.

The burly man Black had met at orientation greeted him welcome flashing his enormous white teeth as he handed him a uniform with one hand while directing him to the boy's locker room with the other. They changed quickly and returned to the gymnasium floor where they awaited instructions. There were only twelve students enrolled. Each wore the required uniform; a pair of baggy dark blue pants with a short cream colored tunic tied with a blue sash. Additionally they donned some light slip on shoes.

The large man stood before them all and for the first time Black noticed his bare feet protruding from under his robe.

The man stretched out his hairy naked arms and announced, "Welcome to my temple!"

Black examined the gym. It was a large rectangular shape. They had entered from one end of the room and to the left and at the far end were empty stands for spectators. Along the right wall was the entrance to the locker rooms followed by an assortment of workout equipment. There were several weights, three punching bags, four ropes hung from the ceiling, a weighted sled, and machines that Black couldn't determine the use of. The center of the gym which they now found themselves in had a dirt floor and was encircled by a rubber track.

The man crossed his large arms over his chest. "And if you perform the right rituals you will receive her many blessings." He gave a pearly grin. "I will be your shepherd and you, little lambs, may call me Maitre Bulgar."

He stroked his wild beard as he walked past each student looking him up and down. As he passed Black he smiled and raised a fist. He paused for a moment at Gilbert to take in the sight. Gilbert's sash had to be tied at the very ends barely able to wrap around his girth.

Bulgar slapped Gilbert on the shoulder nearly rolling him over and said, "I envy you my friend. Stick with me and your journey will be glorious." He turned to address the entire class. "Today I will evaluate your level of fitness."

Bulgar started by testing their level of flexibility. Each student was required to perform a series of stretches. Bulgar was satisfied with Black's flexibility but Rinx was able to outperform him and surprisingly Damascus was the most impressive. At one point he stood on one foot and extended his other leg straight over his head. Gilbert was barely able to reach over his bulbous belly to touch his knees.

Next they were required to run for twelve laps on the track. Black, Rinx, and Damascus completed this task together. None of the three so much as broke a sweat or were breathing heavily at the end. Gilbert on the other hand had been passed several times before he passed out hitting the black rubber of the track with a wet smack. He laid in a pool of his own sweat until Bulgar simply rolled him off the track. Once they had finished, Bulgar gave Gilbert's belly a few good nudges with his foot until the boy regained consciousness.

"Nap's over," Bulgar stated. "Time to test your strength." He pointed to the various free weights.

Gilbert heaved himself off the ground with a whimper and loped to the other students gathered around the equipment.

"I'll carve a man out of you, my friend," Bulgar called to Gilbert.

Black found that he was able to lift the most weight in each exercise but Damascus was very close behind him. It was a sobering thought for Black. He felt like he was at quite a disadvantage with his magical prowess compared to the other students. Black had hoped to find some sense of comfort in the physical activity but in the end it did little to ease the disappointment of the day. Perhaps it was the fact that physical ability was seldom seen as a great accomplishment in their world or perhaps it was because his new friend was every bit his physical equal.

At the end of their tests Bulgar announced, "I am very satisfied with everything I've seen. You all have shown heart which is the most important test of all." Gilbert struggled, breathing heavily and occasionally breaking out into coughing fits. Bulgar continued, "Now hit the showers. The real work begins in the next class." He thrusted a finger at Gilbert and said, "You, stay behind for a minute, my friend." Gilbert affixed a look of terror on his sweaty face.

The rest of the students did as they were told and proceeded to the locker rooms. Afterwards the three friends waited for Gilbert. After a few minutes he waddled from the locker room looking like a giant penguin.

"What did Maitre Bulgar want from you, Gil?" Rinx asked.

Gilbert shook his. "He just wanted to give me some advice."

"Well I'm ready for lunch," Black proclaimed.

Damascus passed by Gilbert and gave him a slap on the back as they proceeded to the dining hall for their break.

After lunch Black parted ways with the other students for his final class of the day, 'Beginner's Enchantments.' He strolled into the class to find a cramped dusty room. Each desk of which there were only a dozen, six on either side of the room, had a drawing board affixed to it and on each drawing board was a lamp. There were several large stacks of paper and boxes of paint, bottles of ink, quills, and paintbrushes. At the front of the room was situated an easel with a large tablet of paper. Next to that was a desk and chair not much larger than the students'.

When it was time for class to start a small man in an ink smeared yellow robe squeezed down the central lane to the front of the class.

The man had immensely bushy eyebrows that he pushed together when he spoke. "Only three this year," he said, taking count of the students. "It's fewer and fewer every year."

He introduced himself as Maitre Gogh.

"Show of hands," Gogh asked. "How many of you have any experience in enchantments?" Only Black raised his hand. "I guess I shouldn't be surprised." Gogh put his hands on his hips with a roll of his eyes. "Well," he raised a hand towards Black. "Let's see what you can do. Grab some paper and produce your best enchantment."

Black attempted to turn his lamp on but when he finally found the switch nothing happened.

"Oh one moment," Gogh said, rummaging through his desk and extracting a small square of parchment with several geometric patterns printed across it. He reached into the hood of the lamp and pulled out a similar looking slip of paper replacing it with the new one. "I made these enchantments to power the lamps but the charge runs out after a week or so and needs to be replaced. Try it now."

Sure enough the lamp flickered on when Black twisted the switch. He then reluctantly pulled a sheet of paper from a nearby stack and commenced with producing an enchantment. It took him the better part of thirty minutes. While the other two students looked on he delicately wove his magic into the characters. After he finished, Gogh examined the work.

Gogh played with his long brown goatee as he made his evaluation. "Runic style. Standard water spell from the looks of it. Simple technique but you have good form. You could use a little improvement on the more precise markings." He stood back and gave it one more long look. "Ok," Gogh said as he grabbed an empty waste paper can from near his desk. "You have good presentation, I'll hand it to you but only one thing really matters; how the enchantment performs."

Black stared at him blankly.

"Well go on my boy," Gogh held the bucket at chest level with both hands a few feet away from Black. "Let's see the fruits of your labor."

Black took the paper in his hand and turned it toward the Maitre. He gave one final look of uncertainty but Gogh only nodded reassuringly. Black gripping the sheet on either side channeled the required magic. There was the slight illumination of the runes followed by a strong jet of water that blasted the maitre directly between his bushy eyebrows. He began stumbling backwards gasping for air before he remembered the bucket in his hands but by the time he had raised it Black had already stopped the spell. In the end the Maitre and a good part of the tiny room was soaked and the inside of the bucket, bone dry.

Everyone stood in shocked silence as the Maitre coughed up a big spurt of water. Black finally opened his mouth to speak but was cut short.

"My boy,"Gogh choked. "I will need to speak to the administration about your display today."

Black felt a lump rise up in his throat but despite his panic he managed to swallow it down to speak. "I-" Gogh raised his hand to silence him.

Gogh set the bin down while at the same time wiping water from his eyes. "You will need to have 'Beginner's Enchantments' stricken from your schedule," he continued. "And I'll ask that you are credited and listed as attending 'Novice Enchantments' going forward."

It took a moment for the Maitre's words to set in. Black remained speechless with his jaw hanging low.

"Your time would be wasted with a beginner's curriculum. I'll need to give you more advanced lessons," Gogh confirmed after reading the boy's confused face.

The remainder of class was spent mostly wiping up the water that had splashed about the room but when it was over Black strode out of that tiny room with his head held a bit higher. Enchantments weren't very popular but it was something that left him walking down the hall with a smile on his lips.

His classes were completed for the day but he still had his first session for the Combat Tournament club. Normally he would have a half hour before he needed to be back in the gymnasium but he was feeling energized. Black made his way directly to the gym at almost a jog hurrying around the other students in the halls.

Black arrived to find Tom and Maitre Brunel already waiting and they quickly greeted the boy. Brunel was wearing his usual faded blue robe but Tom wore an unusual dark blue outfit. Black could recognize it was something likely from the Earthen Realm but wasn't particularly familiar with it. The outfit was two parts, a pair of loose fitting bottoms with a zip-up jacket on top. The steel zipper was only raised halfway up Tom's torso so that it was opened from the chest up. On the left breast was embroidered Tuatha Dé Academy's moon and star silver logo. Under the jacket was a simple white shirt.

Tom caught Black examining his uniform. "Pretty cool, right?" Tom asked Black as he tugged at the bottom of the jacket to smooth it out.

Black hesitated and then nodded.

"Our team captain three years ago took a trip with his family to the Earthen Realm and brought some of these back to replace our old uniforms," Tom explained as he played with the zipper. "He wanted to give us a more Earthen or 'modern' look he called it. Since then we've had Ronald at Ronald's Robes start custom making them for us." He slapped Black on the shoulder. "And don't worry, I have some extras for all of you already. Oh and I heard your wind magic is going to be pretty useless," Tom said casually. Black shot a quick accusatory look at Brunel. Brunel simply shrugged his shoulders and forced a smile. "But don't worry about it, we'll find a way to make it work," Tom continued.

"Make it work?" Came a voice calling behind Black.

Black turned to see an older girl approaching. She wore the same outfit as Tom and she had her brown shoulder length hair pulled back in a tight ponytail. She took her place next to Tom with one hand on her hip. She was easily as tall as Tom and looked down at Black with her lip twisted in disgust.

Black felt the little confidence he'd fostered from his last class begin to fade away.

"We already have one kid that can't perform magic at all plus another just as useless," she shoved a finger at Black. "This is the best we can get from the first years." She now swiveled her head to Brunel.

Brunel raised his hands in defense. "Astrid, you know as well as anyone that the best spells are useless if they aren't backed by fighting spirit." He gestured to Black.

"I can certainly vouch for his fighting spirit," Tom said with a nod.

Astrid rolled her eyes at Tom. "Oh, shut up." She then made her way to the inner ring of the track and began jogging away from them.

"Always a lovely character," Brunel sighed as they watched her come out of the first turn picking up speed.

Tom brushed his hair back. "She'll start to grow on you, I promise."

Some of the other members were arriving and taking to the track as well. It wasn't much longer before Damascus and Rinx arrived.

"Great," Brunel said with a clap of his hands. "Now we can go over the basic rules of CTC."

Brunel proceeded to explain the Combat Tournament Club. The basic objective was to submit or incapacitate your opponent in a one on one bout. Each year of students had a three person team. Two out of three wins earned one point and three wins earned two points. The points at the end of the match would be added up to determine which school was the victor. With six total teams that meant you could accumulate a total of twelve points. Victory could be obtained by way of magic or physical attacks.

"What's to prevent people from getting hurt," Rinx asked.

Brunel exchanged glances with Tom. "Well, we do have two referees that are experts in barrier magic ready to step in should things get too dangerous," Tom said with a cough. "And of course another two medical mages on the sidelines for emergencies."

"Look," Brunel cut in. "There usually are only a couple of serious injuries a year and hardly ever any fatalities so you guys will be fine." Brunel closed his cerulean eyes as he nodded. "I've really got a good feeling about you three."

There was a beat of silence filled finally when Tom said, "Okay! So I have some uniforms over here for you three to try on."

They each found a uniform that fit although it took Damascus two attempts since the first size was too big. The three of them came back from the locker rooms to find the other members waiting for them in the center of the track.

Damascus leaned into Black, "You noticed that Brunel wasn't late for a change?"

"Oh no," Black replied. "The guy was early. I guess we know where his priorities lie." They all three laughed.

Tom introduced the three latest members to the club. Some of the members seemed more enthusiastic than the others giving a warm welcome. Astrid bit her lip while shaking her head.

Tom waited until everyone was finished welcoming the newcomers and continued, "Welcome back everyone else. I know we have some big shoes to fill losing a full team of sixth years but I am feeling really good about this year."

"You say that every year," shouted one of the boys and they all laughed.

"Well this year I really mean it," Tom laughed with them. "But this week we will start purely with getting our stamina back. Some of you are looking a little soft." He pointed a finger at the boy that had previously called him out and they began laughing again. "So today I want to see you all running and then hitting the bags." He pointed to the three rookies. "Except for you three. I want you to stretch, run two laps to get warmed up, and then we're going to see what you can do."

The three students did as they were told and after the two laps they returned to Tom and Astrid. Brunel had taken a position on the sideline watching.

"Alright," Tom said, licking his lips and grabbing Black and Damascus by the shoulders, shoving them to the inner circle. "I want to see what you two can do first. When I give the signal you two can begin. But remember," he gave them both a big smile." We're on the same team here so don't try to kill each other."

"Let's see that spirit," Astrid said as Tom returned.

With a side glance to Astrid, Tom shouted, "Go."

The two boys circled each other slowly sizing up the other. They were both aware that all the other members had stopped what they were doing to watch.

"Good luck to you," Damascus said. Black replied with a nod.

Black raised his fists but the smaller boy continued to circle with his hands at his sides. Black stepped in to attack but found himself pulling back at the last minute when Damascus still didn't raise his hands. Black couldn't explain it but as he looked into Damascus dark eyes he could feel something like a stone settling in his gut. They continued to circle.

"Come on already," Astrid shouted.

As if at Astrid's command Black dove in again but this time committing with a swing of his fist. He hit only air passing a hair's breadth in front of Damascus's nose. Black followed up with another miss. Then a kick only to miss again. All the while Damascus kept his hands at his side. Black pressed the attack. Swing. Miss. Swing. Miss.

Suddenly Black felt the eruption of pain in his ribs as he moved in for another attack. Damascus had stopped him cold in his tracks. As Black buckled over in pain Damascus grappled him by the back of his head pulling his own body up to deliver a knee to Black's face. Black managed to get his arms between the knee and its intended target while shoving the boy off of him.

The pit in Black's stomach was beginning to dissolve into something else. Damascus now had his hands up. Black went on the attack again swinging just over his opponent's head and following up with a knee of his own. Damascus pushed himself off of Black's knee creating some space between the two boys as he launched backwards into the air. The curly haired boy landed like he had springs in his shoes, immediately propelling himself forward quickly setting Black back on his heels. He bombarded Black with a combination of kicks and punches that Black barely managed to block.

Finally Black was able to dig his heels in and the boys were exchanging blows. Black was vaguely aware of a smile etching its way across his face. Each boy was dodging or blocking the others attacks in a stand still until slowly Black was beginning to push Damascus back. Damascus seemed on the verge of being overwhelmed. Black swung catching air again and Damascus wrapped his hands around Black's arm leaping up to lock the larger boy in an arm bar.

Black stood erect with Damascus's body wrapped around his right arm, his full weight pulling him to the ground. Black in a fit of brute strength raised Damascus into the air before sending him hurtling back towards the dirt. Damascus sensing the sudden rush of earth racing towards him released his grasp to cushion his fall. At that moment Black seized the opening, pinning him to the ground and preparing to deliver a fury of punches.

"That's enough," shouted Brunel making his way to the combatants. "Great job you two," he said as he rubbed his peppered chin. The two boys climbed to their feet. "I've given some thought to how we can try to compensate for your lack of ability with magic." Both the boys were breathing hard. "Damascus, the Order of Homme are known for their skill with a sword. I assume you've been trained."

Damascus nodded, still catching his breath.

Brunel held his hand at his side with the fingers spread, palm down. Abruptly some broad leaves sprouting from the dirt and from the center of the leaves grew a wooden shaft directly into Brunel's grip. He held the finished product out in front of him. A length of dark wood in the shape of a long blade and handle.

"Steel wood," Brunel said, handing the sword to Damascus. He reached down to grab a second growing up from the tuft of leaves. "You can't fight in CTC with a sharp blade so I've dulled the edge." He handed the second sword to Black. "I think you'll find it still delivers a smart blow."

Damascus spun the weapon in his hand getting a feel for the weight and length. Black gave a couple practice swings switching hands to see which was more comfortable.

"Well it looks like you two have had enough of a break. Let's start again." Brunel turned and strolled back to the sidelines.

Damascus took a stance with the sword in his right hand extended in front of him. Black tried to mimic his posture. Tom shouted "go" again and in a blur Black's sword was propelled from his hand and a crack to his head planted him on his back.

Damascus stood over him, rotating the sword in his hand again as Tom came jogging over with his usual big smile.

"Well done both of you," Tom said as Damascus extended a hand to Black.

Black hesitated for a moment before taking his hand and being pulled to his feet.

Tom turned to face Rinx and waved her to them. "You said before that you two used to spar together. Do you think you can go another round?" Tom was facing Black again.

Black nodded in response. "Sure." He unzipped his uniform jacket, folded it neatly and set it on the sidelines with the others.

Black's head was still throbbing as he took his position across from Rinx. Tom shouted "Go" and they began going through the familiar motions. Rinx began an incantation but Black wasted no time in closing the distance. Now armed with his new weapon he swung it widely but the sword was too unfamiliar and Rinx to agile for Black to land a blow. Rinx delivered a solid kick to Black's gut stunning him while at the same time propelling her back. She was already beginning another spell before she even landed. Black managed to dodge the first fireball hurtled at him but it was quickly followed by another. He swatted this one with the steel-wood sword showering sparks all around him. Rinx kept her distance lobbing more projectiles at Black.

Black decided to take a gamble and when an opening presented itself he flung the chunk of wood directly at Rinx. The sword spun end over end as it closed in on its target. Rinx dove to the side with a one handed cartwheel using the free hand to fling another fireball but it was widely inaccurate. Black stole the chance to use his totem's hybrid form, closing the gap at incredible speed. Now face to face with Rinx she had no choice but to use her totem as well.

Black felt more comfortable fighting unarmed and was beginning to overwhelm Rinx. They danced across the dirt ring Rinx avoiding most of Black's blows but the ones that were connecting began to take their toll. She was finally able to get another spell off which Black blocked with his forearm. This slowed him enough for her to create some space and follow up with another fireball. With Black at a distance she was again able to commence another bombardment while keeping the distance. However, Black was relentless in his pursuit.

Black pressed on dodging what projectiles he could and blocking or striking away those he couldn't. Her fire spells had a little extra power when she was using her totem and Black could smell his own burnt hair as it sizzled on his hands and arms. He tried to never let them hit the same place consecutively but his arms and hands stung, looking pink like from a bad sunburn.

He was nearly upon her again when she suddenly changed tactics. Leaping high in the air she directed a kick straight to Black's face only just missing. Her leg came down on Black's shoulder where she sat for a moment. Black looking up could see both of her hands were engulfed in flames and crashing towards either side of his head. He reached up quickly, snatching her by both wrists in time for both fireballs to pass right by either side of his face. Black felt the radiating heat as they both passed.

Letting go of one wrist he flung the girl over his shoulder. Rinx hit the ground and rolled twice before landing right back on her feet, already launching another spell. Black turned too late to guard and the fireball hit him directly in the chest. He landed flat on his back with the wind stolen out of his lungs. Before he could scramble back to his feet Tom was stopping the fight.

Black stood sucking air. Charred holes peppered his white shirt. *Another failure,* Black thought but there was another feeling that stirred in him. His heart was slamming hard against his chest. He relaxed into his human form and his white hair grew dark again as Tom ran over to him. Black could not have imagined such a wide smile on a person's face.

"That was incredible!" Tom shouted. A couple of the other members were cheering but all were watching. "You didn't tell me you had a totem. Both of you!" Tom grabbed Black on the shoulder and examined them both. "Are you both alright?"

Rinx for her part looked quite battered and was catching her own breath. They were both sweating with a great deal of dirt caked on them and Rinx had a little smear of blood just peeking over the top of her bottom lip.

Brunel had joined them. "Well done you two." He clapped his hands.

Astrid followed behind Brunel. "Well, one of you has some potential at least," she added.

Brunel waved her away. "No, well done," he swiveled his head towards Damascus. "All of you."

Tom instructed them to finish the day with some laps and stretches. Tom allowed them to have a short session this one time. They hit the showers and changed back into their usual academy robes. The three of them met up with Gilbert for dinner. The banquet hall was filled to max capacity with all the students from every year gathered in one place. The four children sat at the table designated for first year students. The Maitres and Maitresses had their own separate room to eat attached to the banquet hall and rarely shared a meal with their students.

Gilbert looked on with wide eyes as he listened to the other three recount the events from CTC.

"I've heard that almost all the students that participate in Combat Tournament Club end up being recruited by the Guild of Ravens as Battlemages," Gilbert said after the other students had finished their account of the events. "Is that what you all want to do after you graduate?"

Rinx shrugged her shoulders, "I haven't really decided what I want to do."

"Yeah, I can't say that I've given it much thought," Black added.

"I think it's safe to say they won't be recruiting me," Damascus laughed and they all joined in.

Later that night after a long first day, Black and Damascus were settled into their beds. Black's arms had stopped stinging but the bump on his head still ached as he laid on his side and it pressed against his pillow.

As they were lying in the dark Damascus spoke softly, "why didn't you use your totem when we fought?"

Black was startled at first by the sudden sound of the boy's voice. "I don't know," Black replied and thought about it. "I think that I wanted to beat you fairly."

There was a long pause before the soft voice came again. "I can handle it. Don't underestimate your enemy."

"But you're not my enemy," Black whispered.

"You know what I mean," Damascus said sharply. "It's not always going to be a game."

Neither boy spoke a word the rest of the night but Black remained trapped in thought. He considered Damascus's words and the events of the day. He was concentrating on his own ineptness when suddenly he was struck by the reality of Damascus's situation. Black had felt like an outsider but Damascus truly was one. He was the only one that Black was aware of that couldn't use any magic at the academy. Black suddenly knew better than anyone how badly Damascus must want to prove himself.

***

Present

Jack pulled his wool coat tight against the rain as he rounded the corner. He passed a group of young women in short skirts on the corner before he slipped into the alley. Even pissing rain the parties didn't stop on a Saturday night in Soho. Jack sloshed down the alley illuminated by a single pink neon light. The sign buzzed as he approached the entrance to 'The Pink Barracuda.'

Jack pushed open the door and had to shut it behind him. The mechanism that would normally pull it closed had been broken as long as Jack had been coming there. Nearly every Saturday night for the past five years. The regulars knew to close it and it was rare some drunk or dumb kid that didn't know any better came stumbling in. He crossed the room to the bar passing around a little round table with two chairs.

The lights were already set low so Lucy would be warming up in the back. The place reeked of cheap cigarettes and cheaper beer. The bartender spotted him coming. A giant of a man with a bald head, a white buttoned shirt with the sleeves rolled up his enormous black arms, and a tiny bow-tie clinging to his neck.

"Hey Jack, wha' it be tonight? The usual?" The bartender asked, already reaching for the tumbler.

"You bet, Max but make it a double. I gotta feeling something heavy's coming my way tonight," Jack replied, sliding a couple coins across the bar.

Max took the bottle off the shelf and poured. "Double whiskey neat. You go' it."

Jack took the drink and found his booth on the far wall with a good view of the stage. He slid into the booth across the worn cushion with the three tiny holes burned into it. He pulled the ashtray closer to him and pulled an unopened pack from his inside pocket carefully removing the plastic wrapper and discarding it in the ashtray. He slid one out and lit it up savoring the first drag before chasing it with a sip of whiskey.

Up on the stage James was settling down on the piano bench and massaging the first few notes out of the keys. There were a handful of regulars situated around the room nursing their drinks as Lucy took the stage. Her voice cut like a dagger through the smoky room. Her very presence demanded their attention as she crossed the stage in a red sequined dress. Her pale bare arms brushing over James's shoulders as she passed behind him. Her bright red lips articulated the words as the melody rose and then fell. She was really warmed up now, Jack thought.

Jack drove his cigarette butt into the ashtray and finished off the last of his whiskey as the first song came to a close. He sat the glass down feeling the liquid warm his belly as he joined in the applause. Jack was vaguely aware of the club's door banging shut during the lull between songs and it was only when Lucy cast a gaze at him and then over his shoulder that he became aware of someone standing next to his booth.

"If you're going to occupy my time during the show you should at least buy me a drink, Amadeus," Jack said without ever taking his eyes off the stage.

There was a hushed exchange difficult for Jack to make out since Lucy was starting in on an upbeat number.

"Make mine a double," Jack added.

Black slid into the booth with his back to the stage careful not to block Jack's view. "How's it going Jackie?"

Jack could just barely make out Black's silver eyes in his peripheral. "Could be worse, I suppose."

He picked the pack of cigarettes up off the table, slid one out but before he could light it a flame snapped in front of his face. The flame burned from between a pinched thumb and forefinger. For the first time Jack turned his head following the slender arm back to its source, a beautiful woman with short hair of the most crimson red he'd ever seen. Max was standing behind her with a tray and three whiskeys, two on the rocks, one neat, all doubles. With Jack's fag lit Rinx slid into the seat across from him and Max distributed the drinks before walking away.

Jack stared into Rinx's eyes. Even her eyes had a tint of red mixed with the brown. "Did the Guild of Ravens demote you or are you training some rookie now?" Jack continued to stare into the woman's eyes as he spoke.

"Neither. Just a friend that happens to be working on the same case," Black stated.

"Friend? Ah, you must be the Rinx I heard about," *Was there a hint of red now on her cheeks,* Jack thought. The light was too dim to know for certain.

"And you must be Jackie," Rinx asked.

"Jack," he said, raising his glass. "To friends then." They all raised their glasses and took a drink.

"That's an interesting accent to find in London," Rinx observed flashing a smile. "You're a little far from New York I'd say."

Jack pulled a long drag off his cig and turned his head to the side to exhale a plume of smoke. "Aren't we all a little far from home, honey. Besides, I have your friend here to thank for me being here."

Rinx turned her head to Black. "I helped him out of a little trouble a while ago," Black said dismissively.

Jack took another drag. "So what kind of trouble brings you to London tonight?"

Black described the information they'd received from Premier Morgu. Jack leaned back in his seat, closing his eyes. The smoke from the ashtray filled the space between them.

"Yeah I know something," Jack finally said, opening his eyes and leaning forward again. "But I need something from you."

Rinx looked skeptical but Black responded. "I assumed as much. What do you need?"

"I had an item that was pinched from me. A certain relic of moderate power. The details are unimportant but what is important is that it was to be delivered to me before some bastard intercepted it," Jack explained. "And a real piece of work, this guy." He glanced up at Lucy who'd moved on to a melancholic tune. "Sammy Nelson. Fella' has a nasty reputation with women and worse. Surrounds himself with a bunch of goons."

Black stretched out feeling the fake leather creak under him. "Come on Jackie, you couldn't handle this guy?"

"He has some kinda ward that is blocking my hexes and I don't have the raw magical power you guys have. Remember, I'm what you guys call 'Earthen born.' And like I said, he's got a lotta' goons." Jack ground another butt in the ashtray.

"We don't have time to waste," Rinx chimed in.

Jack's left arm brushed the piece concealed in a holster tucked against his ribs. "I'm ready when you are."

Black gave a nod and each of them slammed what was left of their whiskey and climbed out of the booth. As they made their way for the exit Jack detoured to the bar.

"Tell Lucy I'm sorry I missed the rest of the show." Jack gave a glance back to the stage and caught her green eyes on him. "Business," he said to Max. With a nod he joined the others in the rain.

They followed him through the winding streets until they came to a Chinese restaurant painted completely red. Just to the left of the restaurant was some stone steps leading to a basement entrance. They could hear the music before they even took a step off the cobble stones.

They followed Jack to the basement door. Jack gave the door three hard knocks before and an enormous man in a studded leather jacket, several facial piercings, and a neon green mohawk swung open the door.

The man pushed his round chest against Jack forcing his way outside while bending down to avoid hitting his mohawk on the door frame. "I thought Sammy told you not to show your face around here Jack," the man said. The giant glanced over Jack's shoulders at the two individuals accompanying him. He looked up and down both of them. One was wearing a black poncho and the other a red poncho and each pulled their hoods off almost in unison. "You and your mates can fuck off."

Music blasted from the open door. Jack pulled his right hand from his coat pocket brandishing a set of brass knuckles. Before the man had a chance to see them Jack was already breaking his jaw leaving him to fall to the wet ground in a heap.

"Gods!" Rinx exclaimed.

"You said we were in a hurry," Jack responded. "No need for small talk."

Black sighed and they stepped over the unconscious man shutting the door behind them. Inside the music was deafening. There was a sea of punks jumping and dancing to the band screaming on the stage. The lights flashed overhead as they waded through the chaos. Eventually they came to another door guarded by a couple more tattooed and heavily pierced men. As they approached, the men recognizing Jack, moved to intercept but this time Black and Rinx stepped in to block their attempt. One of the men tried to shove Black but was grabbed by the arm breaking it in multiple places before being tossed into the mosh pit of the crowd. The other man grabbed Rinx by the shoulder and promptly received an uppercut in the chin knocking him out cold.

Jack had already pushed through the door before they'd finished. Black and Rinx followed in after him. They moved down a corridor lit by red overhead lights until coming to another set of doors. Jack busted through them and they entered a brightly lit large office. Directly in front of them a man was sitting at a desk bent over a pile of white powder with a rolled up twenty pound note in his nose. He stared at them for a moment and then finished his line. He sniffed, wiped his nose, and stood up smoothing his slicked hair.

Around the room were at least twelve women in skimpy outfits eyeing them and three men in suites. Their skin was pale and looked tight across their features, almost paper thin. Black surveyed the room, noticing that some had their lips curled back in a snarl and their gums seemed to have eroded away revealing too much of their teeth. The man who'd been bent over the pile of drugs and was sporting an expensive looking beige suite moved around to the front of his desk.

"O' Jack you really jumped o'er the candle stick this time," the man said.

"But Sammy, it's you who's about to be burned," Jack replied. "You have something that belongs to me."

Sammy gave a laugh and pulled a small medallion from his pocket. "Quite the powerful protection charm," he said with a smile. "I guess that's why you needed the extra muscle." He regarded Black and Rinx for a moment. "I'd tell you to take it back. Hell, I'd tell you to take any item from my collection." Sammy gestured to the several wooden crates and boxes piled around the office. "If I thought it'd send you on out the door, but I know that's not why you're really here."

Jack stared into Sammy's inky eyes. There was a cold resolve in his heart and he knew all along what he came here for. He started across the office toward Sammy. At that the scantily clad women descended on them. Black and Rinx held the glassy eyed women at bay in an all out melee. Jack casually strolled toward Sammy leaving the brawl to his entourage.

Sammy confidently smiled knowing that the charm would protect him from whatever spell Jack could throw at him and surely those two couldn't punch their way through his people. He leisurely commenced an incantation.

Suddenly Jack with a burst of speed was on him and the cold steel barrel of a .357 magnum clicked between Sammy's teeth cutting his incantation midway. Sammy's eyes were like golf balls in his head. Black and Rinx were still beating on the body guards. Sammy mumbled but Jack pushed the barrel further into his mouth, the sight scratching the roof of his palette filling it with more metallic flavoring.

Jack wore a crazed look as he stared into Sammy's eyes. "Abra-cadabra, asshole," Jack said before the hammer fell, painting the back wall and ceiling with Sammy's brains.

The people Black and Rinx had been knocking around the room all collapsed to the floor in fetid piles. The putrid smell was upon them instantly. The paper-like skin on their faces and hands took on a jelly-like composition and began to slough off from the bone. Rinx wretched stepping back from the cadavers strewn about the floor.

Black held a hand over his nose and mouth. "Necromancy," he said searching for Jack.

Jack pulled the medallion from Sammy's inside pocket and turned to face his peers with a couple of specks of blood on his face.

"This is a hell of a mess here," Rinx said with her forearm pressed hard under her nose.

Black shot Jack a cold look. "Wipe the blood off your face and let's get out of here."

They returned to the Pink Barracuda without speaking. Once inside the three slid back into Jack's booth. Jack caught Max's attention and held up three fingers before lighting up another cigarette. This time he had to dig around his pocket to use his gold flip-lighter. Max arrived with three drinks and they each downed them in one. Lucy had already finished her set before they returned so it was just some jazz record tumbling out of the speakers.

"Another, Max," Jack said, trying to direct his smoke away from the others.

Max was gone and back again with another round in time for Jack to light up another fag. This time the drinks sat in front of their respective drinkers.

When Max returned to his post Jack leaned back in his seat and said, "That was pretty fucked up."

"Yeah, I'd say that was pretty fucked up," Black concurred as he eyed Jack from across the table. "Explain to me how we went from retrieving your stolen merchandise to executing a man."

Jack took a sip of his fresh whiskey. "The guy had it coming. You saw the dead bodies he had reanimated. God knows what he did to those girls before they died." He reached for his drink again while Black eyeballed him, catching the slight tremor in his hand. "Or what he did after."

"This isn't how we do things," Black insisted.

"We can't all wait for the old magic police to swoop in and save the day Amadeus." Jack leaned forward. "These streets are full of people like Sammy that never end up on the Guild of Ravens' radar. And you talk to me about 'how we do things.' I've seen you soaked in blood." He leaned back again and tucked his cigarette into his mouth. "I know how you do things."

Rinx watched Black out of the corner of her eye. She could see his eyes narrow and even in the dim light she caught the rapidly pulsing vein at his temple.

"You intended on murdering him from the start," Black said through clenched teeth.

Jack waved away his comment and turned his head so as to not meet Black's stare.

"We did our part," Rinx cut in. "Now just tell us what we came here for."

Jack explained how a man had been recruiting some people for a serious ritual. "Rookies mostly. Some young wannabes just barely seen real magic." He explained that there were few details on what the ritual was actually meant to do. "Vague promises of power. The kind of shit you've heard before with these cult-like weirdos. It stunk to high hell." Despite the vague information he knew of where it was to take place. Jack described an old building in the Limehouse district. "You'll know it when you see it. Right next to the water, rundown, storage building for the docks. But my understanding is it's been out of use and condemned for years. Just follow the rats and you'll find it."

"Anything else?" Black's temper seemed to have cooled a bit.

"Yeah one more thing. The man sniffing around, he called himself Hannibal. Should be easy to recognize. He had some gnarly scarred hands." Jack buried his cigarette butt in the ashtray. "That's all I've got."

"Thanks," Rinx said bluntly as she slid out of the booth.

Black followed her before pausing. Standing at the end of the table he turned to face Jack again. "What happened tonight. That's the same kind of stuff that forced you to leave the states."

Jack stared into his empty glass with a bored expression but meanwhile in his mind he wondered if he'd gotten all the blood off his face. He felt like maybe he missed some under his chin. He rubbed at it automatically. *Nothing,* he thought.

"It's not like that," he replied to Black as he wiped at one of his cheeks.

Black watched him for a moment and then said, "Take care of yourself, Jackie," and then they were gone.

The underground offered Black and Rinx a break from the London rain as they made their way to the neighborhood of Limehouse. It took them most of the way but it wasn't long before they had to leave the dry, lit refuge of the tunnel system to make the rest of their voyage on foot.

As they followed the brick-paved roads towards the river the rain was beginning to change to sleet. They each had their hoods pulled tight. There had not been time to change into more Earthen appropriate clothing before they used the travel gates to teleport into the London area. The old cloaks they'd received all those years ago had grown as they did so that they still fit into adulthood. Normally cloaks would have made them stand out in an Earthen city but on a night like the one they found themselves in, they were thankful to have the protection from the elements.

Black and Rinx followed Jack's directions and found the building easy enough. It was a large warehouse with boarded up windows. They searched around the exterior of the building before they discovered a door with a heavy padlock attached. Black threw his shoulder into the door tearing the latch off and nearly all the hinges. He stumbled through the doorway into the inky blackness of the structure. He could detect the faint scent of something that had been burning and animal urine. Rinx summoned a light from behind him and as it illuminated the darkness three large brown rats scurried to safety further into the darkness.

The caverness building appeared to be empty from what they could see in the glow of Rinx's spell. The frozen rain pelted the roof high overhead as they creeped their way into the center. On the dirty stone floor the edge of something began to take shape as they approached. There was a coarse white powder spread across the floor and as Rinx raised her flame to better survey the pattern they could make out that the powder formed a large pentagram. There were several sigils encircling the pentagram and at the end of each point was a waxy residue, splattered with what the pair recognized immediately as dried blood.

"Well, we found the ritual sight," Rinx whispered.

"Let's split up and have a look around," Black suggested.

Rinx nodded in agreement and Black recited the spell needed to summon his own flame for illumination. They both started off in different directions. Black made his way to the back of the building stepping around a puddle pooling on the concrete from a leak in the roof. He discovered an office with the door missing. The office protruded from the back wall and had several broken windows. Inside he found a desk pushed against the wall directly across from the door and a cot at the very end. Black inspected the cot and could see it had recently been slept in. On the desk was an old tome opened to a particular page and some notes scattered about. Black examined the text on the aged and yellowed paper of the book but was unable to discern exactly what it said. He collected the notes and folded them into the book, stuffing them all into a pouch that hung at his hip.

Black exited the office and followed the wall making his way clockwise from where he had started which was the normal procedure taught to Battlemages when investigating in pairs. He slowly made his way down one wall stirring up dust that floated about the dim light of his flame. Black passed tall metal shelves that were bare aside from the occasional wooden skid stacked under them. Nothing unusual stood out to him and eventually he found his way back to the front of the building. From there he returned back to the ritual site where he could see Rinx's light hovering in the blackness.

"I found a lot of nothing," Rinx stated with one hand on her hip.

Black opened his mouth to speak, "I-" he cut himself off.

Both Rinx and Black twisted their heads towards the entrance of the warehouse. They each leaned in instinctively to hear what sounded like someone speaking low. Suddenly a pin-prick of light appeared in the doorway. The light threw harsh shadows on a large hooded figure looming in the entrance.

It suddenly clicked in Black's mind what was happening. He extinguished his light and swatted Rinx's out of her hand in one swift motion. Black wrapped an arm around Rinx's body and dove as far as he could out of the path of a violent eruption that ripped through the building. Debris from the roof crashed down on the pair.

A moment later the debris was thrown clear. Black and Rinx stood in their hybrid forms, their clothes tattered. Each of Rinx's hands were blazing with fire. With their totem-enhanced eyes they were able to see a little clearer in the dark. The figure was gone.

"That explosion," Black said. "I think we found our murderer."

Like a fiery comet Rinx blurred past Black and was out the door. He lingered a moment in the rain, now pouring through the ruined roof before chasing after her. Outside he surveyed the area but found no sign of anyone before he heard the slow splash of someone approaching in the gloom. It was Rinx, red faced and her jaw clenched hard.

"He's gone," she stated. "We had him and he slipped away, damn it!" She slammed one of her fists into the palm of her hand. "We have nothing."

Black felt the bulk of the tome against his thigh. "Maybe not."

Chapter 8

Past

A few weeks after Black began his courses he'd begun to slip into a familiar routine. He was still struggling with his element and Maitre Brunel had assigned the task of learning a second spell in their affinity by midterm. It felt like a daunting task for Black but his other classes progressed just fine. Maitre Brunel had spoken with Maitre Bulgar and since then Bulgar had Black and Damascus practicing swordplay in almost every class in addition to some normal workouts. Maitre Bulgar was thrilled when he discovered they were members of CTC and watched in delight as the two boys dueled.

One of Black's other classes, Mysteries of Nature, which he shared with Gilbert had been assigned a group project. Black and Gilbert had the misfortune of being placed in a group with Darius who they also shared the class with. Their assignment was to find a particular kind of flower called an asphodelus. Any group that could find one would be exempt from the next exam.

Darius had been sitting in front of them and turned back, his beady green eyes on them, "we are finding that flower."

A couple days later on a Saturday morning Black sat with Rinx and Damascus at breakfast. They had all finished their meal when Gilbert plopped down with a plate full of eggs and a tall glass of milk.

"Late again," Rinx said.

Gilbert's face was a light shade of red.

"What do you get up to every morning," Damascus said, eyeing him suspiciously.

Gilbert averted his eyes and began greedily stuffing some eggs into his mouth. "Nothing, really."

"Well we need to meet up with Darius in a bit to find this flower so eat up quick," Black advised.

"Yuck, what a creep that kid," Rinx said as she grabbed her throat and feigned throwing up.

"That's unlucky for you two. Be careful with that one," Damascus added, looking at Black.

Black nodded his head. "We'll be fine, but thanks."

After Gilbert had quickly finished his breakfast they said their goodbyes to Rinx and Damascus. Black and Gilbert took some sausages wrapped in napkins and muffins from the breakfast spread.

"We can eat this for lunch if we are out for a while," Black said.

"I'll take some extra for Darius just in case," Gilbert stated as he piled a couple more sausages onto a napkin and rolled it up.

They took their cloaks and a couple of backpacks from their rooms before meeting up with Darius at the front entrance of the academy. Black wore the cloak he'd received from Mazurus and the other two had the academy branded dark blue cloaks.

"Cool cloak," Gilbert said admiring the image on the back.

Darius made a face and rolled his eyes. "Let's get going, we don't have all day."

The three set out walking for several hours. The sun hung high in the sky and the cool September morning had turned into a warm afternoon. Darius and Gilbert had removed their cloaks a couple of hours earlier and stuffed them in their bags. Black enjoyed the constant comfortable temperature provided by his elven mantle. They'd followed the same path due North since they'd set out to not get lost. At the beginning they'd followed an obvious path through grassy fields but soon the path faded away and the odd copse of trees became a forest. The canopy wasn't so thick that the sun couldn't break through the leaves in regular frequency. A gentle breeze gave the branches a little sway in the canopy and carried a coolness that hinted at autumn. The occasional chipmunk or squirrel would scurry up a tree as they approached and twice they caught sight of a rabbit running for refuge.

They had spoken little since they'd set off opting for the almost constant song of the birds and typical forest sounds but suddenly Darius broke their silence, "This is such a waste of time." They had been marching in a line with Darius leading the way. He stopped next to a fallen dead tree. "I'm sure fatty is getting hungry. Let's take a break and eat some lunch," he said as he swung off the bag from his back and hopped up on a log to sit.

Black who had been following behind Darius, gave a glance back at Gilbert. "Sure," he said, finding a mossy spot under a tree to rest.

Gilbert took a seat between the two in the dirt. He wiped the sweat from his forehead and pulled a bottle of water out, taking a long drink. Next he pulled the sausages from his bag. Darius took a drink from his own bottle and pulled a small meat pie from his bag.

"We took extra sausages from breakfast this morning for you too if you want some," Gilbert said with a slight quiver in his voice.

Darius hesitated for a moment looking at his pie and then said, "Ok, I guess you can take one of my pies. I took them from dinner yesterday." He pulled another from his sack and handed it to Gilbert who exchanged it with three of the sausages. "Thanks," Darius responded.

Gilbert broke the pie in half and passed one part to Black. Black nodded in gratitude.

"Well at least it's a beautiful day," Gilbert said, unwrapping some of the greasy sausages from the napkins.

Darius grunted in agreement as he chewed on the crust of a pie.

They finished their lunch without much discussion. Darius was laying on his back with the back of his head cupped in his hands on the log. Black was nodding off with his back resting against the tree and Gilbert had a book out examining a patch of small yellow flowers next to him.

Gilbert had one finger pressed against the page of his book. "Creeping buttercup," he said quietly to himself.

As if stirred by Gilbert's words, Darius set up on the log, slid down, and started to stroll further into the forest.

Gilbert raised up to his knees. "Where are you going?" he asked.

"I'm just going to take a piss," Darius continued. "I'll let you know if I need a hand," he chuckled as he disappeared into some thicket.

Gilbert settled back down and turned his round face towards Black. "I guess we won't be able to skip that next test, huh?"

Black raised his drooping head and stretched his arms yawning. "I guess not, but it's nice to get out and have some fresh air. I wouldn't call it a waste." he said, glancing in the direction that Darius had disappeared.

Suddenly there came a call from the forest, "AMADEUS- GILBERT!"

Black jumped to his feet and Gilbert heaved himself up.

"It's Darius," Gilbert said, pulling his backpack over his shoulder.

"AMADEUS- GILBERT!" Darius shouted again.

Black bolted through the brush hurdling a bush as he went, leaving Gilbert behind. He rushed forward in the direction he heard the shouting before he broke into a clearing. He found Darius standing in the clearing with a large grin on his face. Darius stabbed a thumb over his shoulder. Black's eyes followed Darius's thumb. On the other side of the clearing was a rocky hill with a sparse cypress tree hanging over the entrance of a gaping hole. In the center of the clearing were half a dozen conical stalks with pale flowers blooming from them.

"Asphodels!" Gilbert shouted, crunching out of the tree line carrying Black and Darius's bags.

They each took a flower from one of the stalks and delicately placed them in their sacks. Darius was inspecting the hole in the hill.

"What do you think's in there," Darius asked the others.

Black stood beside him. "I don't know but," he sniffed. "There's a foul air from it."

"Let's take a look," Darius said as he began rifling around in his bag.

"I don't know if we should go in there guys," Gilbert stated.

"Of course you don't," Darius replied, pulling a lighter from his bag. "You're a coward." He opened the silver lighter and flicked it alight. "I stole this from my dad," he said as he extinguished the flame and lit it again.

Darius started into the cave. Black turned to Gilbert and shrugged before following Darius in. Gilbert lingered a moment before shuffling after the other two boys.

Inside the cave the smell was so strong that even Darius and Gilbert could smell it. They followed the faint glow of Darius's lighter around an immediate bend and then down a gentle slope into the earth. There was the occasional root that hung down brushing through their hair or against a shoulder. Black looked back past the bulbous silhouette of Gilbert to the fading light of the entrance. After a few minutes of walking the path opened up to a cave. The only sound as they pushed on into the room was the faint shuffle of their feet on the rocky floor and Gilbert's heavy breathing.

The smell in the cave was almost unbearable and they were all now covering their noses.

Black put a hand on Darius's shoulder. "I think Gil is right. We shouldn't be in here," Black whispered.

Darius shrugged Black's hand off. "Just a little further," he replied in a hushed tone.

Black could no longer see the path behind them. Darius inched his way forward until there was a loud crunch followed by something skittering across the floor. They all froze huddled close in the limited glow of the lighter surrounded by impenetrable darkness. Darius lowered the light down to look at his feet. Crushed beneath his right foot was half the ribcage of some small animal. The other half still had the remnants of desiccated skin clinging to it. He stretched his arm out from his body still trying to keep it low to the ground. To their horror were several more animal corpses in varying states of decay as far as the light could reach.

Gilbert began to gag. Darius took a step back bumping into Black. He turned quickly and pushed past the other two boys in the direction they had come from. Darius had just passed Gilbert when he froze again. There was a rustling sound like something dragging across the floor.

"Something's in here," Gilbert murmured. His face was twisted in terror and his heavy breathing had stopped.

They were all to some degree aware of the thumping in their chests. It felt like their hearts were threatening to escape through their throats. The dragging sound grew closer.

"It's between us and the exit," Darius whispered, his beady eyes now bulging from his skull.

They all now held their breath as they stared into the darkness. Slowly something resembling a human face emerged from the shadows. The faint light shimmered off one milky eye that protruded from the socket. The other looked deflated in the creature's head with a crusty trail down the paper-thin skin of the cheek. The nose had been torn off leaving only two slits in the center of its face and the lips were missing like the nose. The gums had retreated back making the teeth appear much longer and there were a couple gaps where some were missing. The creature shambled forward, its pale naked body was fully visible. The waxy skin drooped so that in some places the bones were so clearly seen and the belly was bloated, sagging down between its thin thighs.

It took one more step forward on its nobly legs dragging one foot across the ground before it stopped and let a groan rise from its agape mouth. Its tongue slipped over its teeth rapidly making a moist slurping noise. It raised one boney hand out in front of itself. What fingernails remained were jagged and caked with filth.

Suddenly it let out a scream and rushed forward. All three boys fell into each other, adding their own screams to the creature's. The monster fell upon Darius knocking all the boys to the ground. Darius was on his back and the lighter had dropped from his hand landing near his head on the stone, miraculously staying lit. The other two boys instinctively scooted away from the walking horror which had climbed onto Darius. Darius continued to scream as the monster's maul closed in on his face.

Darius grabbed the creature by the throat holding its crooked teeth at bay. The monster's putrid breath filled his nostrils and saliva was running onto his face as its teeth clicked shut. Despite Darius's efforts the creature's rancid mouth was growing closer. The flame flickered causing the shadows to dance across the thing's grotesque features.

Black finally reclaiming his wits changed into a wolf, rushing forward and grabbing the thing by the ankle in his jaws. He pulled with all his strength but the creature was incredibly strong despite its emaciated visage. Black could feel his fangs driven down to bone and a liquid oozed into his mouth. It took everything he had to not let go out of pure revulsion.

The creature was snapping only an inch from Darius's nose when suddenly a stoney hand plunged itself into the creature's mouth. It continued to scream and chomp on the stone encrusted hand and some of its teeth splintered and chipped. Gilbert had the monster by its jaw and was pushing it back. His face was full of panic and appeared crazed but somehow he and Black together managed to pull it off of Darius.

The creature was back on its feet and the momentum combined with a hard push from Gilbert sent it stumbling back over Black. Black released the creature as it fell back against a wall. Unfortunately in the confusion the momentum also caused Gilbert to lose his footing falling onto his side.

The creature locked its gooey sights onto Gilbert, screaming as it pushed itself off the wall. It shambled forward with both of its gnarled hands groping for its next victim before a row of icy spikes erupted from the floor pinning the monster to the wall. Black and Gilbert looked up to see Darius on his feet with the lighter in his hand.

"RUN!" Darius shouted.

Gilbert scrambled back to his feet as Darius passed him leading the way with lighter. They all ran up the narrow pathway with Black bringing up the rear. They burst into the daylight and were back in the clearing. The creature continued to howl from deep within the earth.

Gilbert struggled to call out between his labored breathing, "Wait-," he cried. "Wait-," he buckled over putting his hands on his knees but turning in a way so that he could still see the entrance to the cave. The others stopped running and looked at him. "It's a ghoul." He took two more heavy breaths. "It's a ghoul so it can't come into the sunlight." Two more breaths. "We're safe."

Darius fell back on his butt, his face pale and his eyes red. Black changed back into his human form and immediately wretched, throwing up part of his lunch. They remained in silence for a little while letting the adrenaline left work its way out of their system. Black pulled his bottle out to wash the vomit taste from his mouth. The ghoul eventually stopped howling.

Finally Darius spoke, "That was insane." He looked at Gilbert. "You put your hand in its mouth. It must smell awful."

Gilbert looked at his hand and back to Darius. "It can't smell any worse than your face after you finished kissing it."

"Kissing it?" Darius said and then burst into laughter. The other two boys joined in.

After they finally stopped laughing Gilbert said, "We really should start back. After seeing that thing I really don't want to be outside the academy walls when the sun begins to set."

The other boys nodded in agreement and stood up to begin the trek back.

As they walked Darius asked Black, "So you can turn into a wolf?"

Black nodded.

"Is it a totem?" Gilbert asked.

"Yeah," Black answered.

"Awesome," Darius stated.

The three were climbing the steps just as the sun was beginning to kiss the horizon. The coolness of the evening had begun to set in and they were feeling exhausted from the events of the day.

They heard a voice from the top of the stairs and they looked up to see Mr. Bayer's crooked nose pointed at them.

"So I saw you three had quite an adventure today," Bayer smiled, revealing his stained teeth.

He snorted and spat a brown glob just in front of Gilbert's feet. Gilbert jumped back a step. A pigeon was perched on his shoulder. Its head twisted from side to side alternating its beady eyes, watching them.

"You should be careful out there," Bayer started past them. "It can be dangerous for some young pups like you lot."

Bayer headed off in the direction of his post at the academy wall.

"Thanks for the advice," Darius shouted after him and then said quietly to the others, "creepy old buzzard. Doesn't look much different from that thing in the cave."

Gilbert gave a nervous laugh and they all three passed through the wooden doors. They made their way back to the dorm to drop their things off.

"Well, see you guys around," Darius said before he made his way to Newton who was lounging on a sofa in the common area.

Black and Gilbert decided to drop their bags in their rooms and immediately go to dinner. When they arrived in the dining hall they found Rinx and Damascus had just sat down to eat. The two boys took their dinner and sat down with the other two kids.

Black recanted the adventure they'd had that day avoiding the more disgusting bits of the story on account of not wanting to put them off their appetites. The other two students listened in muted shock and at times horror.

"And Darius actually stepped in to save you?" Damascus asked, looking to Gilbert.

Gilbert shrugged and responded, "yeah, I guess so."

Black slapped the round boy on the shoulder. "To be fair, Gil did save him first." Black mimicked grabbing himself on the mouth. "He covered his hand in stone and grabbed the thing mlike mmmiss."

"Wow, that must have taken a lot of courage," Rinx stated.

Damascus added, "You could even call it heroic."

Gilbert's face was completely red. "Noooo, I think Black did most of the work pulling it off of him." He shuffled uncomfortably in his seat.

"I can't believe they would allow a creature like that to roam the grounds," Damascus said. "Seems quite dangerous to me."

"No kidding," Black added with a chuckle.

"Well we know why they don't allow students outside the academy at night now." Rinx confirmed.

Soon the conversation turned to class work.

"So what are you two planning to do for your second elemental spell in Maitre Brunel's class?" Gilbert asked Rinx and Black.

"Well," Rinx began. "I already know how to ignite some objects on fire so technically I think that counts but it's not very exciting so I think I'm going to try and learn another spell."

"You're going to learn a third?" Gilbert asked, obviously impressed.

"I think so," Rinx admitted. "I think I'm going to try and learn the 'Dragon's Breath' spell. Breathing fire could be fun plus it leaves my hands free in a fight." She punched the air.

"That does sound useful," Black agreed.

Rinx forced a smile. "Have you decided what you want to do, Deus?"

"I'm not sure yet," He admitted, trying to keep his head up in front of his friends.

"I'm sure you'll figure something out," Gilbert stated.

After a short silence in the conversation Damascus turned the attention back to Gilbert. "What about you, Gil? What are you planning?"

"I started working on a barrier spell, 'Stone Wall.' It does exactly what it sounds like." Gilbert pushed some peas around on his plate as he explained. "It's a pretty basic earth spell. I think all sorcerers with an affinity to earth learn it pretty early so hopefully it's not too difficult."

"Sounds like a good defensive spell," Black admitted, nodding his head.

"But," Gilbert raised his head as if he just remembered something. "Damascus, what are you doing?"

Damascus stretched back in his chair. "Oh, I have to take a regular boring written test." They all accepted this as obvious. "I'm surprised Brunel would even take the time to make one, honestly." They all nodded their heads in agreement.

Later after they had gone back to their rooms for the night Black settled into his bed with the large book of basic elemental spells he'd brought with him from Rinx's home. He turned to the section containing wind spells and ran his finger down the list reading the description of each and the level of difficulty. The problem he kept running into was that all the most useful spells were either above his current ability or required massive amounts of power to make them effective.

He read to himself the description of a spell called 'Wind Blades.' Project a blade formed from wind with a wave of your hand. Capable of slicing through barriers and enemies. Caution; the spell is incredibly dangerous when wielded by a powerful sorcerer, able to cut like the keenest of swords. Level of difficulty. Black whispered the word aloud, "Master."

Black picked out another spell that sounded interesting; 'Tornado.' Manifest and direct a tornado that pulls in surrounding debris creating deadly projectiles, Black read. The size and power of the tornado is only limited by the sorcerer's control and available magic. He pointed to the level of difficulty again and let out a sigh. Expert.

Black finally settled on a spell ranked 'Novice' which was one step above 'Beginner.' It was a spell that according to the information in his book could only reach its full potential after the sorcerer learned to maintain a steady but powerful stream of magic. What gave Black some hope was one line in the description; can alternatively be useful in select situations where control is lacking but only for short durations and with a moderate risk of physical injury. Black continued to read. In this alternate form 'Levitate' is commonly referred to as 'Propel' instead.

Black let a smile spread across his face and turned to Damascus who was in his separate bed reading a book on undead creatures titled, 'Undead Dangers.' Feeling Black's eyes upon him he looked up from the pages of his tome.

"Well, what are you grinning about?" Damascus asked.

"I think I found my next spell," Black responded.

"And?"

"I'm going to learn how to fly."

***

Present

After Black and Rinx failed to find Hannibal they returned back to Tír na nÓg. They decided that the safest place for them to decide their next step was within the Order of Homme at the home of Damascus. Damascus had welcomed them back warmly assuring them that all his current guards and servants had been personally vetted.

"I can promise you that there is no safer place in all of Tuatha Dé," Damascus declared.

They had arrived late but none the less Damascus had been prepared for their return and already had rooms ready for them. The pair were exhausted from their day and the potion that Damascus had provided Black in the morning had worn off quite some time sooner leaving him with an unusual feeling. He felt hollow like at any moment his body could cave in on itself and he wanted nothing more than a comfortable bed to sleep in. After some brief greetings the pair were off to their separate rooms.

Black was asleep almost as soon as his head hit the pillow. His body was in a state of complete rest and recovery but his mind was drifting in a state of dream and something else. In this state he found himself as that little boy Mazurus had found in the forest all those years ago. His black hair hung down to the middle of his back. He smelled the old familiar and comforting scent of the trees, grass, and dirt but suddenly another smell filled his nostrils. It was a sickening sweet smell of decay and sulfur.

"That smell," suddenly came many voices speaking in unison. "Is the smell of brimstone."

Black saw now in the sky above him an inky orb staring back with several feathered wings spread out behind it. The wings encircled the eye and rotated at differing speeds. Some clockwise and others counter-clockwise.

"A great darkness looms just behind the horizon. I have seen what can not be. You know the evil that waits just behind a paper-thin vale. It yearns to break through and bring ruin on this world. It will be a calamity." The eye continued.

"Corvus," Black whispered. "It has been a long time since we've spoken."

Suddenly the forest all around Black erupted into flames. The smoke was bitter in his nose and lungs, causing him to cough. The trees popped and crackled in the intense heat. Soon the trees fell away and it was burning buildings that rose up around him. It was Tuatha Dé that was burning and all manner of grotesque and horrid creature roamed the streets. Naked men and women were impaled on spikes lining the alleyways. The awful screams of people echoed through Black's ears as he witnessed the demons dragging people from their homes kicking and screaming. There was a large wooden cage full of children and the brutes were lining up. Some enormously obese monster with the head of a horse grinned like a man as it reached into the cage and passed out the terrified children. Some of the brutes were unhinging their jaws and swallowing the children whole while others were taking wet crunching bites. Black heard those that could, cry out for their mothers as they slid down the demon's throats.

Black's attention was suddenly caught by the sight of a naked woman climbing across the rooftop with a baby in her arms. The woman walked to the edge, swayed for a moment and then flung herself with the baby into the open air. Black closed his eyes just before the impact but he could not shut out the sound of the crunch on the stones below. When he opened his eyes all the demons had turned casually to look at the mess and began to laugh. The laughs were like someone feverishly working at a violin that was out of tune. Black's mind raced back to that terrible day all those years ago. The day of the Great Calamity as it had come to be called since. The terror, helplessness, and pain of that day filled him ten fold.

Black was beginning to feel his head spin and the pure spirit of madness was set upon him. He could feel his visage locked in a state of horror and although he was screaming no sound was escaping his throat. He suddenly felt the compulsion to tear his own eyes out removing the horrid sight before him. He began clawing wildly at the orbs set in his head. He tried not to close his eyelids so that he could get every last gooey bit scooped from his sockets.

And again he was back in the green forest with the scent of pine and both his sanity and eyes intact. The black eye of Corvus still loomed over him.

"You see what is to come if you fail," Corvus demanded.

"You're a trickster," Black found himself saying. He was crying and had to swallow the sobs that were rising up in his throat.

"You have been fooled but not by us," the spirit responded.

Black had tears running from his eyes when he awoke the next morning. He set up in bed letting the blanket slip from his chest. His body glistened with sweat in the orange-red morning light that poured through a gap in the heavy forest-green curtains. Black wiped his eyes clean of the tears and crust and slid to the edge of the bed to allow his bare feet to fall onto the cool wooden floor.

Black sat alone in the mostly dark room but he still felt the presence of that all seeing black eye hovering over him. His nightmare was already beginning to fade but the meaning was set firm into his consciousness. Black stood, crossed the room to the window and threw the curtains open. The morning was bright but a dark armada of clouds were beginning their advance on the rising sun.

Another dark day, Black thought. *Maybe the darkest day before its over,* came another thought he couldn't be certain was his own from somewhere deeper within his mind.

A pitcher of water, basin, and small towel sat upon a dark stained wooden table. Black used this to clean himself and then found the familiar linen clothes he associated with the Order of Homme neatly folded on a green cushioned chair near the window. He slipped on the linen clothes.

Dressed, Black crossed the room to the door but stopped just before grabbing the handle. He could hear voices in the hallway and recognized them as Rinx and Damascus.

"You don't know how badly I want that," came Damascus's voice.

"If you want it so badly then why don't you just do it?" Rinx pleaded.

"We've discussed this before and you know it's not that simple. I-" Damascus was cut off.

"-Have an obligation to tradition, blah blah blah," Rinx finished his sentence. "What about your obligation to us? To yourself? To me? Doesn't that mean anything to you?"

Black clumsily grabbed the door handle making as much noise as would seem natural. He stepped into the hallway finding his two friends standing in Rinx's doorway staring at him. He noted Damascus's hand falling away from Rinx's as it took its usual position folded behind his back.

"Good morning you two," Black smiled. "I'm starving." He rubbed his belly.

Damascus gestured down the hall in the direction of the stairs. "Breakfast should be prepared."

"Great," Black responded.

"I'll be down in a bit," Rinx stated.

After a quick exchange of glances with Rinx, Damascus said, "I'll join you, my friend."

As they descended the stairs Black asked, "Is everything alright?"

Damascus let out a sigh and for a moment his demeanor shifted. His face as well as his shoulders seemed to drop before he re-composed himself.

"I found myself in a very difficult situation." Damascus admitted. "I'm torn between what duty demands of me and what my heart desires."

"You've always managed to do what you believe to be right," Black advised. "I think you should trust your instinct."

"And you have always been a good friend," Damascus stated.

Black patted him on the shoulder as they entered the dining hall. "So have you."

They stood at the bottom of the stairs. Black started for the dining room but stopped when Damascus hesitated.

"And you, my friend," Damascus raised an eyebrow as he asked. "These past years you have grown more solitary. Is that what you believe is right?"

"I–" Black struggled to find his words and struggled even more to look his friend in the eye. "I believe– I have seen too many people hurt." Black opened his mouth as if to say more but didn't.

Damascus gave a nod and moved to the dining room as he added, "The Order of Homme has always believed in strength through unity. Alone we are easily broken."

Upon the dining table was an assortment of sliced meats, cheese, and smoked salmon. As the two ate Black described in more detail the events of the previous day and finally mentioned the book along with the notes they had discovered in the warehouse.

"I've had a chance to briefly review what was written," Black said.

"And," Damascus inquired.

"The book is in a language I am unfamiliar with but the notes I presume are a loose translation of at least some of the passages," he replied.

Damascus listened intently.

"I'm convinced this is a spell for opening a portal to hell," Black continued.

"As Premier Morgu suspected," Damascus shook his head.

"Yes, but it's strange," Black added.

"How so?"

"Something about the way it ends," Black explained. "And the wording. There seems to be more on the marked pages of the book than what is written in the notes. They seem incomplete."

Damascus rubbed his chin. "So there is more to this spell?"

"I think so," Black admitted.

"Do you think Morgu may be able to offer more insight into this? She strikes me as a woman that knows more than she lets on," Damascus raised an eyebrow.

"Probably," Black agreed, sitting back in his chair while folding his arms across his chest. "Or possibly. I think we should at least inform her of what we have found."

"Then I would send word to her," Damascus said while simultaneously snapping his fingers summoning a servant to his side.

The servant quickly returned to them with a pen and stationary. Black wrote out a message to Morgu explaining the situation. Damascus sealed the note in an envelope before calling over a guard.

"Make sure this letter is delivered to Premier Morgu herself, understood?" Damascus informed him.

"Yes sir," the guard stated before he was on his way.

Two hours passed before the guard returned, reporting that he had brought guests. The three friends had been speculating on what the next move should be but the conversation immediately died as they moved to the foyer. Standing just within the entrance was Premier Morgu and Barnabus.

Damascus moved to greet the pair while extending a hand. "Premier Morgu and Premier Barnabus what a pleasure to meet you."

Morgu took Damascus's hand delicately while Barnabus's bronze mechanical arm remained at rest by his side.

Damascus's hand lingered for a moment in front of Barnabus before he finally retracted it and said, "Of course, I am at liberty to state that I welcome you both as an individual and not as a representative of the Order of Homme and that the Order will not have any official involvement with whatever transpires here during your visit."

"That goes without saying," Morgu agreed with a slight upturn of her lips. "The Order would not want to be seen as too friendly with the Guild of Ravens."

"Let's get this over with," Barnabus wheezed. "You dragged me here Margret so let's skip the pleasantries."

"I'll be respectful of your time," Damascus responded and gestured to the adjacent room. "Right this way."

Damascus led the two Premiers into the dining hall. As they passed, Black and Rinx gave a respectful nod before falling in behind them. They took their seats around the table and after a suspicious glance at Barnabas's masked visage Damascus ordered a servant to bring refreshments.

A log crackled in the nearby fireplace as it burned.

Black had remained standing and quickly spoke up, presenting the leather bound book and notes he discovered in the warehouse. "As outlined in the letter we sent to you Premier Morgu, here is the tome we discovered." Black passed the book and notes to her as he spoke. "Unfortunately the book is written in a language we do not recognize."

Morgu silently opened the book to the pages marked by the hand written notes. She examined the text of the book before passing it to Barnabus and turned her attention back to the loose sheets. Barnabus's yellow eyes quickly scanned each line as he turned the pages.

After a long silence Morgu said, "Unfortunately I can not speak to the content of the book but I brought Premier Barnabus in the hopes that his expertise in ancient languages may be of some use. However, in regards to the notes here," she said, raising the papers for everyone to see. "I can confirm that this is a rather complicated ritual for opening a doorway to hell and I'd say that it does seem to end quite abruptly giving the impression that it is incomplete. Furthermore, I have seen this hand-writing enough to recognize the owner."

Morgu paused again, scanning the notes before she continued. "I am certain that these notes were written by Premier Valen himself."

Black leaned forward placing his hands on the edge of the table and surveying the others. "So the big question still remains; what was this spell supposed to do when completed?"

Barnabus cleared his throat as Black rose from his seat again standing. "I may be able to answer that question," the Premier stated. "It's an old language but one I am familiar with, though I haven't read it in an age. According to the text here the spell is meant to open the portal to hell as you've deduced from the notes." Barnabus exhaled a long wheezing sigh from his mask and his mechanical arm whorled as the fingers delicately turned a page. "And then expel the inhabitants from said plane."

There was another long moment of silence and Black wore a dumbfounded look upon his face before he finally regained his composure and spoke. "The spell is meant to force the demons into our world!?" He exclaimed in disbelief.

"Indeed," Barnabus confirmed. "but it requires a tremendous amount of magical power and a site uniquely constructed for the ritual, so not a spell easily performed."

"Like the power accrued from several soul pacts," Black said at almost a whisper.

Morgu nodded. "Another Great Calamity." She thought for a moment. "No, this would be on a scale that would make the Great Calamity all those years ago look insignificant. I believe you two are in a unique position to appreciate the scale of such a thing better than anyone else here."

Black and Rinx exchanged looks.

Barnabus continued, "And I suspect that the previous attempts were simply meant to test the efficacy of the power accumulated considering that the text states the second half of the spell could only be completed on the night of a full moon and based off your description of the site you investigated. It would not have been able to facilitate the second half of the spell."

Black recalled his encounter three nights ago in this very house with the werewolves. "A full moon like tonight," he said flatly. His statement hung in the air as they all slowly absorbed it.

"This makes no sense," Rinx blurted out and shot a suspicious look from Barnabus to Morgu. "Premier Valen was researching this?" Her face was a clear mixture of confusion and anger. "By both of your accounts, he hated demons."

Black interjected, "There must be something we are missing."

Barnabus turned his bronze visage to Morgu. "I was asked to translate and that is what I've done. Do what you will with the facts."

Black looked to Morgu who was pursing her lips together. "You know something," Black accused.

She set the papers down. "Valen had a large estate outside of the city that not many people knew about. I was suspicious as to how he was wrapped up in this so I had one of my people keep an eye on it." She placed her elbows on the table and folded her hands in front of her mouth as she continued. "They reported this morning dozens of suspicious people arriving at the estate. Considering what we know now and the complexity of the spell, this is likely where they've been preparing to perform the final ritual from the start."

"And with the full moon tonight…" Damascus trailed off.

"We need to act quickly," Rinx shouted, banging her fist against the table.

"We need time to rally a force against these," Morgu grinded her teeth searching for the word. "Lunatics," she spat the word out. "I'm afraid our response may be too slow." She stood suddenly. "I must go now if we are to have any chance." Barnabus casually pushed his chair out standing. She leveled her gaze at the three friends.

Black folded his arms across his chest and furrowed his brow. He pictured in tattered detail the vision Corvus had shown him. "Tell me where to find this estate. I'll leave immediately."

Rinx leapt to her feet. "Are you insane?" She screamed and as if startled by her own voice adopted a calmer tone. "You heard what she said, right? Dozens of these cultists. It could be a small army."

"Jack told us Hannibal was recruiting Earthen born amateurs so it's unlikely that they are all much of a threat," Black said looking away from Rinx. "Maybe I can buy us some time. Disrupt the ritual long enough for the Guild to send aid."

Rinx clenched her fists so tight that her nails nearly drew blood. "Then I'm coming with you. I'm seeing this through to the end."

"Of course," Damascus said, drawing all of their attention to him. Still sitting he continued, "Of course the Order of Homme will be unable to participate in a joint operation with the Guild of Ravens without some serious deliberation." He slowly rose from his seat shaking his head before letting his brown eyes settle on Rinx and then slowly to Black. "I however, wouldn't mind an outing with my old friends," he finished with a broad smile spreading across his dark face. "What could happen? Who could say?"

Black shook his head. "This is too dangerous. It will likely be suic-"

"Suicide for you," Rinx shouted. "Stop trying to do everything alone!" Silence lingered in the room. "We're in this together."

"She's right, my friend," Damascus added.

Black knew there was nothing he could say to deter them. "If something happens to-"

"We're in this together," Rinx repeated.

Morgu bowed her head as she spoke, "Then we are counting on you three."

The two Premiers wasted no time in departing. Damascus had quickly changed into his leather brown and green uniform, tying his black curls back. He emerged from his quarters strapping a belt around his waist equipped with a short sword and three small leather pouches and on his left arm he wore the most valuable item in the Order of Homme, an Aegis.

The three stepped through the front door of the mansion out into the gloomy open air. The atmosphere was oppressive and they had little to say to one another but Damascus spoke up.

"We have no time to waste and I'm now very aware that I'm going to slow you two down," He said, frowning as he spoke.

Black looked into the dark gray clouds that continued to build overhead. "I will take the sky," he said. "I'll have a better view from up there. You two can decide how you want to proceed."

Black raised an arm up to the sky and starting from his hand, feathered wings erupted and beat against the air. Shiny black ravens rose up towards the clouds from his body until there was nothing left of the man who had just been standing there. The birds circled overhead.

"Shit," Rinx said, rolling her eyes and throwing her hands up before they came to rest on her hips.

"Do you think that-" Damascus was cut off as red fur burst from all over Rinx's body.

She quickly took the form of a large fox easily as big as a small horse. Her bushy tail whipped through the air as she turned her head back towards Damascus. The fur starting from her lower jaw down her chest and disappearing under her belly was a contrasting white. Rinx's orange red eyes with black slitted pupils narrowed in on Damascus and her massive mandible lowered revealing ivory teeth and a large pink tongue.

Rinx let out a great sigh, "Just climb on."

Damascus raised a hand to his face trying to conceal his smile as he did what he was instructed. Guards looked on in shock as the great fox bearing their leader kicked up dust and tore out of the neighborhood towards the main gate of Tuatha Dé.

Chapter 9

Past

Black's courses continued to be steady and mostly uneventful. In his Enchantment's class he was slowly but surely improving their potency. He occasionally shared some advice with his other two classmates and Gogh had explained the advantages and disadvantages of enchantments to them.

"It is said that enchantments provide shortcuts for spells," Gogh professed. "But that is a very simplistic way of looking at them. They take dedication and talent to create, something that few can muster. Which is why they often can be a lucrative craft." Black noticed for the first time the several precious rings on Gogh's fingers. "But they are not perfect copies," Gogh continued. "You may be able to skip the use of an incantation but in doing so and channeling your magic through a foreign medium like a scroll, you lose some of the potency of the spell and thus require more magic to match the incantation's power. Additionally the advantages and disadvantages of a particular affinity are also lessened." Gogh tapped his chin scanning the class before continuing. "For example, someone with an affinity for water spells will have less of an advantage using a water enchantment but at the same time will have less trouble with a fire enchantment than if they just tried to cast the fire spell outright." He searched the room again. "Is that clear?"

All three students nodded their heads in unison.

They had begun occasionally taking their classes outside when the weather was good so that they could test their enchantments without fear of destroying the classroom. Gogh continued to be impressed with Black's basic water and fire enchantments. Gogh assured Black that his wind enchantment was performing well for his level but since it was even weaker than his normal incantation Black seldom spent time making them. His real difficulty was his earth enchantment. It had improved but because of it being contrary to his affinity, continued to lag behind the others.

For Maitre Brunel's Elements class, Black had been practicing his 'Propel' spell for the upcoming midterms. After weeks of practice he was getting varying results. Sometimes he would feel a sudden gust of wind rise up from under him and other times he'd feel nothing at all.

Once during CTC practice when he was sparring with Rinx, he tried to leap clean over her using 'Propel' to accelerate himself. After completing the spell in mid-air he felt his feet flung over his head resulting with him landing flat on his back and the wind knocked out of him.

Most of the teammates including Rinx that had witnessed this spectacle were thrown into hysterics and Black was certain he caught a glimpse of Astrid shaking her head in disgust.

A week later Black was sparring with Damascus during their practice when Astrid approached them.

She watched them for a moment before speaking, "This is an embarrassment." Both the boys stopped lowering their wooden swords. Astrid pointed to Damascus. "You have an excuse for not using magic, but you!" She stuck her finger into Black's chest. "You have no excuse and yet I still haven't seen you perform a single useful spell."

Black was speechless and knew that she was right.

"That's not fair," Damascus came to his defense. "His swordplay has improved immensely."

"CTC isn't meant for sword fighting," Astrid returned. "It is meant for mages to duel one another. I don't expect you to understand how pathetic this is."

Damascus glared back at Astrid and for the first time since Black had known him, he could see anger rising to the surface of his face. Astrid gave no indication that she either noticed or cared.

"We have one week before the first tournament and you are far from prepared," Astrid had begun to shout.

Tom had been overseeing two others sparring when he heard Astrid shouting and made his way to where they were arguing.

Tom wore an awkward smile on his face as he spoke, "whoa guys, what is going on here?"

"I think it's time this one-," Astrid said, jamming her finger in Black's chest again. "Learned what a real CTC match is like."

"I don't think that this is such a good idea," Tom shook his head with his hands held up in front of him but Astrid had already turned and walked away taking her place as if a match was about to begin.

Tom and Black exchanged looks and Tom shrugged. "She seems to be in a particularly bad mood today," Tom whispered. "Are you ok with this?"

Black felt everyone's eyes on him.

"Well what are you waiting for, Tom?" Astrid shouted. "Get out of the way!"

Black felt he had no choice but at the same time there was a growing anger within him that wanted to be set loose. He nodded to Tom.

"Alright," Tom said, grabbing Damascus by the arm and leading him to the side. "Take it easy," Tom called to Astrid. "We are all teammates here."

Black looked across to Astrid who scowled back at him. Black gripped his wooden sword tight in his hand and tried to recall if he'd ever seen Astrid use her magic. All he knew was that her and Tom trained privately after the others finished practice each day. He had no idea what to expect but he knew his major weakness was distance so he'd need to close the gap quickly to have any chance.

"Ready," Tom shouted with his hand in the air.

"Of course," Astrid yelled back.

"Ready," Black replied.

"Fight!" Tom's hand dropped like he was chopping the air.

Black wasted no time breaking into a dead sprint and immediately summoning his totem. As he charged forward he could see Astrid's hand in the air and her lips were moving. Black became vaguely aware that it felt like he was running in sand. He raised his sword over head which felt heavier than usual. He was over halfway to his opponent when her hand dropped.

She's fast with her incantations, he thought but also at the same time felt that everything was slowing around him. His eyes darted searching for where the attack would come from and expected by her hand gesture that it was likely from above.

He cast his gaze up while still keeping her in sight but saw nothing. Suddenly he felt his whole body slammed by some invisible force. First the sword slipped from his hand over his shoulder dropping point first to the ground and before he could think his body was pinned hard to the ground.

Black's bones ached as he tried to push himself up from the ground with little success. He strained his neck trying to turn his face towards Astrid, getting dirt in his mouth and one of his eyes as he did. She stood sneering at him with one hand held palm down out in front of her.

"Pathetic," Astrid said quietly. "How do you beat someone with your sword if you can't get close to them?" She continued to sneer.

Black felt the rage building up within him and he pushed with all his strength trying to raise his body from the ground. Every limb felt impossibly heavy. Black began recanting the 'Propel' spell.

"Oh, what's this?" Astrid said in feigned concern.

He completed the spell and felt himself rise slowly but the weight was even more intense as he finally managed to get his chest off the ground. He felt squeezed and all the air was pushed from his lungs like he was smashed between two boulders.

Astrid looked genuinely annoyed by Black's continued resistance. "Enough," she said with a small waive of her extended hand and Black was slammed hard against the earth again.

What precious bit of air was left in his lungs got knocked clean out of him with a crack. Astrid apparently felt that she'd made her point and released her spell while Black remained on the ground trying to breathe with tears in his eyes.

"Gods, Astrid," Tom cried out. "That was too far!"

"Better he learns now then in a real match," she growled back.

Damascus was already at Black's side and Rinx had quickly joined them.

"Is he ok," Tom asked as Astrid walked away.

"I'm not sure," Damascus answered while Black continued to try and catch his breath.

Astrid was gone and Black was on his back with one arm wrapped around his torso when suddenly they heard another voice from behind them.

"What has happened here?" It was Brunel. "I come to check on your progress and this is what I find?"

There was a moment of silence filled by Black's labored breathing. He managed to push some words out, "I think I broke my ribs." Black was wincing in pain with each word.

"How did this happen?" Brunel demanded.

"Well-," Tom began.

"It was an accident," Black strained to say. "I pushed myself too hard and my body gave out, I guess." Black was furious but the bulk of that fury was directed back at himself.

No one else spoke a word until Brunel finally said, "Well, let's get you to my sister and have her check you out."

The five of them made their way to Abigail's classroom. With every breath a sharp pain would explode on Black's left side nearly knocking the wind out of him all over again. He leaned against Damascus until they got out of the gymnasium when Black decided he could do the rest of the walk under his own power.

They entered Abigail's room to find her still at her desk grading papers. She looked up from the stack of documents and fixed an annoyed face on her brother.

"What do you want?" she demanded.

Maitre Brunel affixed a huge smile to his face. "Oh dear sister," he exclaimed. "Wonderful sister, I knew I'd find you still working."

The room was large and very tidy. There was one wall full of books and another one full of tiny drawers. There were several island tables surrounded by tall wooden stools.

"What do you want?" the Maitresse asked again, tapping her finger on the desk.

"This poor student has suffered an injury," Maitre Brunel informed her.

She kept her gaze locked on her brother. "Then take him to the infirmary."

"Well the thing is, he has his first tournament next week and well," the Maitre ran his hand through his hair. "It would be great if he was in tip-top shape for it."

Abigail closed her blue eyes and let out a long sign as she pushed away from her desk and stood up.

Walking around her desk with her white robe flowing around her, she pointed to one of the island tables and said, "You, lay down there."

Tom and Damascus helped Black onto the table. He grunted in pain as he laid back flat. Abigail held her hands over Black as he tried not to breathe in too deeply, avoiding the pain that would come with it. She closed her eyes and recanted an incantation that made the palms of her hands faintly glow.

After they stopped glowing she opened her eyes and said, "You have two cracked ribs, a sprained wrist, and several inflamed ligaments aside from some minor cuts and bruises."

"That doesn't sound too serious," her brother chirped.

Abigail let out another long sigh and said, "I'm going to give you something a little more advanced."

The Maitresse turned from the group and glided over to the wall of drawers at the end closest to her desk. There was one with a bronze plate and keyhole just below her eye level. She reached into her robes and pulled out a small bronze key attached to some brown leather band around her neck. Sliding the key into the hole and turning there was a quiet click and the drawer slid out. From within the drawer was a faint silvery glow. She reached in and took something out before sliding the drawer shut and locking it back. After she returned the key back into the confines of her robe and glided back to them.

She opened her hand revealing a small vial with just a drop of a luminescent liquid. The substance glistened with a silver-white light. The children were craning their necks to have a better look at the vial.

"It's beautiful," Rinx whispered.

"It's the sap of life," Maitre Brunel stated.

"A diluted version of the sap of life," Abigail corrected. She held the vial up in front of her face between her forefinger and thumb. "It should be more than sufficient to heal all your injuries by this evening."

"Incredible," Damascus muttered, tilting his head for a better look at the contents.

"Yes, my sister is quite the healing prodigy," Maitre Brunel beamed.

The Maitresse ignored the compliment and uncorked the bottle. At the same time Black sat up carefully on the table. He pushed some air between his lips making a hissing noise and tightly closed his eyes as he did this. The Maitresse passed the vial to Black who held it delicately in his left hand.

"Drink it," The Maitresse commanded.

Black inspected the contents a moment longer before slowly placing it under his nose. He sniffed the substance but found that it had no fragrance. After one more glance at the glowing liquid he threw back his head and poured the contents into his mouth.

Although the liquid seemed to slip quite easily from the vial when it hit his tongue, it coated it with a thick sticky layer. This coating continued all the way down his throat before filling his belly. It felt warm and the warmth began to spread throughout his body.

"How does it taste," Rinx asked.

Black smacked his lips letting the flavor spread around his mouth before smiling. "It's really sweet," he confirmed. "It tastes good."

The warmth continued to fill him and the sharp stabbing pain in his chest already felt slightly dulled although he continued to move with caution.

"Thank you Maitresse Brunel," Black said earnestly. "I think I feel a little better already."

"That would be the anesthetic properties of the sap taking effect," Abigail explained. "But you should still take things slowly for the rest of the evening to be safe."

Rinx suddenly perked up. "Oh we forgot our things in the locker rooms."

Damascus volunteered to retrieve Black's things for him so Rinx and Damascus hurried back to the gymnasium. Tom agreed to accompany Black back to the dorm just in case he should need any assistance.

As the group made their way out of the classroom Brunel called back to his sister, "Thank you Abigail."

Abigail simply waved her brother away as she returned to her desk and work. Brunel returned to the gymnasium following the other two children while Tom and Black walked slowly back to the boy's dormitory.

Before they entered Tom stopped and asked, "How are you feeling?"

"It's hard to say," Black responded. "It still hurts a lot but I don't think it's as bad." Black rubbed the tender area on his ribs as he spoke.

Tom raised a hand to slap Black on the shoulder but then thought better of it. "You're doing a great job and win or lose next week, I think you will perform splendidly," Tom said and then looked away as if momentarily lost in thought. "You know, Astrid and I began CTC at the same time. I don't think you would have recognized her then. She was much more carefree." He glanced around as if making sure no other students were in earshot. "She was reckless, honestly and when she had her first match it ended in a loss. And a crushed leg. We didn't have the benefit of Maitresse Brunel's miraculous healing abilities then and it took her two weeks to fully recover in the infirmary." Tom took one more glance around. "During her recovery her mother passed away as well."

Black suddenly felt a strange pang of sympathy that dissolved some of the resentment that had been growing in him. "What happened," He inquired.

"I don't know the details," Tom replied. "And I never asked. But I can say it all definitely changed her. She threw herself into CTC with an intensity I've never seen from anyone else." Tom's sullen face suddenly shifted back into cheerfulness. "Anyways. Don't let her discourage you. Keep up the good work." Again Tom raised his hand to slap Black on the shoulder coming so close that Black flinched in anticipation before Tom stopped himself. "And if you could maybe keep this talk between us."

Black agreed and he retired to his room while Tom made his way back to the fifth year boy's dorm.

The sap worked just as expected. By the time Black was ready to sleep the pain had completely vanished and he felt like a new boy. He had the deepest sleep he'd ever experienced that night. Just to be safe the next day he refrained from any physical exercise although he was quite confident that he'd completely healed the prior night. The practices the week leading up to the first tournament were spent with much lighter sparring and exercises to avoid any injuries.

Finally the day arrived and their first tournament was nearly ready to begin. Each student of Tuatha Dé Academy wore their black CTC uniform as they stood on the inner ring of the track that encircled the battlegrounds.

Across the battlegrounds from the Tuatha Dé students stood their opponents from the Ashter Academy. They were dressed in more traditional rust colored robes. All but one had a hood pulled up. Black assumed by his age and how he walked down the line speaking to each of his teammates that he was likely their team leader.

Black recounted the rules in his mind. Each year was allowed to submit three students to battle one on one against the opposing year students. Two out three wins would score you one point and three out of three wins would score you two points. At the end of the tournament all points would be tallied and whichever team had the highest score won the tournament.

The stands were packed on all sides with spectators. Black examined the crowd behind him and spotted Gilbert. Gilbert caught his eye and with a large smile raised a fist in the air before looking around nervously and lowering it back to his lap. Not far from Gilbert sat Newt and Darius. They spotted Black at the same time.

Darius cupped his hands around his mouth and shouted over the raucous, "Don't embarrass us!" The pair laughed to each other as Darius pointed directly to Black.

Black felt like a hummingbird was flitting around in his stomach and his palms were damp.

Rinx leaned in close to Black so that she could speak to him over the ambience of the crowd. "I'm nervous," she confided. "What about you?"

"Nah, I'm fine," Black lied.

"There's a lot of people watching us," Rinx looked around the gymnasium as she spoke. "I hope I don't make a fool of myself."

Black didn't respond. He watched as Tom entered the center of the dirt ring with the Ashter team captain and two adults Black didn't know. The two adults were wearing the same style of robes. The whole left side of the robe was black and the right side white. Tom and the other teenager shook hands after a brief exchange and Tom returned back to their team with a sheet of paper in his hand.

"The match-ups have been drawn," Tom said, holding up the sheet of paper. "I'll let you all know who you'll be facing off against in a moment but first I'll discuss it with the first years."

Tom approached the three first year students. "Okay, so as usual we go in order based on year which means you guys are up first," Tom said loudly. "What order each individual fights and against who is random." He shook the paper in his hand. "And first up is you Amadeus." Tom said it like Black had won a prize. "Following you is Damascus and then Rinx, third."

Tom must have read the apprehension on Black's face. "Don't worry," Tom assured them all. "You've all been training very hard and I know we've all been impressed."

Except Astrid, Black imagined them all thinking.

"Plus," Tom added, pointing down the sidelines. "We have a prodigy medical mage in case someone does get injured."

In the direction of Tom's protruded finger was Abigail conversing with her brother and looking annoyed as usual by the experience.

Black did take a bit of comfort knowing her near miraculous abilities first hand.

"Now," Tom continued. "First year combatants can be a bit of a wild card since none of us have seen them perform in previous years but they are rarely too impressive and sometimes you luck out and get a guy who can't really do anything."

Tom did his best to reassure them. "That's really all there is to say except-," he leaned in closer to them trying not to speak too loud. "Go out there and kick these guys' asses." Tom shoved his thumb over his shoulder towards the other team. "The Ashter team captain is a real jerk."

Tom went down the line informing each student of their placement and providing some advice where he could. Black and his fellow first years began stretching and trying to warm themselves up in preparation.

"I'm excited," Damascus said to no one in particular. "I can't wait to see what I can do."

Rinx and Black would not have known he was excited looking at him. He looked as collected as always.

Tom returned and informed them that it was nearly time to begin. Shortly after one of the men wearing the black and white robes began shouting through a megaphone over the crowd.

"We are prepared to commence the first Academic Combat Tournament of the year between Tuatha Dé Academy and Ashter Academy. Starting with the first year student from Ashter, Mikail Malkovich." A short hooded student from the other team approached the man speaking in the center of the gym.

Black unzipped his dark blue jacket and threw it to the side before picking up his wooden sword.

"You've got this my friend," Damascus said, slapping him hard on the back.

"And from our very own Tuatha Dé Academy, Amadeus Black!" The man with the megaphone gestured in Black's direction.

The crowd behind Black cheered as he jogged out to the center of the battlegrounds and he could faintly hear Rinx shouting "Good Luck." The adrenaline had really started to flow by that time. He felt awkward in his own body and a little off balance. The man who called him referred to himself as a referee and asked to inspect Black's sword. After he carefully ran his thumb up the blade's dulled edge and seemed satisfied he handed it back. Black noticed the other referee standing at the edge of the ring had begun casting a spell. A faint shimmering dome encased them within the fighting area.

Mikail lowered his hood revealing his face. He had short orange hair with green eyes and freckles peppered his nose and cheeks. Mikail extended a hand to Black and they shook before they parted and took their positions several feet from each other.

The first referee stood between the two boys until he received a signal from the other. The referee then raised his hand to the sky and backed up leaving a wide open space between the boys.

"On my mark you begin the fight," the ref called to the boys.

They both nodded in comprehension. Black planted his feet ready to move in any direction while raising his sword in front of his body.

"Ready," the ref shouted with his hand still raised. "FIGHT!" The ref's hand dropped, chopping through the air.

Black immediately evoked his totem as he kicked off trying to close the distance to Mikail. At the same time Mikail initiated a spell. Mikail with his right foot drew a line in the dirt and in response a wall of flames burst from the ground a few feet in front of him. The flames roared about ten feet in front of Mikail and divided the ring in half. Black slid to a stop several feet in front of the wall of flames. The fire was so tall that he struggled to find Mikail on the other side.

Suddenly another line of flames rushed past Black on his left side, colliding with the barrier behind him and missing him by a large margin. Black's muscles were coiled tight anticipating an attack at any moment when a third wall burst from his right. Again the flames completely missed him. They climbed nearly fifteen feet into the air when they collided with the referee's barrier.

Black was vaguely aware of the crowd roaring over the sound of the flames that remained dancing all around him. Another wall erupted to his left but closer than the first. The heat combined with the adrenaline sent rivers of sweat running down Black's face. He suddenly felt claustrophobic and his mind raced as his situation took shape in his head.

It had finally hit him. He was being boxed in. Again flames raised past him on his right side and again they were closer than before. Black had very little room left to move or to dodge. He felt as though a noose was tightening around his neck as the fiery walls closed in around him.

He took several deep breaths driving away the creeping panic that was rising like the flames in every direction that he looked. A memory combined with Rhiss's words played in his head as he began the same useless spell he'd recited time and time again. With his free left hand spread out in front of him a powerful gust collided with the wall of flames separating him from Mikail. The flames bowed against Black's spell, showering Mikail in sparks and dust. Mikail raised an arm to shield his face from the debris.

Black seized the opportunity, rushing forward, sword in hand leaping over the diminished flames. As he took to the air he spit out the spell to further propel him higher purely on reflex. A flash of pride pulsed through him for a brief moment, realizing he'd just successfully used his 'Propel' spell. He easily cleared the fire with his sword held high over his head, descending on his prey.

Mikail squinted up at Black through bloodshot eyes. The lower half of his face was still hidden behind his arm. As Black dropped into striking range his ears detected the faintest of sounds coming from Mikail. Before he could react the incantation was completed and with an upward thrust Mikail delivered a fireball directly to Black's chest. His momentum reversed, Black was sent flipping end over end backwards through the flame wall before his head came to a hard stop on the earthen ground.

The next moment Black was setting up straight, his head pounded as the crowd was roaring. He took a beat, piecing together what was happening around him. Black was sitting on the side lines with the team's backs to him. The other members were clapping and jumping up and down as Tom came sauntering out of the ring with his usual simple grin plastered on his face. Black climbed to his feet. On shaky legs he saw Abigail spot him from the left, approach, and extend a hand to steady him.

One of the referees cried out, "Tuatha Dé has won the tournament!"

"How are you feeling," Abigail asked.

Black rubbed the back of his head and watched the team swarm around Tom. Even Astrid was smiling and congratulating him.

"My head hurts quite a bit," Black responded.

"I'm not surprised," Abigail confirmed. "You had a concussion but you've already been treated and should be feeling better in no time."

Black was still rubbing the back of his head when Rinx and Damascus finally caught sight of him in the chaos. The pair ran over to him. Rinx had a tear in her dusty t-shirt exposing her navel but was otherwise intact. While Damascus looked like he just put a fresh uniform on. This prompted

Black to look down at his own clothes realizing for the first time that he was completely shirtless.

Rinx following his gaze said, "Ah, yes your shirt was pretty burnt up after your fight so Maitresse Brunel just threw it away. Are you ok?"

"Yeah, just a headache," Black said.

Damascus held a sword in each hand. "I grabbed your sword for you," he said, extending it to Black handle first. "Great fight! A shame he hit you with a lucky shot."

Black stared down at his sword in both hands as he spoke, "Thanks. And how about you two?" Black raised his head.

They both nodded.

"I got lucky," Damascus admitted. "My opponent could only spray water at me before I broke his jaw. But Tom's fight," Damascus added, looking genuinely impressed. "Was absolutely amazing."

Before they could speak any further the team had crowded around them.

Tom, still receiving slaps on the back and congratulations, asked, "All good, Amedeus?"

Black managed to assure him that he was fine before some fans from the stands rushed them and pulled Tom away. Black caught a brief glance of disdain from Astrid before she was lost in the growing crowd.

There was a great deal of celebration that evening. Black did his best to wear a mask of joy for the team's victory. He was desperate to hear the retelling of everyone's fight during the reverie and by all accounts both Tom and Astrid put on amazing performances. The Ashter Academy team had left shortly after the conclusion of the tournament and the fans had joined the team down on the ground. At some point food and drinks began to be passed around.

Black's head had long since stopped throbbing when he caught a glimpse of Astrid leaving the gymnasium. He excused himself and ran after her. Black caught her halfway down the hall outside the gym.

Black called, "Astrid, wait!"

Astrid spun around and looked annoyed when she saw who was approaching her. "What do you want," she demanded.

"You were right," Black blurted out.

Astrid placed a hand on her hip and maintained a steady gaze on Black.

"I was unprepared for the fight tonight." Black suddenly, overcome by an anger he hadn't expected, raised a finger and continued. "But don't think I'm not taking this seriously."

Whatever Astrid was thinking she kept to herself and her face remained unchanged.

Black lowered his hand back to his side and clenched his fists tightly. "I'm going to win next time."

Astrid turned her back on him and started back down the hall. Black's rage was rising again and he took a step after her.

"You did alright today considering," Astrid said walking away. "But wind magic sucks. Tom says you're an enchanter, find another element."

Astrid turned the corner and was gone.

***

Present

Rinx raced across the countryside with Damascus on her back while Black soared overhead. The land was blanketed with gently rolling hills and marked with the occasional rocky outcropping and copse of trees. A single raven glided alongside Rinx and Damascus allowing Black to easily relay information to them should he spot something from above. The dark clouds were beginning to spit a fine mist of rain as they closed in on their destination and the smell of the coming storm was strong.

The accompanying raven informed the two on the ground that Black had spotted a villa in the distance. He pushed on, flying ahead to scout the area. The daylight was beginning to dim as he circled high around the white three storied home topped with red-orange tiles. He could count two dozen figures in heavy robes patrolling the grounds. Black turned and came back to a copse of trees atop a hill overlooking the villa. Rinx was standing in her human form next to Damascus concealed in the brush. The ravens converged, taking again the shape of a man. Black described what he had seen.

"There are likely more inside," Damascus said what they'd all been thinking after Black had given his report.

Rinx turned her face to the sky as rain started to fall more in earnest. "We don't have much time before the moon has risen. Hell, maybe it's already begun. Hard to say with these clouds."

"We just have to buy time," Black reminded them. He watched between the branches as some of the robed figures milled around. A few of them pulled their hoods up against the rain. "Perhaps if we can create a distraction and draw them out one of us can sneak inside and disrupt the ritual site."

There was a long period of silence. Black weighed the possibilities; distraction or infiltration. Neither option was favorable. The distraction team would need to entertain an overwhelming number of enemies and the person infiltrating could find themselves trapped inside with no means of escape. Black finally decided that at least the distraction team had the benefit of being able to retreat if needed.

"I'll sneak in," Damascus volunteered.

Black had no doubt that his friends had come to the same conclusion he had and he could see the look of dread on Rinx's face when Damascus spoke up.

"No," Black placed a hand on Damascus's shoulder and although Rinx tried to hide it he recognized the faintest hint of relief sweep across her visage. "Rinx can create the most mayhem from a distance and your Aegis is the best tool for keeping her safe." Black turned towards the villa. "I'm going."

Damascus opened his mouth to protest but instead simply nodded his head in agreement.

"We have no time to waste," Rinx cut in. "I'll draw their attention so be ready to rush in."

"Right." Black broke apart into a feathered mass that rose into the sky.

Rinx pushed her way through the thicket so that she stood with a clear line of sight on the villa. Damascus stood to her right removing two vials from one of his pouches. He swallowed the contents of both and returned the empty containers. He inhaled deeply and shuttered, squeezing his eyes tight.

Rinx waited a moment and asked, "Ready?"

Damascus exhaled at the same time he drew his short sword. "I'm ready." His brown eyes dilated and his breathing became deep and steady.

Rinx extended a hand out in front of her, palm up. A golf ball sized red flame sprung into existence. She began reciting an incantation slowly, taking extra care to articulate each word clearly and precisely for maximum effect. Rinx ignored all distractions, closing her eyes to focus all her attention on the spell.

Overhead Black held position simultaneously watching his friends and the movements of the enemy. He could see the pinprick flicker of light from Rinx's spell below. One of the hooded figures closest to Rinx and Damascus seemed to go stiff. The opening of his hood was pointed in their direction. It was beginning to get dark and with the falling rain it would be difficult for human eyes to make out much at the pair's distance but the light casted by Rinx's flame was another story. The hooded figure was moving closer to investigate.

The rain sizzled as it landed on the small ball of fire. Damascus stood like a statue with his shield raised and sword at the ready. Rinx raised her hand over her head and with the final word of the spell the red ball collapsed in on itself before rapidly expanding and changing to a deep blue sphere of swirling fire. The mass had the diameter of a full grown man.

Black saw the sudden manifestation of what looked like a small sun. The hooded figure spun around to flee in the opposite direction but lost his footing in the mud falling twice. All attention was now on the blue hot-burning orb that was sent hurtling toward the struggling figure. There was a short cry before he was overtaken and disappeared. The orb continued on its trajectory towards the villa. Many of the figures tried to scramble out of the way before it finally collided with the earth in a massive explosion just outside the mansion.

The blue flames erupted and many of the people below were caught up in the fire and were almost instantly turned to ash. A handful of the more talented mages managed to protect themselves but from what Black could make out, few of them even managed to make it through unscathed. Black kept his distance as a fiery plume rose into the sky from the impact spot. Debris was falling down with the rain and presented its own hazard to the people on the ground. It became hard to see what was happening as smoke and dust spread out. It was however easy to spot the swaths of earth that burned brightly.

Rinx observed the carnage with a certain amount of satisfaction. Her head begun to spin and she caught herself.

"Are you ok?" Damascus asked.

"I'm fine," Rinx confirmed. "It just took a lot out of me. I won't be able to do that again for a bit." A normal size fireball materialized in her hand. "I'll need to keep it simple for a bit." She spotted a man discarding his flaming robe and falling in the mud. She flung the fireball at the distracted man and ignited his torso.

***

Black had a bit of hope. Perhaps with the smokescreen Rinx and Damascus had a better chance than he had originally thought. However, his hope quickly died when a swarm of mages poured out of the entrance of the villa. It resembled a river flooding the smoke covered yard. Black estimated that there were well over a hundred people. He had a moment of hesitation before committing again to the plan.

The unkindness dove towards the entrance of the villa. As Black closed in on his target an unsettling feeling came over him. There was a sudden cry from deep within him.

STOP!

Black turned away from the entrance at the same time a barrage of spikes burst up from the ground narrowly missing him. The spikes crossed one another creating a wall that rose up the facade of the building. They continued to encase the house, leaving no way that Black could see to enter.

Damn the gods, Black cursed to himself.

He had no time to waste and decided to change his tactics. Dispatching one raven to deliver a message to Rinx and Damascus. He would fight. Black wasted no time resuming his human shape already in his hybrid form directly behind the mass of confused enemies. Before anyone had a chance to detect his presence, his sword was firmly gripped in his right hand while his left was leveled at the backs of his foes.

Activating the rune on his hand a bolt of lightning whipped through the crowd burning holes through those directly in its path. Many more people standing adjacent to the main bolt were hit by smaller tendrils that dropped them in heaps on the ground either dead or badly injured and unconscious.

***

Rinx and Damascus looked on in despair as the throng of mages began to emerge from the smoke before a spiked wall encircled the villa. A moment later they witnessed the white-hot flash streak through what remained of the smoke. As the raven arrived to deliver Black's message they already knew what it was going to say.

"I couldn't get in. I'll draw their attention for as long as I can while you escape and wait for reinforcements," the raven called before tearing back to the battlefield not waiting for an answer.

***

Most of the fire had been extinguished by the rain and the stink of burnt debris was thick in the air. Some of the figures in the crowd close enough to see through the haze were brandishing weapons. Before Black could muster a second lightning bolt one man rushed him with a club in hand. Black managed to deftly side step the attack, severing the attacker's head at the same time.

Almost immediately a second man was before him swinging a short sword. Black blocked it with his own sword and while he was struggling with the swordsman he spotted a woman to his left. Her arms were outstretched towards him as she prepared a spell for attack. Before she could finish, Black's raven dove from the sky scratching and pecking at her eyes. Black pressed the swordsman back with brute force before delivering a quick kick to his enemy's knee. As the man collapsed in pain Black whipped his blade across his throat and kicked him to the mud leaving him to die.

Black then charged towards the woman still flailing blindly at the attacking raven, burying his sword in her chest up to the hilt. The raven folded itself into Black's shoulder at the same time he pulled his sword free. He felt a small burst of energy as his body was made whole again. With that he let out a cry as he waded into the rising smoke cutting down three more robed individuals. He soon found himself on the defense with attacks coming from all directions. His only saving grace was a combination of rain, smoke, and the growing darkness of night obscuring him from the overwhelming number of enemies trying to catch him.

Black could hear the cries and curses of pain from the gloom and the occasional flash of magical attacks lighting up the darkness. He found himself fighting off two men with daggers when he caught the sound of someone screaming in pain directly behind him. The smoke was beginning to burn the back of his throat a bit and after dispatching the two dagger wielding men he spun around coughing hard and anticipating another attacker.

Out of the haze stumbled a man with his hands wrapped around a long icy protrusion from his chest. A gurgling sound rose up from the man's throat followed by a stream of blood before he fell over on his side dead.

Suddenly Black heard the sound of someone rushing him, again from behind. He spun around this time to be met by a broad shoulder man swinging a sword at his head. He blocked it but struggled to over power this one. From the corner of Black's eye he caught sight of a shimmer. At the source of the shimmer, suddenly the smoke and rain seemed to separate as an invisible conical force rushed towards Black. On pure instinct and panic Black used his speed enhancing runes and blurred backwards. When he came to a stop it was just in time to see his attacker fall forward into the path of the force and erupt in a spray of blood and bone. A concussive shockwave from the impact rippled out hitting Black in the chest and knocking him back several more feet. He struggled to keep his feet under him and began to fall before his back slammed against a wall, allowing him to regain his balance.

The blast had cleared the smoke in the vicinity and as his eyes traced the attack back to its source he could see several others writhing on the ground that had been caught up in the explosion. At the end of the clearing stood a man with salt and pepper hair and beard. He stared at Black with green eyes full of pure malice. He had two scarred palms held up with the fingers spread out before him.

"Hannibal," Black said the name like a curse.

Chapter 10

Past

The days after Black's defeat in his first Combat Tournament seem to rush by. He felt that there was so much to be done in so little time even with the next tournament months away.

A month after the first tournament all the students were granted two weeks off for the Saturnalia holiday. Rinx and Black returned home to spend the holiday with Rinx's family and Mazurus. They arrived to find the house festively decorated. It was the first time they'd been home since they'd begun their studies at the academy.

Black demonstrated how he'd improved on his enchantments to Mazurus and used it as an opportunity to discuss how to utilize them best in combat. The key, as Mazurus explained it, was to create space between you and your enemy. The time spent reciting a spell was replaced with the time spent withdrawing a scroll and unrolling it. This proved to run counter to how Black normally fought. Usually he tried to close the distance between him and his opponent as quickly as possible so this felt unnatural to him.

The bulk of Black's time however was spent with Mhimo. Black hadn't realized how much he'd missed the boy until he saw him again. Mhimo was taller than Black had remembered but seemed to be just as shy as always and would seemingly appear out of nowhere. Black loved recounting his time in class, CTC, and showing off his new sword skills with the boy. Mhimo rarely left Black's side during his time at the Quint home.

Black had never seen the boy so excited as when Rinx convinced their mother to come to their next Combat Tournament. The next Tournament was against their biggest rival academy from Tristendale. The city of Tuatha Dé was holding a celebration on the day of the tournament in honor of the rivalry. Rinx successfully persuaded Rhiss that it would be the perfect time to visit.

After they returned to the academy Black resumed improving his 'Propel' ability. Even though he had managed to successfully use the spell for the first time during the tournament, the defeat left him feeling unsatisfied by the spell. He continued to perfect mostly out of need to pass his upcoming midterm in his 'Intro to Elements' class. Maitre Brunel, while not overly impressed with the spell, awarded Black a passing grade.

With the midterms out of the way and only about a month to go before the next tournament, Black focused almost all his free time to becoming more proficient with scrolls. He needed to be able to alternate between his sword and a scroll. For this, Black inquired to Maitre Gogh on how mages used scrolls effectively in combat.

"They aren't considered very practical in fast paced combat," Gogh admitted, stroking the hair on his chin. "But in the past when they did-" Gogh turned abruptly and began rummaging around in a trunk that was tucked away in the corner of his classroom. "They normally wore one of these and used a springed umbilicus." Gogh held in one hand a leather belt with two conical pouches and in the other hand a short rod.

"Observe," Gogh instructed.

The rod clearly had a wooden handler at one end and a rod with a slit down the length of it. Gogh took one of Black's enchantment papers and threaded the end into the slit. He twisted the tip of the rod which seemed to secure the parchment in place and began wrapping the paper around the rod. Once he was finished, Gogh grabbed the handle and with his free handle took the parchment by the exposed lip, unwinding the parchment until it was fully on display. He let go of the lip of paper and with a metallic whorl the paper retracted back around the rod.

"Much easier to handle," Gogh proclaimed. He passed the contraption and belt to Black before turning back to his chest and finding a second umbilicus. Gogh slid the second rod into one of the pouches on the belt in Black's hand. "I presume that you are planning to use these in the next Combat Tournament?"

"I am," Black confirmed.

"Oh how interesting," Gogh stroked the hairs on his chin again. "I don't believe I've ever seen a student use enchanted scrolls in a tournament since I've been here. I'm sure it will be quite the sight."

Black was now able to access two scrolls in the heat of battle with ease having them holster around his hip. During training both of them sat on his right side with their wooden handles easily accessible. Now he needed a way to switch from scroll to sword. For this he went to Maitre Brunel who supplied him with a sheath and belt that affixed the sword to his back with the handle protruding over his right shoulder.

With the help of the Maitres he felt he had the tools he needed for the next tournament. Next, he spent the remainder of the month leading up to the tournament practicing alternating between scroll and sword. Rinx and Damascus aided him in developing the muscle memory required to perform this task under pressure.

While sparring with Rinx he alternated between hand-to-hand combat and a water enchanted scroll to counter Rinx's fire spells. One day after they had concluded their bout Black glanced over to see Tom and Astrid watching them. It was only for a moment but Black thought he caught the tiniest hint of amusement on Astrid's face before she turned back to her conversation with Tom.

The day of the tournament finally came. That morning Black, Rinx, and Damascus met in the dining hall for breakfast. Gilbert arrived after they had nearly finished, carrying a large plate of eggs and a tall glass of milk as had become usual.

Damascus turned to Gilbert. "These two are going to be meeting up with Rinx's mother later," Damascus said while jabbing a thumb in Rinx and Black's direction. "Maybe you and I can head into the city for the tournament festival too and meet up with them later." Damascus looked Gilbert up and down, taking note of how his robes seemed to pool around him on the bench. "And maybe we can stop by Ronald's Robes to have your's tapered in a bit."

Gilbert, who had just taken a huge gulp of milk, went red like a tomato. "Uh, sure," he said as he choked on his milk. Gilbert looked down at himself and then asked, "You think so?"

"Oh yeah," Black chimed in, exchanging a smile with Damascus. "It must be the 'Body Fortitude' class."

Damascus seemingly on cue added slyly, "Unless you have some secret?"

Gilbert was overtly flustered as the two boys laughed.

All the students were granted the day off from classes in honor of the festival being held in town. Later that day Rinx and Black changed into their CTC uniforms as well as their cloaks since it was still somewhat cold. The pair made their way to the academy gate and as planned, waiting for them on the other side of the gate was Rhiss with her crimson hair gently flowing in the wind. There were some other students passing to and from the city as they greeted Rhiss. Rinx gave her mother a big hug and then looked around.

"Where's Mhimo," Rinx asked.

"He is shopping in the city square," Rhiss stated. "He wanted to purchase a gift for each of you but I wasn't supposed to tell you that." She held up a finger. "So you better act surprised."

The children nodded and began the trek towards the city square. Despite the lingering winter chill the sun shone brightly and warmed their faces as they walked and talked.

Black asked about Mazurus and Rhiss replied, "He wanted me to apologize for not being here today. He had some business that was going to keep him away for a while."

Black nodded understandingly but not without a great deal of disappointment.

Rhiss inquired about their classes and finally how they felt about the upcoming tournament.

"I'm a bit nervous," Rinx admitted. "The first tournament was tough but the worst part is not knowing who you'll be fighting and what they can do." She shrugged.

"Unfortunately," Rhiss said. "That is what it is like for those that decide to make fighting their calling." She peered down at Rinx from the corner of her eye. "And what about you Amadeus?" she said, shifting her attention.

Black stared at his feet as they walked and ran his fingers through his dark hair. "I just don't want to lose again."

Rinx, watching Black chimed in, "he is really getting good at using his enchanted scrolls, mother." And then she spoke directly to Black. "I think today you are going to show everyone what you can do."

The three continued winding their way down the cobblestone streets nearing the square before they spotted Darius and Newt hovering around a stand selling sweets. The pair of boys spotted the trio approaching. Rinx let out a sound of disgust as they neared the two.

Darius called out, "Look who it is. I guess we should be thanking you for us having the day off? Or rather Combat Tournament Club." Darius and Newt both laughed.

"Yeah, you're welcome," Rinx responded coldly.

Rhiss paused for a moment before saying, "I'll go find Mhimo and you two can meet up with us after you've finished talking with your friends."

Rinx rolled her eyes and turned to correct her mother but she was already several feet away.

Darius held a small sack of red candy. He extended the bag to Rinx and said, "Want a sweet, friend?"

Rinx scoffed and shook her head.

Darius turned to Black and added, "Sorry, but these are only for winners."

"Yeah, maybe if you win today you can have one," Newt suggested and started laughing.

Darius continued a bit more seriously, "It was actually impressive before you got knocked out. Try not to let the team carry you this time."

Darius glanced at Rinx before deciding to offer the bag of sweets to Black despite his previous mocking. Black hesitantly took one and popped it in his mouth. It had an artificial cherry flavor.

"Thanks for the advice," Black replied, rolling the ball around in his mouth. "And for the candy."

"Good luck," Darius called to them as they parted ways.

They hadn't made it but twenty feet when Black was hit by a sudden sharp pain in his head. His stomach began to roll with a bout of nausea and he spit the hard candy out of his mouth. With one hand clenching his stomach and the other on his head he turned back toward Darius and Newt expecting to see them in hysterics. The two boys were simply looking over the other sweets on display seemingly unaware of Black's predicament. A groan came from beside him. He noticed that Rinx was slightly bent over with both hands clutching either side of her head obviously in pain as well. Black looked again at Darius and Newt and now saw them staring in their direction but their gaze was upwards toward the sky. Then came the sound of cloth ripping but at an impossibly loud volume. Black witnessed a shadow rolling over everything and as he spun back around, the pain lessening he witnessed dark clouds manifesting and spreading out overhead.

The nausea had faded and the pain in Black's skull had reduced to a dull throbbing. Rinx too seemed to have recovered and was standing upright again watching the growing darkness in the sky as she massaged her left temple. Darius came running up behind them followed by Newt.

"What the hell was that sound," Darius demanded.

Black turned back to the pair. Newt stared into the sky with his jaw slack as Darius too stared past Black and Rinx.

"Are you two OK?" Darius asked with a look of confusion on his face, finally taking notice of their distress.

"Suddenly my head–," Rinx mumbled.

Then there came a rising cacophony of screams.

"It's coming from the city square," Newt said to no one in particular as they all turned towards the sounds.

They looked on uncertain of what was happening. There was the occasional person rushing past from the direction of the square. Darius tried to call out to a woman running by but she just ignored him. The screams, some of them so guttural and painful sounding were getting louder and closer. All four of the children had a sense of ice water running down their spines.

Newt spoke up, "Maybe we should head back to the academy."

Despite Black's elven cloak he could feel a chill making him shutter. They all stared down the street leading towards the city square and from the corner of Black's eye he realized that Rinx was in her hybrid form. To his own amazement he then noticed that he too was standing in the middle of the street in his hybrid form.

"Guys–," Newt was cut off by the sound of someone screaming nearby and just out of sight around the corner.

Their feet felt suddenly cemented to the ground. A few buildings down from them a man wearing a seafoam green robe stumbled out of an alleyway. He fell sprawled out on the ground and scrambled to roll onto his back. He sat up staring in the direction he'd just fled as he muttered to himself.

Suddenly he turned a blood streaked face towards the children and croaked, "help."

None of the children made a move but instead watched on as the man turned his attention back to the alley he'd escaped from. He began to shake and whimper with tears leaving thin trails on his bloody cheeks. There then came the soft patting of bare feet. The children followed the man's gaze back to the source of the sound. From around the corner a naked woman emerged. She walked seductively towards the weeping man. Her skin was very pale and wet. She ran a hand from below her navel slowly up to her large, glistening breasts while pushing out her pouty crimson lips. Her black hair reached down to the small of her back. From out of her thick hair on the back of her head extended a long black cord stretching all the back into the alley. The woman closed in on the man and extended her arms as if to embrace him at the same time letting out a low moan.

The woman lowered herself down onto the trembling man's lap straddling him. She let out another moan before kissing him. He continued to whimper even as the woman kissed him. The children watched in horror as she extended her arms out on either side of the man and long boney spikes extended from the inside of her arms. Suddenly she embraced him tightly simultaneously wrapping her legs around him. The man's screams from having the spikes driven into his body were muffled as the woman kept smothering his mouth with hers. With a wet slurping noise the cord attached to the back of the woman's head was drawn tight and the pair were dragged back into the alley, the man's legs kicking all the way. There was a slimy residue mixed with blood left in their wake.

The children watched wide-eyed as the muffled sounds of the man's screams faded and the subtle sound of numerous taps on the cobblestone drew closer. From around the corner came an enormous, eyeless, worm. Its skin was slimy and flesh colored. It moved on an innumerable number of legs like a centipede. It turned one end in the direction of the children and looked to be sniffing the air slowly inching its way towards them.

None of the kids had ever felt such a primal form of fear. None of them spoke or moved. It was as if a spell had been cast upon them. They were encased in fear. Turned into living statues by it.

The grotesque worm moved closer still. There was a strong fetid odor that emanated from it. Black could feel that he was on the verge of retching when without warning a man came running out into the street from behind the creature. He came sliding to a halt when he saw the monster. The worm whipped what could only be assumed as its head in the direction of the man.

The man brought his hands up to his face in horror and cried, "no no no," as he turned and ran back the way he'd come.

From the end of the creature's head a large orifice opened and out slid feet first the naked woman from before. There was a wet slurping sound and splatter as her feet hit the ground. She extended her arms and let out a moan as she broke into a dead sprint following after the terrified man. The large worm skittered in pursuit, trailing behind the woman connected by the long black cord. They both slipped around the corner and out of site.

All four of the children seemed to exhale at the same time like the spell had been lifted.

"What the hell was that," Darius blurted out in a shrill voice.

Newt's long legs buckled under him and he fell to the ground.

"I don't know," Black struggled to respond. His hands shook uncontrollably.

"We should go back," Newt mumbled, still sitting on the ground.

There was a sudden eruption of blue flames in the distance, rising high into the sky.

"My mother and brother are in that direction," Rinx whimpered.

There were screams coming from all around them now.

"What do we do," Darius said, looking at Black. His eyes pleaded for an answer.

"We should go back," Newt repeated but made no move to stand.

Rinx took an unsteady step forward. "My mother," Rinx whispered.

Black felt pulled in two opposite directions with equal force and consequently didn't move either way.

They all froze again as a sudden clop like hooves on stone came from the same alley the worm had crawled from. Between the sounds of clops was the sound of something dragging across the ground. Stepping into the street came a large hairy man. His height was twice that of a normal man and his head was crowned with two long straight horns rising up from just above his brow. His legs bent back like a goat complete with the hooves they had heard approaching. In one large fist he dragged the headless body of some unfortunate victim leaving a smear of blood in its wake. The other hand raised something up to his mouth. Its jaws opened revealing a row of blocky teeth. It was at this point Black realized that this was no man and the thing in its hand was a severed head. With a loud crunch the beast took a bite like from an apple, smacking its lips as it chewed.

It was then that the beast turned towards the children. Its eyes were set wide on its long and narrow face. It smiled at them before cramming what was left of the head into its maul with another revolting crunch. Blood and gore trickled down its pointed chin. The beast let the body slip from its grip as it marched in their direction. Its hooves clicked on the cobblestone with each step and its long hairy arms swung casually from its broad shoulders as it grew nearer.

Black took a step back which seemed to set everyone else into motion. Rinx spun around with a mask of panic on her face, her eyes settling on what was happening just behind Black. Black following her gaze, turned to see Newt still on the ground with tears running down his face while Darius was trying to pull up his dead weight. Newt's mouth hung open like he was screaming but the only sound was his panicked breathing.

Black leaned in to aid Darius but before he could came the voices.

Several voices speaking in unison, dominated by one very deep, rose up from behind Black. "Oh, sweet children," the hulking beast purred. "Don't run. Won't you play with me?"

Black turned slowly to see the monster marching closer to them. His hand groped for the scrolls at his hip only to find empty air. He didn't have the scrolls or his sword. He was completely unarmed. Rinx must have had the same idea because she began reciting an incantation. At almost the same time Darius sprung up next to Black with a wild look in his eye as he begun his own spell.

Rinx launched a fireball directly into the monster's face. Darius followed up with an eruption of icy spikes that started from just in front of the children ending with a crisscross of jagged ice locking the beast's right leg in place. The monster barely slowed as its leg seemed to effortlessly crumble the ice to a pile of broken shards with its next step forward. Its face emerged from a cloud that hung in the air around its head caused by the fireball's impact. The face was now bisected horizontally by a large toothy grin.

The monster began a loud monotone laugh, of which Black could feel the bass vibrating in his chest. The laughter filled his ears and was rising to a deafening volume as the creature closed in. Suddenly the laughter stopped and the monster stood motionless. In the silence they could hear all of their heavy breathing and from behind them someone chanting a spell.

They all turned to see dressed in her CTC uniform, arm extended out in front of her and her brow pushed together in a look of determination, Astrid.

***

Present

Black stood with his back against the stone wall separating him from the villa, locking eyes with the sneering Hannibal. The smoke that had been cleared away by the explosion was beginning to fill the open space again. Black could see the flashes of fire occasionally through the haze and the cries of battle. Hannibal was preparing another spell for attack. Having witnessed what the last spell was capable of and the damage Hannibal was willing to do to his own comrades, Black could not risk drawing the blast in the direction of his own allies.

Black held his ground until the final moment he caught sight of a small spark ignited between Hannibal's gnarled hands. The environment blurred past him as he used his speed enchantment moving directly to the right. As his vision snapped back into focus he raised his arms to protect himself from flying debris caused by the impact of Hannibal's spell hitting the stone barrier protecting the villa. Black was knocked down into the mud. He struggled to climb back up to his feet slipping in the muck as flashes of spells lit up the encroaching darkness of night. As Black finally got his feet under him he saw in a sudden flash the wild face of Hannibal towering over him.

"You won't stop this," Hannibal roared as he grabbed Black's sword arm just below the elbow.

His grip was strong and in the mud Black fought for the leverage to pull away. Black heard a sudden pop like a large lightbulb just went out. At the same time pain shot up his right arm and his sword slipped from his grip falling into the mud with a thick splash. In a move of wild desperation Black reeled back before slamming his head into Hannibal's face.

Hannibal let go of Black's arm and each of the men stumbled back from each other dazed. Smoke rose from Hannibal's hand that had held Black a moment ago. His other hand clutched his face. Black looked down at his forearm to find a bloody lesion surrounded by scorched skin. He tried to make a fist but the pain was nearly unbearable.

"This is a holy crusade," Hannibal growled through bloodshot and tear filled eyes. Blood diluted by the rain ran from his nose into his mouth giving his teeth a pink hue.

Hannibal raised his hands palms out at Black to begin another incantation. One palm looked blackened with soot. Black rushed forward in an attempt to disrupt the spell. As he got into striking distance he caught the pink flash of Hannibal's smile before a hand reached out groping for Black's neck. Black kept his injured arm tucked close into his body as he recoiled out of reach of Hannibal's hand. Another hand grabbed at Black's face but he knocked it away with his left arm. Black was on his heels pedaling backwards as Hannibal tried to grab hold of him.

Off balance Black found himself falling backwards landing flat on his back. Hannibal came down directly on top of him with both his hands wrapping around the neck of his foe. Black instinctively latched his left hand onto one of Hannibal's wrists. Hannibal's wild green eyes bore into Black as the pink grin widened across his face.

"I finally got you," Hannibal taunted.

There was a smell of ozone and a crackling sound as Black unleashed his lightning bolt enchantment into Hannibal's body and almost instant unimaginable pain as it surged back into Black. The two men were locked in place staring into eachothers hate filled eyes as the electricity cooked them from the inside. After what felt like an eternity, darkness closed in on Black's vision and he lost consciousness.

Hannibal sunk down, coming to rest on Black's chest. They remained motionless like that for a time in the mud while the rain fell on their still smoking bodies.

Get up, came the husky voice of Fenrir. You aren't dead yet.

Black suddenly felt himself gasping for air and his body ached with pain. His left arm especially felt like thousands of needles were being drilled down to the bone. He coughed and noticed the heavy weight on his chest was Hannibal. With difficulty he managed to push Hannibal off him. Black laid in the mud for some minutes before he was able to sit up. The smell of burnt meat filled his nostrils as he examined the body next to him. Hannibal's right arm was almost entirely black from the elbow down and his eyes had been burned out of their sockets.

Black found his way to his feet and stumbled to the stone barrier. He supported his weight against it as he walked, finally coming to a stop at the section that had crumbled against the impact of Hannibal's second attack. He rested for a moment still hearing the cries of pain and flashes of spells in the darkness.

There was a scream very close to him and an eruption of fire. From the smoke a man came tumbling across the ground. Right behind him was Damascus delivering a killing blow with an already bloodied sword. A sudden plume of fire erupted and in the light Black could clearly make out Rinx walking backwards and two figures engulfed in flame, flailing.

Damascus caught sight of Black and called out, "Amadeus!"

He looked Black up and down and his question was clear on his face without him needing to ask it. Black nodded his head to say he was ok although he felt far from it. After the two figures still aflame came to rest on the ground, silent,

Rinx joined Black and Damascus standing in front of the shattered portion of the barrier.

"You really thought –," Rinx began, raising her index finger to Black. "Gods!" The battered sight of Black hit her all at once.

Black waved her away with his left hand and said, "Hannibal is dead."

"Well done," Damascus said as he scanned their surroundings.

There were still the sounds of battle, flashes of spells, and death screams in the surrounding darkness.

Having composed herself Rinx said, "Premier Barnabus's, uh, whatever they are showed up out of nowhere."

She wasn't out of breath but she looked tired. Damascus, blood streaked but alert, was as focused as ever.

Black collected his thoughts. "Hannibal's dead but that doesn't mean we've stopped the ritual." He rubbed his aching head. "The site must be inside."

He tried to close his right hand into a fist again and it felt like the skin was tearing off his forearm and the searing pain intensified for an instant. Blood had run down from the open wound, mixed with the rain, and dripped off his knuckles. Black felt exhausted and every part of his body hurt. The other two looked at him as if waiting for direction.

"We have to find it and make sure the ritual isn't completed," Black stated, looking in Damascus's eyes and then Rinx's. "I can't do it alone," he added, dropping his gaze down to his mangled arm.

Damascus nodded and led the way stepping over the rubble of the wall to the villa. His Aegis was held up in front of him and his sword at the ready.

Rinx with a smirk on her face said, "Of course you can't," before gesturing for Black to follow behind Damascus leaving her to bring up the rear.

Chapter 11

Past

Beads of sweat were forming on Astrid's forehead as she held firm. She continued reciting her incantation on a loop between quick short breaths with both her arms extended out in front of her palms down. The brutish demon held by her spell shuttered under its own immense weight. The smile that had momentarily faded returned to the monster's face. The children looked on in horror as the beast slowly and carefully raised its right leg to take another step towards them. The stones beneath the demon's hoof were cracked to pieces by the combined weight of the monster and the force of Astrid's spell. The younger children still standing all inched backwards as the demon progressed with another steady but careful step. Again the demon shattered the stones beneath it, sending up small plumes of dust and debris as its clove hooves connected with the street.

Between Astrid's monotonous chanting quickly came one clear word; "Run."

Rinx, Black, and Darius turned their heads, never fully letting the demon out of their line of sight. They observed Astrid's determined look as her breaths were becoming more rapid and the beads of sweat had begun to run down her face. Astrid's command to run was reflected clearly in her eyes. With no further hesitation Rinx and Darius lunged at Newt's gangly limbs. They finally had him heaved up to his feet. An instant later they were half dragging him past Astrid. Newt's legs were like rubber underneath him and didn't seem capable of fully supporting his weight.

Black watched as the three kids fled past the sweet stand Newt and Darius had so recently been perusing. Black turned back to the demon that was slowly gaining ground on them and then back to Astrid still holding steady. She was looking more and more fatigued by the strain of her sustained spell. For a moment it was as if they could read each other's thoughts. Black could see Astrid's face fixed in an expression that said, "Run, stupid. I can handle this." Answered by Black's expression that read, "I can't. I can't let you die here." Followed again by Astrid's face arranging itself into a desperate plea.

The demon was nearly upon them Black stood between it and Astrid. He returned his full attention back to the monster. It was towering over Black still wearing that maddening grin highlighted by blood congealed around its lips and gums. At that proximity the smell of the beast nearly made Astrid and Black gag. It was a stink of rotten eggs and stale death.

Black felt locked in place by an overwhelming sensation of fear and indecision. He felt powerless and he was powerless yet couldn't bring himself to abandon Astrid. He had no plan though his mind was racing in search of a solution. He was physically no match for this behemoth and he knew it. He could find options that ended in them walking away from this. The only kernel of peace in this whole mess was knowing that the others had escaped. *They should have had enough time to run and maybe hide somewhere,* he thought. Another rock shattering step and the demon was close enough it could reach out and touch him.

Suddenly Astrid's chanting stopped and at the same time a hand grabbed the back of Black's collar, yanking him back. He stumbled backwards off balance and barely managed to keep his feet under him. Astrid now stood between him and the demon.

"Run you idiot, run!" Astrid shouted while panting for breath.

Their eyes locked in what was only a moment but felt stretched out over the span of Black's short life. Astrid's face was twisted into desperation while his features were a mix of helplessness and fear for what was about to come.

Released from Astrid's spell the demon easily and swiftly drew up its long hairy left arm and swung in a backhand motion ripping Astrid off her feet in a sickening crunching sound. Her body flipped through the air before tumbling across the stony street coming to rest in a heap against a wall. Black opened his mouth for only a squeak to escape.

The demon's wide set eyes kept both Black and Astrid's still frames in its line of sight as it pressed on towards its next victim. Black's legs were shaking beneath him as he was fully gripped by the horror of what he had just seen. His eyes were opened so wide they looked like they were nearly going to fall out of his head as he stared at the looming monster.

The demon slowly extended one hairy hand towards the boy. Black remained frozen by fear as he watched his doom reaching for him. Without warning there was an explosion of thick rope-like tendrils from the ground at the beast's feet. The cobblestones were flung in all directions as the vines rapidly spiraled up the demon's legs then his torso and finally shot out to its thick forearm. The grin dropped from the beast's face once more as the tendrils snapped tight and began slowly pulling the monster's arm against its body, away from the paralyzed boy.

Black regaining a small amount of his senses, turned in time to see Maitresse Abigail Brunel, fist clenched out in front of her standing several feet behind him. She was cloaked in her usual white robe and her eyes held a gleam that could kill. Charging ahead of her was Maitre Brunel with a wooden sword held low to one side clenched tight in both hands. He sprinted forward and when he was only a few feet behind Black a wooden log erupted from the ground directly under Brunel's feet. Angled towards the monster the log propelled Brunel high into the air in a blue blur. The momentum easily carried him over the demon's left shoulder and as Brunel passed he made a single strike with his sword at the beast's neck.

Brunel landed behind the demon, rolled, and was back on his feet with the sword now held casually in one hand at his side. The demon let out a croke from deep in its gorge before vile black blood began streaming from its neck and over its shoulders. Its body went slack and was pulled down to its knees by the still tightening tendrils. The impact of hitting the ground sent the demon's head tumbling from its shoulders where it landed on the bloody stump of a neck at Black's feet.

Black also fell to his knees staring down at the wide set eyes and long face of the demon looking back at him. Its thick tongue hung from its slack jaw. Black thought he caught a slight flicker in the eyes and then nothing. The demon was dead.

The demon's body remained held in place by the tendrils. An odor fouler than before emanated from the gooey black blood like rancid meat. Abigail sprinted to Astrid's limp body crumpled against the wall. At the same time Brunel strolled to Black giving the demon's body a generous birth. Brunel crouched down next to Black who was still staring at the monster's large horned head.

Brunel planted the tip of his sword into the narrow gap of two cobblestones and asked, "Are you hurt?"

There was a long pause while Black continued staring at the monster's long face. He finally acknowledged Brunel's presence and turned his head slowly to meet his gaze.

Without any warning or control tears began pouring from Black's eyes. He grabbed onto Brunel tightly and buried his face hard into his shoulder. The Maitre wrapped his arms around the boy firmly and letting him sob against him.

After a few short minutes when Black had finished crying he pushed away from Brunel and answered, "No." Black's blood shot eyes moved to Abigail crouched next to Astrid. "I'm not hurt."

Brunel followed Black's gaze before standing upright, smoothing out his powder blue robe, and helping Black up to his feet.

Abigail slowly walked back to them. As she approached her face was set firmly. Her eyes moved from the dead monster, to Brunel, and then briefly to Black before her face softened and her eyes flicked back to her brother.

"There was nothing I could do," Abigail said. There was the faintest hitch of pain buried in her monotone response that betrayed her, revealing how she felt despite her attempts to hide it.

Black stared across the empty space at Astrid's lifeless body. He felt like a shell of who he had been. Now just an empty husk. He fingered the wooden ring Mazurus had gifted him long ago and wished he was there now before wiping the rest of the tears from eyes and cheeks.

A handful of the city's guards ran down the street past the trio only slowing down to briefly examine the decapitated demon and then rushing in the direction of the main square.

"Perhaps we should follow them," Abigail suggested. "There could be others that need help."

The siblings both looked at Black considering what to do when there came a cry from behind them. They all turned to see a short round man with receding brown hair running as fast as his stubby legs could carry him. Following closely behind him were two city guards.

The chubby man sprinted to where Astrid's body had come to rest and fell to his knees crying her name. He pulled her to his chest and moaned, "My baby girl! No gods, not my baby girl!"

One of the guards reluctantly implored the man, placing a hand gently on his shuttering shoulder, "Premier Valen please, we need to get you to a safe location."

Valen pushed the hand from his shoulder and clutched Astrid tighter to his chest and sobbed. Black felt numb as he stared at the father's heaving shoulders.

"Amadeus!" Black heard another cry behind him and turned to see Rinx fully in her fox form bolting towards him. As she approached him she stood back up on her hind legs fluidly regaining her human form.

She looked at the wreckage of the demon and then at Valen clutching Astrid. Black could see the weight of what had happened wash over her.

She looked in shock and spoke dumbly, "I came back for you after we found some guards. I told Darius I could move faster by myself." Rinx examined Black and then seemed to regain some of her composure. She looked at Brunel and Abigail. "My mother and brother were in the city square." Her eyes were fixed with an expression that was begging them for help.

Maitre Brunel regarded the two with an icy expression. "I don't think we should," he trailed off, exchanging a look with his sister. An unspoken conversation seemed to play out between the two before Abigail turned and started towards the city square. Brunel turned back to the children with a cold look in his eyes. "Stay close to us and do exactly what we say."

As the four proceeded to the city square Black gave one last look over his shoulder at Valen rocking back and forth with his forehead drooped down against Astrid's head.

They carefully made their way allowing Maitre Brunel to lead. Whenever they would come to a corner the two children would remain with Abigail while her brother would peak around the corner and advance several feet checking that it was safe before returning to guide them. They passed several bloody scenes and the occasional dead demon along the way. They were passing more and more guards as they got nearer the square.

When they finally entered the square it resembled a warzone. Guards were lining up bodies of the victims or what was left of them down one side of the square. The four could easily estimate that there had been over a hundred casualties in the square alone. A handful of survivors were being treated by a few city guards. Abigail left the other three, rushing over to help the wounded. A couple of the buildings surrounding the square had been reduced to rubble. Several large forms were scattered around the square. Two of them were charred down to the bone. Just large smoldering horned skeletons remained. A third resembled a carapace like that of an enormous insect with a large chunk blown out of it and plumes of smoke rising up from the hole and gaps in the armor. It appeared it had been burned out from the inside. Many more were littered about in varying forms of destruction.

The kids spotted the slender frame and crimson hair of Rhiss as she made her way through the chaos of the scene towards them. Her white robe had black stains all over it. The right sleeve was completely missing and the exposed arm was covered in soot all the way up to the shoulder. Her face looked much older and had ashes smeared across it. Black and Rinx ran to her. Immediately Rinx hugged her tight, Black just stopping short. The numb feeling he'd recently experienced washed over him again, renewed.

Rinx pulled away from her mother, looked around, and asked, "Where is Mhimo?"

Rhiss looked down at her daughter. She opened her mouth and closed it again.

"Where is Mhimo?" Rinx asked again with a rising panic in her voice.

"I can't find his scent anywhere," Rhiss paused for a moment, selecting her words carefully. "I can't find him anywhere." She stopped short as if she wanted to say more but couldn't bring herself to do it.

Rinx shook her head in disbelief.

"I'm sorry," Rhiss said with a trembling voice, almost a whisper.

Rinx burst into tears and buried her face against Rhiss's filthy robe. Rhiss held her daughter firmly against her body and stroked her crimson hair. Black watched silently. His eyes were damp and still stung from crying earlier but no new tears fell. He had simply been a spectator to the events that unfolded. Black had been unable to help in any way. He'd never felt so powerless or so dependent. Astrid had saved his life only to die for it, for him to be saved again by the Brunel siblings immediately after. There was a dark pit inside him and from that pit bubbled up an acidic bitterness. Black resented his weakness and himself.

A firm hand fell on Black's shoulder, shattering his thoughts and making him jump. It was Maitre Brunel. Brunel looked down at the boy and forced a reassuring smile before pulling his head in against him. The Maitre held Black in a side hug while they watched the mother and daughter comfort each other. Except for the sounds of Rinx's sobs they all stood silently for a time. All the while Black's bitterness continued to burn him from the inside.

***

Present

Black followed Damascus over the rubble of the wall with Rinx closely behind. Hannibal's blast had smashed in the front of the villa. Three mutilated bodies laid strewn around the broken boards and stones that had previously built up the entrance. The intricately decorated red and white rug in the foyer was soaked from the rain blowing into the gaping hole punched through the front of the building. Their feet sloshed over the carpet as they cautiously but quickly made their way into the home.

There was a low creak from the adjacent room bringing all three of them to a stop in their tracks. There was a long pause as they listened. The villa was severely damaged so it didn't seem unusual for it to groan and creak but still they waited.

Finally Damascus, Aegis and sword at the ready carefully glided toward the adjacent room. He moved like a panther. Each step exuded an air of grace combined with coiled muscle ready to pounce. Damascus reached the doorway and hesitated just for a moment. In that moment sprung from around the corner a tall lean man with gray thinning hair.

The man landed directly in the doorway, barring their path while another man emerged from another hiding place behind the first. Both men were cloaked in brown robes. The first man let out a hiss, spraying a stream of clear liquid from his mouth while the second man commenced a spell. Damascus's sharp reflexes quickly intercepted the liquid with his Aegis and in such close proximity the substance splashed back into the first man's face.

The thin man let out a howl of pain, clutching his smoking face as his skin sizzled. In the narrow space of the doorway, Black and Rinx were helpless to assist. The second man finished his spell and a jet of flame erupted from his right fist taking the shape of a sword. Damascus bashed the first man in his screaming face, knocking him further into the room. At the same time the man with the flaming sword held high charged Damascus. Again Damascus's Aegis intercepted. As the conjured weapon connected with the shield it simply fizzled away. The sudden dismissal and lack of impact threw the robed man off balance, stumbling towards Damascus. Damascus in anticipation already had his short sword rising up from under his shield piercing the man's abdomen just below his sternum. The blade smoothly slipped up behind the ribs towards the heart.

Damascus pulled his blade free and spun towards the first man. The tall man raised a hand from his melted face in surrender but it was too late. His head was severed from his neck. Damascus had already returned to his coiled, panther-like prowl through the room before the body hit the floor.

The room was long with some furniture. Table, couch, and a couple of chairs. Some debris from Hannibal's explosion had been scattered about. Only a couple of what appeared to be electric lights at the far end illuminated the space. To the right was another doorway and likely the place where the second man had been hiding. The doorway entered into a dark room and as the three approached they were able to make out more detail inside.

The room had a musty smell emanating from it. The floor was a large stone slab with a square hole cut into it. In the hole were stone steps that descended down about thirty feet. There were a couple of torches on the wall leading down that were unlit. By the smell of smoke in the air the three could assume that they'd likely been blown out in the explosion. At the end of the steps was one torch still burning, revealing that the steps turned sharply to the right and disappeared behind a wall.

Damascus gave a glance back to the other two. Without a word he continued on down the stairs with the other two in tow. After the three reached the bottom of the first stretch of steps they found another stretch like the first with a burning torch about every fifteen feet. The stairs were well lit. The path was narrow and seemed to be cut into solid rock all the way down. They made twelve turns descending the stairs in total before they finally made it to the bottom. During the last four flights of stairs they'd begun to hear the echoes of someone speaking deep within. It got louder and louder as they approached the end of their descent. They could recognize it as an elaborate incantation.

At the bottom of the stairs they passed through a stone doorway and entered into a large natural cavern. Stalagmites were barely visible and the ceiling was completely lost in the gloom. What little light there was came from several feet ahead. There was the flickering of many candles. As the three quietly approached they could make out a cloaked figure. From a distance they were able to see heaps on the ground next to each cluster of candles. As they silently drew nearer they soon realized that the heaps were bodies. The cloaked figure unaware of their presence continued reciting his incantation. He stood in the middle of a pentagram made of off-white powder and more complex than the one they'd discovered in the warehouse. At each point of the pentagram was a cluster of candles and a body with its throat cut. At the man's feet was a dimly glowing orb. Rinx and Black recognized it immediately as a receptacle for storing souls.

The man was short and stocky. Black considered that this could be Nictus Prothers, Hannibal's co-conspirator and the man that had seemed to disappear. The three continued their approach, no longer in a line but fanned out shoulder to shoulder. Black felt he was regaining a bit of strength despite the persistent pain. He pushed forward a few feet ahead of the other two.

Black was nearly at the edge of the pentagram when a sudden force slammed into him buckling his knees and causing him to fall down on all fours. His lungs struggled to push against a persistent pressure on his back. Black's head hung low allowing him to look back at Rinx and Damascus just behind him and to his left. Damascus held his shield over his head while Rinx was clinging tightly to him with one hand gripping the edge of the Aegis.

Rinx raised a hand as if to conjure a fireball but nothing happened. The Aegis while protecting her from the invisible force also prevented her from casting a spell.

Black struggled to raise his head to the cloaked figure. This all felt familiar like he'd been here before. "Prothers," he grunted but even as the name left his mouth he knew he was wrong. "You?"

Rinx and Damascus tried to move closer to Black while clinging to the Aegis but when they stepped forward it was like moving in mud buried up to their necks. The progress was slight and exhausting.

The figure turned in their direction, pausing the complicated ritual while one hand extended towards them and another lowered his hood. "Prothers?" the man asked and chuckled to himself. "No, he served his purpose already."

Black recalled the teeth and bloody gore in Premier Valen's home in the city.

Rinx let out a gasp as the man flashed a jolly smile from his chubby face. "Premier Bartholomew Valen," she said to herself.

"I'd say he got what he deserved," Valen continued. "Consorting with demons. Besides, he made an effective decoy."

"Consorting with demons?" Black repeated. "Hypocrite, what makes you any different?" He was struggling to speak and his body was racked with fresh pain.

Fresh blood trickled down his right arm as his wound was reopened. Black activated the strength enhancing enchantments that ran down his spine and slowly started to rise up. His body crackled as he pushed against the gravitational force, driving one leg up from under him. Valen's spell was several times more powerful than the one his daughter Astrid had used on him all those years ago. Valen with the same hand gesture Astrid had used in their fight, intensified the pressure. With a loud pop from Black's knee and a grunt of pain he was back down on all fours. He no longer had the strength to even raise his arms let alone his body.

"You. Don't. Get it," Valen said with a stern look fixed to his face. "They took my baby girl from me. She was all I had left after..." Valen clenched his other hand into a tight fist as he spoke. He seemed to lose interest in Black and turned his attention to Rinx. "You must understand my pain. I pushed the Guild of Ravens to eradicate this menace. But they– Roth wouldn't take action." A look of satisfaction swept across his face. "Now they'll have no choice but to take action."

Valen's fist relaxed and he extended his open hand towards Rinx. "I always looked out for you as you rose up through the ranks. Like a daughter," he added. "I'm sure you understand." His eyes were misty and imploring.

Rinx shook her head and her voice trembled as she spoke, "not like this. How many others will be forced to suffer for revenge?"

"Revenge?" Valen furrowed his brow and dropped his off hand to his side. "This is a crusade." He shook his head. "I'm sorry it has to be this way. I tried to keep you out of this."

Valen turned back to the orb while the three remained pinned in place. He resumed his incantation with one hand still extended towards them.

Black's mind flashed back to the Great Calamity. The helplessness he experienced as a boy. He refused to let this play out like it did before. He may have been frozen in place but even pinned beneath Valen's spell he was no longer that helpless child depending on everyone else to save him. He would not idly wait for some horror to shamble out and snatch away his friends. Not again. Not ever again.

Suddenly the earth began to shake. Once more Valen stopped his spell and whirled back around. He wore a look of confusion on his face.

"This isn't right," Valen managed before the earth began to crack under him forcing him to fight to stay on his feet. The pentagram was ravaged by rocks that jutted up from the ground, crumbled, and jutted up again.

Black held his body up with his one good arm while his mutilated arm struggled to channel as much power as he could into the 'earthquake' spell he'd enchanted onto the ground with his own blood.

Valen lost his concentration in the confusion and his gravitational spell was lifted from the three. Rinx snatched the sword from Damascus's hand, stepping out from under the Aegis as she did. Black stopped his enchantment at the same time a red blur streaked past. At the end of the blur stood Rinx with the short sword buried up to the hilt in Valen's chest.

Valen stared into Rinx's eyes with a mix of shock and betrayal painted on his face. "My girl," were the only words that escaped from his lips as he slipped off the sword and collapsed to the shattered stones beneath him, dead.

Rinx stared down at the form of Valen at her feet illuminated by the glowing orb filled with all the souls he'd stolen. She finally turned and walked back to Damascus handing him the sword before they hugged each other. They hung there like that in the flickering light of the remaining candles for a time while Damascus stroked her back. Eventually they each turned, remembering Black and rushed to help him.

Black had not moved from his hunched over position on the ground when they pulled him up. Even breathing sent spasms of pain throughout his entire body. It was slow going and although they needed to stop twice for Black to rest they finally made it back to the top of the stairs. By the time they had reached the ground floor, the decimated forces of Valen's cult were being rounded up by a force of guild mages. The rain had stopped and a bright full moon had broken through the clouds. The moonlight revealed a muddy field strewn with bodies. In the chaos they managed to track down a medical mage that had arrived with the Guild of Ravens soldiers.

After some emergency treatment and the guild mage was satisfied that Black was well enough to move, they found Premier Morgu and Barnabus. Premier Geist was also with them and while Barnabus tended to his damaged puppets Rinx and Black described to the other two Premiers what had transpired. Geist was shocked to learn of Valen's involvement in Premier Roth's murder and the conspiracy to unleash hellspawn into their world. Morgu however, looked unsurprised and Black couldn't help but suspect that perhaps she'd already put the pieces together.

After Rinx and Black had completed their report, they all returned back to Damascus's mansion where Black remained for four days while he recovered from his wounds. Damascus provided his special concoction to speed up the recovery and Rinx finally took her holiday to visit her mother promising Damascus that she'd return.

One day while Black and Damascus sat having lunch together sunlight was pouring in through the tall windows in the dining room. They were having soup and Black found himself without much of an appetite so he was mostly pushing it around his bowl. His right arm was still wrapped in bandages and the anesthetic in Damascus's concoction was wearing off since he was starting to feel the dull pain in his knee return.

Damascus looked across the table at Black and said, "were lucky you know? This could have easily been a repeat of what happened when we were kids. Worse really." He studied Black closely as he spoke.

Black set his spoon down next to the bowl and a servant rushed to clear his spot. He examined the enchantment in the palm of his left hand. "Ever since that day," Black started, paused for a moment and then continued. "I've felt two things. One like a dark pit in my guts and the other like a debt I could never repay."

Damascus listened, his brown eyes carefully watched Black trace the markings on his palm.

"Maybe Valen felt that way, too," Black continued. "Maybe Hannibal and all those people felt that way." Black thought a bit more and then said, "You told me before about 'strength through unity.' I think Valen and the others that had been touched by that tragedy all those years ago were left alone by it. Even though they had all these people around them–" he broke off trying to collect his thoughts. "I think they were still alone in their minds." His face lightened. "But who can say for sure, right?"

There was a long silence and Damascus asked, "so what are your plans after you've recovered? On to the next case?"

Black looked up. "No, I think I'm going to take some time off. Gods know I have plenty of it accrued."

He did just that. Taking some time to travel back to where Mazurus had found him all those years ago. He spent most of that time as a wolf, hunting and running through the forest. He felt lighter and freer than he had in years. Almost all his days were filled with sunshine and the smell of the forest.

***

Past

The students were given a month off from the academy following the calamity. There were no more combat tournaments for the rest of the year. An investigation into how the demons had been set loose in the city was conducted but there was never any conclusion.

Rhiss had searched in vain for Mhimo but was never able to discover exactly what had happened to him. She and the others were forced to assume the worst. He'd likely fallen victim to some unnamed horror that they'd never know of.

Black had spent several nights alone during that month in Rhiss's home, awakened in tears by nightmares. Mazurus had returned from wherever he had been and made attempts to comfort both the children as best as he could. Black appreciated his effort but they did little to soothe the children's pain. The image of Astrid being killed by that monster haunted him and the unknown fate of Mhimo may have been worse. At least Black could be certain that Astrid hadn't been alone in her final moment but Mhimo, the thought of the boy who'd looked up to him dying alone at the end was unbearable. One death filled his heart with fire while the other split it in half. At times, it felt like too much.

By the end of the month the acidic bitterness that had been growing within Black solidified into a hard resolution. Black was determined to return to the academy and begin preparation for next year's CTC. After he had made a name for himself in CTC he'd be an easy pick to join the Battlemage class for the Guild of Ravens. And after that, he hadn't decided yet but he knew he needed to be stronger. He needed to be able to take care of himself next time. He would not be helpless again or so he believed.